Call It Magic

JL Pete

she's out of view, I return to my book, burying my head in it like I meant to come here alone and get some reading done. When I see the waitress returning, I put the book in my purse because she is returning on a mission.

She walks the aisle leading to my table with a tambourine under her folded arm, a lighter in her hand and my plate in the other with a pink candle leaning to the side in the dessert.

"Would you like extra spoons?"

"Extra spoons?" I ask.

She nudges her head towards the placemat across from me where an untouched glass of water sits for my no show.

"No," I reply with all my charm school politeness intact. I'd like to sit with the mountain of whip cream that's hiding something I will feel guilty about the rest of the night with just one spoon. Solo spoono. Thanks.

The waitress sets the dessert filled plate in front of me and struggles with the lighter to light the candle. It flickers; she huffs uttering the words "damn it" with a forced smile. The lighter flickers again and finally lights and she lets out a relieved sigh, taking a step back...and it happens. What happens? What always happens. The tired happy birthday song sung by force, including waiters not even waiting tables. Even the busser with a white towel hung over his shoulder has somehow been roped into this.

Where do I stare? God, they all so look unhappy.

Why do we do this? No one likes it. Even children hate it. But here I am, being given the altered version of Happy Birthday with a speed round of clapping and a tambourine shaking at a rapid tempo. I stare into the flame of the candle debating a wish, like the candle holds my fate.

Love. I wish for love. I sigh. Maybe that's too broad. I need to narrow it down. I wish for romance. To be swept off my feet. *Yes. Yes that's it.* To a year of being swept off my feet with romance...or whatever I can get that's close enough. There. Settled.

They're still singing.

What's the polite thing to do when this is over? Just say thanks? Thanks for bringing unwanted attention to my table? Thanks for letting everyone know it's my birthday and I'm by myself? Or thanks for the *oh my god* look on your face ten minutes later, Waitress, as you take the mangled remains of the dessert plate with the candle, *one candle,* lying in the residue, used and unwanted.

Yeah I finished it. I finished *all of it* in less than five minutes. Devoured is a better word.

"Wow! People rarely finish all of this!" The waitress reappears with wide eyes as her hand grips the edge of my plate lifting it with a smile, like she has an unbelievable story tell the cook in the kitchen as she takes it away. I pull the menu from the holder near the condiment tray. I open it and read the nutritional information listed for the dessert I just inhaled, narrowing my eyes at the suggested serving size.

"Number of servings. Four."

Well, fuck me.

I rationalize my indulgence with fairness and honesty. Just like any other girl who ate her weight in cake and chocolate ooze. It's my birthday. This alone has got to be a reason written in some historical birthday handbook somewhere to eat, drink, drink more and end it with a dessert big enough to feed a family.

"When you're ready. No rush," the waitress says, like she's consoling me on my decision making as she slides the bill in my direction on the table. I put the menu back in its holder and reach for my wallet to pay.

Only singles. How fitting.

Why do I have so many singles? Magic show tips. That's right. Magic show TIPS.

Much to my parents' dismay, I'm a magician. Not a teacher or lawyer like them, but a real life, *make that quarter disappear*, magician. They hate answering friends and family about what I'm up to, because unlike my brother, who has dabbled into the world of rehab, jail and teen pregnancy, I'm the black sheep they'd rather not discuss.

"She's still finding herself," they will say or, "She's just going through a phase."

Yes, a phase that has landed me in one of the top magic schools and in sold-out performances. None of which my family will attend.

I place my stack of family shamed singles on the tray with the bill and stand, patting down the skirt of my dress and pulling my purse to my shoulder. As I turn to leave, I take one last look back at the place setting across from where I was sitting.

"You have a great birthday," the hostess calls out to me from behind the host desk as I pass her to leave the restaurant. She's cheerful, and I mirror her with my own forced "thank you" back.

"Have a good one!" the young male host holding the door says as I head outside. I give him a thin line of a grin and repeat, "Have a good one," under my breath with a deep sigh as the cool air hits my skin, almost whispering to my humidity-induced, shape-shifting hair that rain is coming.

Keys in hand, I walk the parking lot just around the corner from the restaurant, passing every car but mine until I get to an open spot. The *only* open spot in the filled parking lot. I'm pretty sure it's not supposed to be empty. I'm pretty sure my car is supposed to be sitting here.

Where is my car?

I look to the ground beneath me, dumbfounded by the empty space I'm standing in. *Am I in the right lot?* I look right and then left, tightening the grip on my keys in hand, spotting the attendant who is sitting in a tiny white booth, unaffected by my sudden panic. He wasn't happy to see me parking in his lot, and I doubt he will be happy with my concern as to where my car ran off to without me in it. I approach the booth, mulling over the right word to put emphasis on, like, "Where is *my* fucking car?" or, "Where *is* my fucking car?" but before I can open my mouth, the attendant begins to repeat the mantra of parking lot attendants everywhere like a broken record.

"We aren't responsible for theft or damage," he says. He hasn't even looked up at me.

"Theft or damage? Well did you see anyone?" I ask.

He continues to stare down at his folded newspaper as if he didn't hear me. So I repeat my question as calmly as a person who just lost the only means of getting around in a city that doesn't believe public transit is a viable means of getting anywhere.

"Where is my *fucking* car?!" I may have shouted this a little louder than I intended, however the emphasis? Right where it needed to be. The attendant does look up finally. He takes a long stare at the street in front of him, taking a deep breath in and turns to me.

"*Lady,* we aren't responsible for theft or damage of any kind."

Oh so helpful. Because nothing sets an already angry person off more than having the same thing repeated with the addition of the polite old-fashioned form of gender reference. I've never punched a stranger before, but tonight may just end that. I take a deep breath in as the attendant goes back to reading his paper and taking a sip of his coffee. I stand defiant in front of the attendant without budging and he points to the sign above the empty parking spot.

"Call them. They probably have answers."

The number is for a towing company and the sign is for a dry cleaner which reads, Parking is for RoRo Cleaners. All Others will be Towed. All others as in, we don't care if it's your birthday and you didn't read the sign. Joe Schmo needs his firmly pressed dress shirts for a client meeting at 8 a.m. and this spot is reserved for him.

Fuck Joe Schmo and his firmly pressed shirts. Where is my car?

I dig in my purse for change to use the payphone nearby and call the number listed, and I'm pretty sure the guy on the other end of the line has a mouth full of marbles while he recites the address to me three times. With each repeat, he gets harder and harder to understand.

"That's five miles from here!" I say.

"That's right little lady." Only it sounded more like, "disth..rigth...lithel...laaath-y."

When I appear back in front of the attendant, I sigh with a loud groan because he doesn't notice me at first. But when he does, I can see his eyes are worn and tired when he regards me.

"Do you have the number for a cab?" I ask.

He stares through me and points to the sign outside his sliding door in a rehearsed manner. I squint and read it out loud.

"We. Are. Not. Responsible. For. Theft. Or. Damage."

Seriously? I'm going to lose it.

"Underneath," the attendant says.

The number for the taxi is listed as Shamu Taxi. I search my purse for more change, but upon first glance, I only find pennies.

I would only have pennies to go with my single theme of the night, wouldn't I?

I find a few singles as well as a square folded ten I use for magic shows, hidden in a pocket of my purse. I hold out the singles in my hand towards the attendant.

"Do you have change?" I ask.

He chuckles as he glances at my dollar bills like Bozo the Clown just made an appearance. I do have a red whiskey nose right now, but that's beside the point.

"No, lady. No change."

Lady.

His smile fades and he returns to his paper. His desk is full of papers and an industrial sized stapler but just to the left of it is what looks like a small black phone receiver.

"Is that a cell phone?" I ask.

He puts his paper down and slides his one hand over the top of the phone shaking his head. "Not for customers, Lady."

"If I can turn this dollar into ten dollars, will you let me use it to call a cab?"

He doesn't reply with any words but his eyes are saying "show me." So I do.

I reach into my purse and grab the already folded ten dollar bill and hide it in my palm as I hold out a flat, crisp one dollar bill. I fold the dollar in half and then fold it again. I fold the dollar down until it resembles a quarter sized square like the ten dollar bill I have hidden. The attendant is probably thinking he should have just handed me the phone right about now, but I carry on despite his deadpan eyes.

I unfold the dollar and show both sides to the attendant, giving him a nod to keep watching, and he does. I fold it again in the same way, holding it tight in my right hand and slipping the already folded ten dollar bill on top using sleight of hand and then snap the fingers of my left. I pull the folded square of the ten dollar bill out and unfold it, showing both sides to the attendant whose eyes are wide with his mouth gaping open. I hand him the money and he hands me the phone in a fluid motion. He stares at both sides of the bill and then back at me.

I acknowledge him with a flicker of my lashes but dial for a cab and then hand the phone back. He's still watching the ten dollar bill like the ink is going to rub off. I assure him its legit legal tender.

"You like magic, Lady?"

I shake my head yes and don't want to talk to him anymore because I know the next question is going to be if I do birthday parties.

"My niece loves magic shows."

Here it comes.

"You ever do birthday parties?"

Yep, knew it.

I give him my card, because a girl's gotta eat regardless of the means to get there, and I walk towards the empty spot like I am going to find a hidden clue to my car's abduction. I've named my car David Copperfield, or D.C. for short, because of its color- copper, and I would bed that magic God named David Copperfield so fast, it's not even funny. But right now, Houdini is probably a more fitting name, and I would not bed him, because he's dead.

I imagine my lost D.C. cold and afraid in a lot full of vehicles that were impounded for crimes like unpaid parking tickets, belonging to drivers who got arrested or becoming evidence in a murder.

Extreme? Hardly.

My sweet D.C. doesn't deserve this. I wait in the empty spot, shooing off a car that wants to park in it because this spot is reserved for me, my body, me and *only* me until the cab comes.

"You need a ride?" A stranger calls from the car next to me with the passenger window rolled down.

"A ride?" I ask.

Oh sure, let's just take a ride from a stranger tonight and see how well that works out because the rest of my night can't get any worse.

"No, but thank you," I say. I peer into the window to see a man leaning his head towards me.

"You sure?" He leans closer to the window, his voice carries louder. "That cab you called doesn't look like it's in any hurry to get here."

"How do you know I called a cab? Maybe I'm just saving this space for my friends." My arms wrap around my torso with one of my legs crossing over the other like I'm in some sort of new yoga pose created for waiting in a parking lot, and I narrow my eyes at the driver.

"You must not have very nice friends if they're making you wait in the rain."

"What rain?"

Oh, that rain. The rain that has begun to tap on my face like a brilliant *fuck you* to cap my night.

"Ride?" he asks again, leaning from the driver's seat and pushing the passenger side door open to a visual of black leather seats and glowing lights from the dashboard. He's wearing a light brown leather jacket that creaks when he leans back in his seat.

"You aren't a serial killer are you?" I tighten my gaze to get a better view of him, tilting my head to the side. His eyes have an innocent boyish wonder to them. His body is relaxed as he answers. One hand is holding the steering wheel while the other is palm down in the passenger seat.

"Is that what's going to get you to take me up on my offer? Telling you I'm not a serial killer?" He's humored by me and his own response, and I shrug because I don't really know if it makes a difference.

"Yes, and maybe a look at your license."

He digs his hand into the back of his jean pocket, wiggling in his seat until it loosens and pulls out a slim black wallet. "Here."

He hands me his license and I take a cautious step towards his car to grab it. Our fingers touch with an electric shock when they meet which makes us both pull back saying, "sorry" at the same time. I bring his license close to my face, squinting to read the name and address but focus more on the picture. Studying the image against the man sitting before me, "Reagan Snow?" I ask.

"That's me."

I look at the picture once more and study him in the driver's seat before leaning in the car to hand it back.

"Did I pass?" he asks while pushing his license back into his wallet and forcing the wallet back into his jeans.

"You passed that question," I say.

"There's more?" he asks.

I debate other questions like, *Why are you just sitting here in a dimly lit parking lot?* but the rain is falling harder and I already know my hair is beginning to do that wonderful frizzy thing it does when water hits it. It's frizzy betrayal taking center focus instead of my instinct that says, *Wait for the cab, stupid.* My instinct is a rude bitch sometimes.

"I just need a ride to the towing yard. I can pay you," I say.

"No need. Besides, I don't trust your magic money."

I'm probably going to die. This guy is way too observant. How does he know about the money? *God, this is how it ends,* me doing a stupid magic trick with a dollar to get a phone call in, *my last phone call,* and this guy who knows everything I've done since being in this parking lot just randomly shows up. If he starts asking me about the dessert, I'm rolling out of this car like an action movie star. I don't even care how fast we're going.

I sit down in the passenger seat and buckle myself in, repeating the address for the tow yard.

"Do you have a Thomas Guide?" I ask.

He furrows his brow and cocks his head to the side. "A Thomas what?"

I don't follow up with anything other than a shy smile as I stare straight ahead at the dashboard and the pine tree hanging from the rearview mirror, taking in the scent I didn't recognize at all until now.

"You like music?" Reagan asks.

I shake my head and realize he isn't looking at me; he's looking at the road *like he should be* so I let loose with a wavy version of "Ye-ah." He reaches to turn the volume up on the radio as Nirvana's Heart Shaped Box fills the car. He bops his head to the beat while turning the steering wheel.

"These guys are great!" I say.

"They're a classic," he says.

"A classic?"

"They're *going to be* a classic. Our kid's kids will talk about them. Like the Beatles or the Stones." He corrects himself and flashes a quick, warm smile my way. A smile that puts my fears of this being my last few moments at ease.

I grin back, realizing again that he isn't looking at me, so I laugh a little too loud. "You ever seen them in concert?" I ask.

He shakes his head no. "Before my time."

"What?"

"Is this it?" He points to the building in front of us as the car rolls to a slow stop. I follow his gaze. *The address is right.* The people outside look exactly how I pictured they would in this part of town, and I'm not sure I want to get my car back now.

Sorry D.C., mama's gotta think of herself now, rest in peace.

"You want me to go in with you?" Reagan interrupts my betrayal to D.C. over safety concerns.

"No, it's fine. I'll be fine." I stare out the front window and startle when a man holding a newspaper slams towards the front passenger side window making me jump in my seat. "Jesus!"

The man yells through the front window, "Can I clean this for a dollar?" He begins without waiting for an answer and as he continues, the window begins to look worse than when he started. Bits of his newspaper are coming off and sticking to the window.

"You sure I can't come in with you?" Reagan asks when I glance at him and back at the man who is now yelling he wants his money. "I'm coming with you."

The man outside the car takes a few steps back when Reagan walks around the front of the car to my side. He opens my door while I struggle to undo the seatbelt like a fool. He reaches over to help, and I lean back, letting him lean over me. He smells like Drakkar cologne and Irish Spring soap, but as soon as I realize this, I hold my breath until he's done.

"Sorry, she sticks sometimes," he whispers with a grunt, unlatching the belt.

I step out and hand the window washer, now standing on the sidewalk, a dollar and he waves it towards me saying, "Thank you, Lady, thank you."

What is it about this city and calling me Lady?

When we step inside the mobile trailer called the office, I recognize Marble Mouth from the way he's talking to another unfortunate car abduction case that's sobbing in front of him. Both are competing with their misunderstood language skills, and if I wasn't worried about how rude I'd look, I'd start laughing at the exchange.

"Next," Marble Mouth calls.

"I'm Harper Adams. You have my car? I called earlier?" I say. Marbles stares at me like he didn't catch a word of what I said, but he responds a few seconds later like a glitchy robot that's come to life.

"Reh-this-athon." But I do not catch this word until he repeats it three times.

"It's in the car," I say. He stares at me like I am the one hundredth person to say this and points to the door where a man shaped like an angry oversized apple wearing a black shirt nods back at him. The man waves for me to follow, and I look at Reagan.

"You don't have to stay. I'll be fine," I say. Reagan glances at me and then at the angry apple man escorting me to my car to get my registration.

"I'll stay until you're safely in your car."

I get my registration and return to the line, reaching the front again where Marble Mouth stares at me like we didn't just meet a few minutes ago.

I hand him my paperwork and he says, "Marbles are in my mouth, I can't speak clearly, sorry." No actually he doesn't say that, that's just what I hear at first. What he actually says is, "That will be two hundred and thirty dollars."

I stare at him like he just told me to go fuck myself, which he kind of did, and he repeats, "two hundred and thirty dollars."

"Can I write a check?" A few other clerks hear me ask and chuckle.

He shakes his head no. I look in my purse like money is going to appear in a thick bundle.

Shit.

"Do you have money?" Reagan whispers. "A credit card?"

"Not one that's going to cover this."

"Here, let me help." He reaches for his wallet and hands Marble Mouth a credit card before I can even get the words out to stop him.

"No, Reagan. God! Now I'm going to have to let you murder me or some weird shit on the way back to my car." He laughs and takes his card back from Marbles, who hands him the receipt to sign.

"You can pay me back, whenever. I'm not worried about it."

"Not worried about two hundred and thirty dollars? God, you aren't from around here are you?"

He shakes his head no with a twinkle in his sideways glance while handing the receipt to Marbles who hands my driver's license and registration back to me. But before Marbles releases them, he does a double take at my picture while giving Reagan a nod.

Marbles smirks at me and says in full marble filled fashion, "Hathy birfday, Harber."

Thanks, Marble Mouth...thanks.

Chapter 2

Reagan 1993

"You think she's gonna notice there's no dry cleaner here?" Gus asks.

I squint at him and wave my arm to the side, motioning for the sign to move left an inch. "Just hang the sign."

Gus and I return to the restaurant through the alley and I take a seat with a clear view of Harper. I stare her way with the occasional blocked view from waitresses getting refills. One eyes me and I eye her back but not in the same way she's looking at me. I want her to get out of the way, and she wants me to...I may have to find out, but for now, I need her to move.

"So this is the girl you're supposed to help, huh?" Gus says, setting down a plate of fries and a burger. I grab a few french fries and take the ketchup from the side of the table. We both look over at Harper who is sitting hunched over a table with her nose in a book, turning her head towards the door each time it opens.

"That's her," I say.

"At least she's a cute one this time."

So, let's get to know each other shall we? You've already met my new distressed friend, Harper, but who am I? Who is this guy giving her a ride to get her car out of tow and lending her money? And why does he think Nirvana was before his time? And who the hell is Gus?

All valid questions, friend. All valid questions.

Reagan Snow. Nice to meet you.

I've been called a few things besides the name that appears on my license. Douchebag, jerk, thief, man-whore, hey you, dude, and Gus' favorite, future boy. But all of them mean nothing except my current title, parolee. You're probably thinking, oh great, he really is a serial killer. But no friend, no. Not quite. I'm currently out on supervised parole for my third public intoxication charge and first DUI charge, and no, I'm not proud. I'm also from the year 2035. Gus, who is dressed like a busser, is my supervising parole officer, and I couldn't be more overjoyed having him serve me food and calling me Sir.

"How about a beer for old time's sake?" I ask, pushing my hands on the table edge, pressing my back against the booth.

"How about I put you back in a cell with Tiny?" he says.

Tiny.

That guy didn't like me much. I don't think I ever spoke a word to him. He just kept commenting on my "stupid pretty face" and how he wanted to smash it. No real reason given. But when your name is Tiny, do you really need a reason to have a chip on your shoulder?

"They're getting ready to sing to her. You should go join," I say with a tip of my head towards Harper.

Gus wants to tell me off, I know he does but he can't because he's a new hire here at this restaurant, and he needs to keep his cover until we're done. He puts on a fake smile, slapping the small white towel over his shoulder and sings Happy Birthday to Harper. She doesn't know where to look while everyone sings, so she stares at the dessert in front of her. When they leave, she blows out the candle and I wonder what she wished for.

"Look at her. Look at her eat that thing." Gus returns and stands with his arm arched on the top of the booth seat, watching in awe.

"I like a girl who can eat," I say.

"You say that now. But it's all fun and games until she can't fit into one of those tight little dresses you like the ladies to wear so much."

I do like a tight dress, and I also like the time I've landed in, the 90's. 1993 to be specific. The era of tight dresses and big mall hair, although grunge is taking over. I can't say I mind that either. Beanies and flannel. If it's done right, a girl can look pretty damn hot, but done wrong, like hippie grunge? Well...it can be a horrible hairy surprise.

"Is the sign still in place?" I ask Gus.

"It's up. Cleaners sure are assholes about their parking."

"...and you called the towing company?"

Gus nods. "You know the guy there can't talk for *shit*!"

Yes, we staged the whole towing incident. But how else was I going to meet Harper? Just walk up to her and introduce myself as the guy from the future who was sent here to tell her life is going to get better, buck up kid? Or how I have to give back to society via time travel as penance for my crimes because that's how they do it in 2035? *Yeah,* I don't think that would have worked as well. But watching her pay the bill and frown at the empty seat across from where she was sitting is making me think the towing idea isn't going to work out well either.

"You better get out there, future boy. She's getting ready to leave."

I follow Gus' stare towards the door. He holds my bill in hand, begging me not to stiff him again. But I stiff him again. *What?* It's not like I'm never going to see him again. He's my goddamn roommate and parole officer for this case.

Before making my exit, I run into the waitress from earlier who was eying me at the drink station. She follows me down the narrow hall leading to the back of the restaurant. I peer over my shoulder with a sly grin and stop walking, turning around to face her when we reach the alcove for the bathrooms.

"I'm just about to go on break." She's telling me this while pulling me by the open zipper of my jacket into a phone booth near the restrooms.

This is no joke, *a phone booth*. I'm not complaining about the location we are in, but a relic like a phone booth is worth a second glance around. Especially when the door slides closed and she pulls the black privacy curtain shut. She's a beautiful blonde with green eyes staring at me the way Harper was staring at her dessert right before she devoured it.

"What's your name?" I ask for absolutely no reason other than I can't think of anything else to say while she's getting acquainted with the button on my jeans and her lips curl around my neck.

"Mary," she whispers, smiling into my lips as we connect.

My one hand curls around the back of her head while the other roams into the opening of her very low cut and easy to unbutton shirt. Her lips taste like nicotine with a hint of wax. A combo that would otherwise deter me if it wasn't for the way she knows how to use her hands as she lowers to her knees. God, she knows how to use her hands and *holy shit,* her mouth.

Before I can admire her handiwork further, I hear my name. It's not sultry or full of hot nicotine and wax. It's full of Gus. It's full of *what part of don't fraternize did you not understand, Reagan?*

I help my talented new phone booth friend up while we both put ourselves back together. Sliding the door open, I'm met with the face and expression I see about ninety percent of the time on these cases with Gus. Mad at me Gus. Disgusted with me Gus. *I trusted you not to pull the same shit* Gus.

Mary squeezes out of the booth, handing me a small slip of paper with her number on it and adjusts her apron tie in the back as she walks away.

"How many times do I have to say it, Reagan?" Gus asks.

"It's technically not fraternizing if it's someone outside the case," I say.

"Wipe that smirk off your face. If I'm not getting any, you're not getting any."

"But Gus, you're a fifty-five year old man. It's different."

"I'm not dead. No fraternizing means *no* fraternizing, you got it?"

I shake my head yes but I do not "*got it*" by a long shot. It seems cruel and unusual to make a man go without sex when it's so...so...available. I mean, look at the way she's staring back at me. All doe eyed and bashful like a naughty school girl in hiding. I picture her in the catholic school girl uniform with pigtail braids while she looks down at her white thigh highs asking me if I want to study.

Hail Mary.

"Stop looking at her like that." Gus intervenes on my fantasy. I still stare. "Stop it or I'm sending you home right now. Tiny misses you."

Mood killed. Killed in a way that only the mere mention of Tiny can do. Gus gestures to the exit through the kitchen where I slip out the back door and into my car, watching Harper from the rearview, then the side mirrors, then alternating between the two. She stands in the empty spot next to me waiting for her car to appear. I almost feel bad for doing this now. Maybe I could have just met her in a coffee shop or book store and bumped into her by accident like all those guys do in the books she reads.

She stomps to the attendant in her combat boots, and I watch in the rearview as her flower printed baby doll dress sways. It's a very nice visual. I want to jump out of my car and help her when I see her on the pay phone, but I wait. I want to jump out and help her when I see her argue with the attendant about change. That is until I see her change a dollar bill into a ten dollar bill.

She doesn't need my help.

She calls the cab from the attendant's booth and begins to pace in the spot her car was in hours ago. Checking her watch, looking up at the road, checking her watch again. She hasn't noticed me yet, so I make her notice me. I offer her a ride, and with a little coaxing, she takes it. I knew she would take it. Is it because I have a charismatic personality? Or the fact that most women find me charming, especially when I flash my boyish baby blues and a smile? Yes, yes and yes. But I think it's more than that with Harper. I want to help her and she doesn't know it yet, but she is in need of being helped.

We don't say much in the car ride to the towing yard, but the music gives us a few seconds of reprieve until I say Nirvana was before my time...*like an idiot*. Truth and time travel are my weakness because I'm a talker and there are rules. Rules about what you can reveal and what you can't, among the other priceless gems we Timers have to follow. There's also a case file the size of a phone book to memorize, and sometimes it's even in different languages!

Everyone studies their case file and answers detailed questions before being cleared to travel. But even with all the backstory and knowledge I have about the time I'm in, this case is different. I recognize it from the second I see Harper, and I realize I'm in trouble. I never get nervous. I'm never stumbling over the time period I'm in or wondering what to say. But with her...*shit.*

She's reluctant to let me come with her inside the towing office to get her car and knowing her personality from the file, I plan for this by scaring her into letting me go, using a homeless companion. *I'm horrible, right?* My friend in travel pulls off his homeless routine without a hitch, and now I'm watching another fellow travel companion who couldn't speak a clear sentence if his life depended on it. He really couldn't. Harper wants to laugh as we stand in line and I do too. How Marvin (Marble Mouth as Harper calls him) got placed in a position where customer service is a top priority, I'll never know.

We get her registration from her car all locked up behind bars and return to the office where Marvin takes my credit card. I don't let his *are you sure* expression throw me. I want to pay for it. I'll probably be eating Top Ramen for weeks because of what I just spent, but it's the least I can do for ruining her already horrible birthday. I hope me being...well... *me*, can make up for it by the end of the night.

"Thanks for coming with me," she says.

"Don't worry about it," I say.

"I'm going to pay you back. I promise!"

"Really you don't..."

"Yes I do."

"No you..."

"Yes I do."

Her wide smile and soft hand covering my lips is the end of my refusal. Harper's hair is still wet from standing in the rain. It's turning frizzy from the humidity as it dries, and unlike her straight-haired pictures in my case file, it now has this slight, just came from the shower thing going on that's not helping my already confused feelings about her case. Her face is shining from the rain that washed her makeup off. She looks better without it. I know guys say this all the time and girls roll their eyes, but she is that girl. *Fuck, what am I doing?*

Harper is cooing at her car when we get to it. She unlocks the driver's side door, sitting down, rubbing the interior like the car has been abused and she's offering comfort. I think she just said the words, "there there." Her car needs someone to put it out of its misery. No lie. It's a Honda Accord hatchback from the 1970's that wants to go to car heaven. Even the horn she just tapped sounds like a dying whale. This car wants out. The wheels are bald; the inside has copper colored seats that look like they are covered in carpet. *CARPET*. I'm not a car snob. I like old cars. I even admire the fact that this car has lasted as long as it has, but Jesus himself would give Harper a distrusting stare down before getting in it.

PETE

Chapter 3

Harper 1993

"When I said I'd wait until you were safely in your car, I didn't know this is what you drove. What is this? Is this even street legal?" Reagan asks.

"You judge, but D.C. has been with me since my freshman year, and he isn't going anywhere," I say.

I crank the engine but nothing happens.

"You could say that again," he says. "Pop the hood, will you?" He takes off his jacket, handing it to me.

"You're a rich, maybe not serial killer who knows cars?" I sit with the driver's side door ajar, placing his jacket on the passenger seat.

"Among other things," he says with a wink.

He lifts the hood gripping it at the top edge, holding his hands steady while I stare at his fingertips. "Try to start it," he yells as raindrops resume hitting the windshield again.

F.Y.I., D.C. hates the rain. It's like a stall inducer that always has my car protesting until I beg and plead into the steering wheel. There's almost always the involvement of tears, or at least the brink of them being unleashed.

I crank the engine again to a click.

"Try it again?" Reagan yells once more, but nothing happens. The engine doesn't turn over and he lets the hood fall. He's soaked when he comes towards the driver's seat. "I think it's the battery," he says.

But I don't hear a word at first because I'm staring at the way his white t-shirt is clinging to his chest. *I don't know, maybe this birthday isn't going to end so bad after all.*

"Harper?"

"Uh...Harper?"

His words haven't registered in my brain, but I do nod while he leans down to squat in the doorway. "I'm gonna go get my car and give you a jump."

I know after a second thought that he's talking about my battery, and I know he's talking about *jumping* my battery but that's not at all what I thought I heard.

"I'll be right back," he says, lifting to stand and leaves out the gate to his car.

But when he returns, he has my newest linguist friend with him. They appear to be heavy in conversation as they get closer. Reagan is leaning his head back and laughing while Marble Mouth continues to talk.

The two men roll my car out of the space with my guidance, steering and braking. Reagan attaches the cables to my battery while Marbles attaches the other end of the cables to the car now aligned next to mine. I rev the engine and D.C. starts right up like the good little God of magic I knew he could be. Reagan thanks Marbles with that bro hug men do, leaning in close with their hands gripped in a shaking position.

It was just a battery jump right? Why are they so "tight" all of a sudden?

"You want a ride to your car?" I ask as Reagan wipes the few wet strands of hair clinging to his forehead.

"I can pay you," he says, mimicking me from earlier.

A fellow smartass. Welcome.

I nudge my head for him to get into the passenger seat, moving his jacket to the back, forgetting that D.C.'s passenger side door is not user friendly to anyone, not even me sometimes. He grips the handle and pulls, only to release the whole door in his hands and to the ground with a heavy thud.

"Um..." He looks at me, no other words falling from his lips.

Dammit D.C.!

I get out and race to his side of the car telling him to, "get in, it's okay" while I adjust the hinge of the door, popping it back into place. "Just push the lock down!" I yell, miming the action with my hand. He's looking at me like I just grew five heads. "Just push the lock down. Just push the...there you go." I nod hearing the lock click.

"Sorry, I should get that fixed." I adjust myself back into the driver's seat. My face? It's on the fiftieth hue of red right now.

"When your car starts detaching itself from its own body...I think it's a sign," he says with a straight face and chuckles seconds later which makes me laugh.

I pull my car out of the lot, both of us wave to Marbles who is sending us off out front on the sidewalk near the entrance for some reason, and I pull up to Reagan's car, letting my engine idle. I rub my hands together and adjust the heat setting...that doesn't even work, so I have no idea why I'm touching it.

"I still owe you...for the tow." I point towards the yard while the cool air from the passenger side door opening begins to seep into the car.

"You don't owe me anything. It's your birthday, right?"

"It was." My eyes drift to the clock in the center of the dash that's partially covered by a small circle of a David Copperfield magazine clipping. *I may be a little obsessed.* Reagan notices it too and stares at it for a second before returning his gaze to me. He taps his fingers on the dashboard.

"Well...I should let you go finish celebrating now that you have your car."

Celebrating.

Here is what celebrating the rest of my night will include. Footy pajamas, a tub of ice cream and the newest romance novel I picked up earlier with Fabio on the cover where I imagine myself as the deprived young heiress. My eyes will drift to the magazines on my coffee table that show David Copperfield and Claudia Schiffer together, smiling, happy and in love. Sadness will grip me as I think about how she could never love him the way I love him, truly love him. Then I'll turn back to my novel and curse that damn stable owner who's caught my heiress eyes with his irresistible but horrible ways.

"Harper?" Reagan calls my name, bringing me back to reality. I stare at him, trying to recall what we were just talking about before I drifted and reply.

"I don't have much celebrating to do. But I feel like I should. I'm twenty-one now!"

"Were you like a heavy heavy drinker or just like a, you know, social drinker?" I ask Reagan why he isn't drinking, and he tells me he stays away from it because he can't handle it. It's a bit more than I was expecting to hear, and usually I would clam up about someone's willpower or lack thereof with the liquid courage, but three margaritas in with a heavy dose of Jose Cuervo tequila, I can't control my mouth. It's a runaway train.

"I ran into some trouble with the law, which sobered me up," he says while raising his glass and motioning to the bartender for another coke. He offered to buy me a birthday drink since I said I turned twenty-one and we've landed in a bar not far from my house.

"Sobered you up? You just told me you've been arrested three times for it!"

"It wasn't the drinking part that got me arrested so much as it was what I did when I was drinking. *Which*, I'm not going to tell you about." He winks while taking a long sip of his drink.

"Not going to tell me? What the hell!? You're going to tell me or we are done here." I smile through my words, watching his eyes as they study my lips from across the table while I take a sip from my straw. *I think he's into me.*

"I'll tell you on one condition..."

"What's that?" I ask, curious of his condition.

He leans in and whispers. "Show me how you did that trick with the money at the parking lot and I'll tell you."

I giggle a little too pitchy for my own liking and nod. I scoot closer so we are sitting side by side, pulling a dollar out of my wallet.

"Give me any bill you have, higher than a single," I say. He gives it to me with reluctance. It's a ten dollar bill with a woman on the face of the bill and I narrow my eyes at him, suspicious of the money.

"Is this fake?" I ask.

"What?" He looks down and takes the bill from my hands, replacing it with a different ten dollar bill and after a few tries of folding and coordination between his hands, he begins to make the trick work.

"How do you know how to do this? *Why* do you know this?" he asks, trying the trick again while I guide his hands.

"Wanna see a card trick?" I ask, ignoring his question as I pull a deck of red playing cards from my purse.

He arches his eye brow as if to say "yes", and I begin to shuffle the cards. They filter from one hand to the next, and I hold half the stack high in one hand, letting it fall in a cascading rush to my other hand in perfect formation.

"If you want more, you're going to have to come to one of my shows. Pick a card." I fan the deck out onto the table and turn my head away while he chooses.

He watches me with the cards as I shuffle them again and pick out a card. "How the fuck did you do that?" he says, staring at the deck like he is trying to figure out how the card he picked without me watching is somehow the one I keep choosing from the deck. He wants more, they always do. But like I said with the attendant at the parking lot, mamas gotta pay them bills.

"Have any change?" I hold out my hand palm up for him to give me whatever change he has in his wallet. He stands, digging his hand into his pocket and pulls out a few quarters and places them in the center of my palm. I make all of them disappear and reappear behind his ear like an old grandpa with a young gullible grandchild.

"So, it's your turn. What does this make you do?" I say, stacking the cards in a neat pile, pushing them to the side and lifting my margarita in the air towards him. I lower it to my lips and he focuses on them.

"The first time..." he says, meeting my gaze. He takes the cards and shuffles them in the most unorganized fashion. "I was outside a closed liquor store and wanted to get more. I was banging on the door, shaking the handle," he mimics with his hands, "and scaring the shit out of some poor night stock clerk who called the police!"

My hands go to my mouth as I laugh. "And the second time?" I ask.

He takes a deep breath in and tilts his head to the side. "The second time...I don't want to say." He smiles but turns his head away from me.

"Tell me or I'm changing all the money in your wallet to dust."

He chuckles as he turns his head back to me, dipping his body in towards mine. "I met a girl at a bar and we got caught in my car," he whispers, leaning back in his chair content with the small nugget of an answer he gave me.

"Doing what? Were you adjusting that sticking seatbelt for her?" I smirk while Reagan's cheeks begin to expand with a red tint. He nods as he takes another sip of his drink.

"What was the third charge for?"

His eyes lose their glimmer and his shoulders pull down as if he was hoping the Q & A about his drinking habits was over.

"The third time..." he turns his head from me to watch the TV above the bar then returns his gaze to mine. His flirtatious smile gone. "I'd rather not kill the mood with it." He looks away and takes his glass to his lips with only ice cubes remaining.

"Oh, the mood?" I grin. "What mood is that?" I ask.

His eyes light back up and study me without a response. He's grinning again and I kinda like it, and I kinda don't. I take the playing cards from his side of the table and shuffle them, doing a few more card tricks, putting Reagan in a state of awe. I get a lot of surprised faces when I do magic, but his reactions feel different to me.

"You're beeping," I say, pointing towards his waistband glowing against his shirt. He looks down and the smile that was racing across his face just seconds ago during my card trick has vanished upon looking up.

"Shit," he mutters, "I gotta go."

The disappointment I feel from his words makes my next sip of margarita taste bitter. He stands, shifting his eyes down towards his waist and back up to me in quick spurts.

"Raincheck?" he asks. His eyes boyish and sweet in their expectant way awaiting my answer.

A raincheck on getting sloppy drunk by myself with a man I barely know who bailed my car out of tow on my birthday? *I think not,* my instinct quips.

He probably has a wife and kids to get back to at home. Look at how nervous he is.

"Sure, why not." I'm pretty sure I just rolled my eyes in the most dramatic way. He ignores my dismissive reply.

"I'm serious. Raincheck?" he asks again, putting cash on the table and sliding it towards me, closing his wallet.

God, he could at least buy me one more drink before he does that thing with his eyes. That thing he's been doing all night. It's making it hard to keep a straight face.

"Earth to Harper?"

"Yes, raincheck, yes."

He gives me a knowing grin. "I'll call you."

I shake my head, watching him make his way towards the exit. I watch other females watch him make his way towards the exit. Of all the people who could have offered me a ride, paid my tow charge and bought me a drink out of guilt on my birthday, I must say, I didn't do too bad.

"Wait!" I run towards the door as it's about to close. "Reagan..." I yell, panting as I run towards him.

I should not be running. How did he get so far, so fast?

He turns around with a half smile, waiting for me catch my breath.

"You...don't...have...my..." I hold up my index finger. "Number."

His smile grows like he was waiting for me to connect the dots. I dig in my purse for one of my business cards and hand it to him.

"Houdini Harper?" He looks up, smirk intact.

"Shut up!" I say. I'm still trying to catch my breath.

He belly laughs, studying the business card again. "I'll call you later this week. Are you free this weekend?"

I almost say I'm free anytime he wants me to be with those eyes doing that thing again, but what kind of girl would that make me? *What am I saying?* I'm the kind of girl who's going home to swoon over a book boyfriend and a magician in love with a supermodel. I'm *that* kind of girl. *Free as fuck.*

"Do you have plans Friday?" I ask, coming out of my stupor. "I have a performance...if you want to come see me in action." The silence between my words and his response is one hundred times longer than I expect. He clears his throat, maintaining that look with his eyes that's been doing things to me all night.

"In action?" he asks. "Okay, Houdini."

I've always been confident and proud with my chosen profession, but right now, I feel like a heel. He gives my card one more glance and motions to his pager and then his car while I follow him. He's parked next to mine.

"You sure you and D.C. are gonna make it home in one piece?" He points to my now unhinged lopsided passenger door.

I nod and then cringe on the inside, cursing D.C. for humiliating me. I walk over to my car of shame while Reagan gets into his. His car *that doesn't* have a door betraying him.

His smug passenger door catches my eye as his car rolls closer. He waves as he passes me while I struggle to adjust my door. His brake lights illuminate, and his car begins to back up towards mine. He gets out of his car and stands next to me, holding my door steady while I adjust the hinge.

"Thanks," I utter with embarrassment laced over every inch of my being. His hands press against the door, making sure it's going to stay.

"I can help you get this fixed," he says as he watches me push against the hinge of the door, and lets out an exhausted sigh.

"Were you just sent here from heaven?" I ask.

"Why, because I look like an angel?" he asks.

Did I… just use a cheesy pickup line by accident?

Did he just complete the cheesy pickup line I used by accident?

"Are you religious?" If he doesn't get my humor and know where I am going with this, I can just say goodbye to that raincheck.

"Because I just answered your prayers?"

We're really doing this? We're really having a pickup line throw down in a bar parking lot?

I place my hand on the upper blade of his back and rub.

"You thought angels had wings?" he asks.

Yep, we're doing this.

"Harper?"

I haven't stopped rubbing his back.

"Yeah?" My voice is husky as I stare at my hand glide over his back, reluctant to meet his eyes.

He takes a hesitant breath in. "I have to go."

I nod, eyes glazed, giddiness in my "okay" back to him before removing my hand.

"I'll call you." He waits for me to confirm and walks back, getting into his car.

I get in my car and drive home singing at the top of my lungs like Whitney Houston and I are soul sisters duetting in an epic one time only performance.

Chapter 4
Reagan 1993

The number that paged me was a six and a zero, which is code meaning I need to leave whatever I am doing or "*GO*" as the numbers spell out, per Gus. I do go. I leave the bar, waving to Harper from my car and head to see Mary from the restaurant. I should feel guilty about the fact that I called her from the bar while I was with Harper, and I kinda did when I returned to the table. I kinda felt guilty when I kissed Mary at her apartment and when we went into the bedroom because her roommate came home. But I felt the guiltiest when each kiss, tug and pull came and went with only one thought.

Harper.

"You were supposed to be here two hours ago! Didn't you get my page?"

When I get in the door, I'm met with a tired, grey-haired black man standing in the doorway of my bedroom with smoke billowing from his ears. That would be pissed off Gus. The one I knew would be waiting for me.

Was it worth it? Well, yeah. Minus the head trip I had the whole time with thoughts of Harper's laugh, her lips sipping her drink and her hands touching mine during her magic trick instructions.

"Reagan, you're going back to the office tomorrow, to regroup," Gus says.

I knew this was coming.

The office. The dingy confines of my fellow parolees who are in trouble like me and their less than enthused supervisors, all of which look like this time travel thing is a boring routine. For me, this is anything but boring. I'm a sci-fi nerd. You know...X-files, Star-trek, Battlestar Galactica? And right now, I'm literally Sam Beckett from Quantum Leap with Gus as my Al!

Gus and I arrive at the office, which is disguised as a library, just before 10 a.m. where a few others are waiting for the doors to open. From the outside, it looks like just another old library. We stand making small talk with the people outside until the doors open and we file our way in, heading towards the periodicals in the fiction section. No one is ever there. Don't believe me? Go to your local library and look for yourself. Empty. Well, with the exception of the old man sitting in a chair with noise cancelling headphones on, pecking away at a laptop one finger at a time.

We stand by a door near the end of one of the racks. Gus slides a white security badge over a sensor that opens the door to an elevator. Once inside the cabin, he pushes a button for the basement and we descend.

"You know, this is for your own good, right?" Gus leans in towards me with a father-to-son kind of stare. "This is your last case, Reagan. After this, you're done. I don't want you to mess this up because you can't resist a pretty face and control the need to get your dick wet."

I nod, and I know. This is my last one, probably the toughest one, and the fact that I'm already having feelings connecting me to Harper isn't making it any easier.

"The rules...." Harper's file is slammed down on the table in front of me by Gus, who takes a seat to my right and across the table from Barney Ballzer, the head of the Timer division who continues to speak.

"I hear you need a *refresher*? A little *reminder* in regards to *priorities* while on the job?" He's asking me but *I'm pretty sure he isn't going to care for my response.*

"I guess."

Wrong answer.

"You guess?! Tell me, who is ...Mary?"

"Mary is..."

"A girl you got to know quite well in a phone booth yesterday! Kelly?" He looks at me for a response but continues to list names without hesitating in the slightest at my attempts in speaking. "Megan?" he continues.

He's really going to go through all of them, huh?

"Michelle?"

I tilt my head with regret on that one.

"Tori?"

Shit. I probably do need to slow it down.

"This isn't a free for all, Reagan. You signed up for this. *This* case specifically. If you want to finish out your probation and stop seeing my ugly mug every six weeks, and his..." He gestures to Gus who resembles a stone-faced statue. "You need to follow the rules."

Barney stands in his grey suit, exposing deep wrinkles in the legs and walks towards a screen that illuminates. *The Rules.* A list displays at the top in big, black, unmistakable, *we are going to go through all of these,* CAPITAL letters.

You know when you were younger on summer break and your parents wrote out a list of chores for you to do each day you were off? You groaned and felt the bubbling of angst in your gut, right? That's me right now.

"Number one." He begins with his grey eyebrows furrowed. "No getting personal or *fraternizing* with anyone during your travel. NO ONE, Reagan! No kissing, no rubbing, no hugging, and for your sake, probably no smiling or doing that *shit* with your eyes!"

I begin to defend my fraternizing choices only to have my words clipped with the next rule being spoken.

"Number two." His voice fluxes. "No bringing contraband with you. I don't want to see you trying to smuggle Hostess Turtle Pies or Bill and Ted's Excellent Cereal in like you did last time!"

What?

They're fucking good!

"Number *three.* No prolonging the assignment. Get in, do your job, get out!"

Some cases aren't a problem. Like my job as a sanitation worker where I helped a guy who fell asleep in a dumpster from being crushed by a trash truck. I couldn't wait to get out of that one. Or working in a nursing home during a heat wave when the power went out and I stopped a sweet older lady from choking. That one was just a heartbreaker.

"Number four. No looking up relatives or loved ones."

Not a problem. They all hate me.

"Number five. No sharing future events or hints about the present *being before your time,* Mr. Nirvana!"

Yeah, I'm an idiot.

"Finally, if I wouldn't do it, *you* shouldn't do it either." His eyes are bulging towards me during the last part.

I imagine there is a lot Barney wouldn't do, which depresses me. He steps away from the screen and takes a seat across from me at the table, leaning in.

"We aren't against you, Reagan. We want you to succeed in this. Once you're done and back home, fraternize all you want, but until then, keep it zipped."

We review Harper's case file and Barney reminds me of the deadline to get it done. Three more months. That's it. He also gives me a sobering reminder in the form of pictures that show my mangled car in an intersection. That day changed everything.

"*This* is what got you here." He points his finger to my car in the picture. "And *this*..." He touches the picture of Harper. "...is what is going to get you out of here. Focus."

I should be thinking about the rules and how I need to get my shit together, but after seeing Harper's case file photos, she's all I'm thinking about. That and my jacket probably still sitting in the back seat of the death trap she calls a car.

I drop Gus off at work, promising to be on time to pick him up and head home to sleep. But there is no sleep. I read through more of Harper's file, the notes I have from the last two months I've been here planting roots, and the pictures. I pull her card from my wallet and chuckle at her name, debating if it's too soon to call.

I don't debate long. I pick up the phone and dial her number, only to get her answering machine.

"Houdini Harper, this is Reagan, your... serial killer. You have my jacket hostage and I was wondering if we could negotiate for its release. I really don't know what I'm saying right now....so...call me." Click.

Guess who's leaving another message because he didn't leave his phone number?

"Harper, so I guess I should give you my number...so *you*... can... call... me... It's Reagan... again, by the way."

Jesus.

I leave both my home phone and pager. And I wait. It's only one hour later when she calls back, and I have to say, I feel nervous, like it's the first time a girl has ever called me. My stomach is tight and my palms are sweating. I'm smiling when she talks...I'm smiling when I talk.

I'm in trouble.

"Come over any time after five to get your hostage," she says.

I can almost see the curl of her lips when she talks.

"The ransom is coming to my show Friday," she continues.

She's a smartass, just like me, and I really like it.

I know I'm at the right place when I see her car outside, passenger door still intact with the addition of duct tape at the hinge. I peer in the backseat but don't see my jacket.

Harper lives in the bottom floor apartment of a house with a private entrance that I walk through, glancing into the main house windows as I pass them. I hear the murmurs of a child talking when I knock. A little boy with blonde hair and dark eyes opens the door staring at me until Harper comes rushing towards him.

"You shouldn't just open the door without asking who it is," she scolds. He looks exactly like her.

"Sorry, come in...come in." She ushers me in with her hand while the little boy holds onto her leg. "This is my nephew Bryson. Can you say hi, Bry?" She stares down at him, and he retracts further into his hold on her leg when I greet him.

"I'm Reagan," I say, bending down to his level and holding my hand out. Bryson turns away but turns his head back to face me after a few seconds.

"He's shy. My brother is supposed to be here to get him, but he's running late. Have you eaten? Are you hungry?" Her voice trails as she walks around the corner. I follow her into the kitchen.

I shrug, taking a seat on a barstool and notice Hostess turtle pies on her counter. Her eyes follow mine and she grins, sliding one towards me.

"You want one? Bryson loves those! I always have them around."

I may already be in love with this woman.

I open the pie and soon have a little shadow sitting next to me. I nudge my head, as if asking if it's okay to share, and Harper nudges her head back at me in the same way.

Bryson and me? We're best friends now.

The doorbell rings and Bryson hops off the stool, running towards the door with Harper trailing after and yelling, "Ask who it is first. Ask who it is."

I step out of the kitchen and watch her grab a backpack and a few stuffed toys. Her hair is tied back in a ponytail that shows off the sculpted curve of her shoulders and neck.

I want to kiss that neck.

"You sure you got everything?" She zips Bryson's backpack, handing it to him and he nods, shrugging the straps onto his little shoulders. He turns his head back towards me and Harper coaxes him. "Say thank you to Reagan for sharing the pie."

She nudges him on his back and I step closer, bending down to a squat, and tell him, "anytime," reaching my hand out for a high five which my new best friend slaps with a proud grin. I make eye contact with the man in the doorway as I stand back up and I recognize him as Harper's brother from her case file. He looks surprised to see me, like we've met somewhere.

"Who's your friend, Harper?" He doesn't look at her when he asks, only me.

"Reagan, this is my brother Chad. Chad, this is Reagan. He's the guy who helped me with my car last night." Chad narrows his eyes towards me and shakes my hand.

"Nice to meet you, sir," I say while noticing the subtle resemblance between him and Harper. Same fair skin and dark eyes. Harper has more of a strawberry blonde color to her hair, while Chad's is all blonde.

"Reagan." He continues to study me. "You know, Harper doesn't have many people over. We're having a small celebration for her birthday Saturday night. You should come."

"Oh, I don't want to intrude..."

"No, no...no intrusion. It'll be here at the house." He points outside the door to the backyard. "Come. We'll barbeque. It'll be fun."

I glance at Harper who looks like she's thinking about the best way to kill her brother. "Maybe I'll swing by," I say, trying to contain my satisfaction in being invited.

"Good. Harper, see you tomorrow. Say bye, Bryson." Both of them wave as they begin to walk towards the main house. Harper waves back until they turn a corner and she closes the door.

"You don't have to come. It's stupid. They forgot my birthday and feel guilty so their making up for it with a party I don't even want." She walks towards the couch, clearing off a few toys. "You wanna sit?" she asks.

"Are you uninviting me? Because I'm pretty sure I got a solid invitation from the host himself."

She shakes her head and clears her throat as if to clear the misunderstanding. "You're still invited, but don't feel obligated. It's just my family. They're so ...*involved* when it comes to people in my life."

I take a seat next to her while she grabs the remote from a small bowl on the coffee table in front of us, turning the TV on and flipping through the channels.

"You're brother lives upstairs in the main house?" I ask, and she nods, turning the channel to MTV. I hear her answer, but I fall short on returning her words when I realize I'm watching *actual* videos on MTV. They *actually* used to play videos!

"You like Snoop and Dr. Dre?" she asks, with a hint of a smirk as she repeats the lyrics from the video now playing on the TV. I can't help but laugh.

"I'm so offended right now," I say with my hand to my chest, feigning shock. "Did you just say you're *mobbin like a mothafucka*?" I laugh even harder as she shakes her head yes and keeps singing. She's pretty damn adorable right now.

The song ends and she laughs at herself, apologizing. "I'm... sorry for my sudden G-ness."

"I'm... sorry for my total whiteness," I say, "and my lack of knowledge when it comes to Dr. Dre." The video ends with commercials for the Real World Season 2.

And so it begins. Goodbye videos.

"Can I use your restroom?" I ask.

Harper points towards a small hallway. The bathroom is at the end of the hall and I pass two rooms with open doors before getting to it. Her bedroom is one and the other has a staircase leading down with a light on at the bottom. I don't snoop, but I do see a table with a red velvet table cloth hanging over it that makes me curious.

"I couldn't help but notice the room you have with stairs. Is that a basement?" I ask when I take a seat back on the couch, trying to sound nonchalant like I wasn't at all totally and completely scoping out her place.

"It's where the magic happens. You wanna see?" She wiggles her brows up and down.

I'm pretty sure the "*magic*" happens in the bedroom, but with this girl, it could happen in a basement. I'm game. I follow her down the stairs to the basement which has a few tables covered in red velvet tablecloths. A set of linked metal rings sit on top of one table, rope and a black top hat sit on another. A few silk scarfs are tied to a high backed chair, and handcuffs with a deck of cards lay on the edge of another.

She wasn't kidding. This *is* where the magic happens.

She shows me some tricks with the steel rings that somehow intersect even though there are no breaks in either of them. She shows me another trick with a scarf that turns into an egg in her hand, and she shows me how a cut rope can be made whole with a few magic words. It's pretty impressive.

"You wanna handcuff me to this chair?" she asks.

I do a clear double take at the question, speechless and wide eyed as she repeats.

"You wanna handcuff me to this chair?" she asks again, raising her eyebrows up and down.

She sits in the chair and puts her hands behind her back. "Grab those handcuffs on the table over there." She wiggles her wrists for me to cuff them.

I hold the cuffs, feeling their weight and have a flashback to my own experiences with these. They're police grade and look legit.

"Put them on as tight as you can," she says with a small smirk.

I walk behind her and bend down to put the cuffs on, squeezing them tight. Then I walk towards the front of her, watching her arms struggle and pull until seconds later, she has the cuffs dangling open from one wrist.

"How'd you do that? Can you show me?" I ask, knowing this could very well come into some practical use in the future.

She gets up and has me sit in the chair. "Put your hands behind your back," she orders, mocking authority.

Hmm...familiar words.

I do as I'm told, but instead of walking around the chair to put the cuffs on, she straddles my lap. I hold my breath when she leans into me to attach the cuffs on my wrists. She doesn't lift off of me. I swallow hard, breathing in and out in the most unnatural way, but I try to look in control while my heart races.

"What's the *first thing* you wanna do right now?" She locks eyes with mine, waiting for an answer.

I'm not a speechless guy, especially with women, but right now, I couldn't even tell you my *fucking* name.

She giggles at my silence, leaning into me again and putting an open bobby pin in one of my hands. Her face is grazing my neck as she guides my fingers on where to hold the bobby pin. I'm pretty sure this isn't the best way to teach me, but I'm also pretty sure I would be willing to learn anything she wants to teach me like this.

"Do you feel how I'm moving it?" she asks.

I feel a lot of things...moving.

I nod, taking in the scent from her perfume. It's like flowers and vanilla.

The cuffs unlatch behind me, and I bring them to the front between her and I.

"You wanna try again?" she asks.

No words still, just another slow head nod from me. She leans in once more placing the cuffs on my wrists, securing them in place. I hold the bobby pin in my fingers, trying to mimic her movements. She's studying my lips, my eyes and my grunts that continue to make her smirk.

"You're enjoying this aren't you?" I ask as my arms shift.

"I am," she whispers.

It's almost too much for me to hold back kissing her while we are this close. Her lips are a beautiful shade of pink, plump and kissable. My hands soften, defeated, still in cuffs and I let out a heavy sigh.

"I can't do it."

She releases her hands from behind me, fanning them flat on her thighs. She tilts her head towards the door and returns her gaze back to me.

"If I locked that door up there and left you in here. I bet you could do it."

"You gonna lock me in your basement?" I ask, but my smile fades from the look she's giving back to me. It's my look.

My fucking look!

Her hands grasp my neck on both sides and her fingers feather my hair up in the back while my eyes flutter closed waiting for the impact of her lips. I have been in some weird predicaments, but this is by far the most exciting one. I feel her breath close to my lips.

God I want her to kiss me. Please, please kiss me, Harper.

She hovers over them and I open my eyes. She's looking down at my lips and then back up. I grin into her smile.

"Harper?" A voice calls from upstairs. It's a female, and it seems to stun Harper when she recognizes it.

"Shit!" She lifts from my lap, scrambling like she is forgetting something to the right, then to the left. "I'll be right back."

"You're not gonna leave me like this are you?" I ask. Heat builds in my neck with the tingling feeling of being caught doing something wrong that I didn't even know I was doing.

"I'll be right back. I promise," she whispers, shushing me.

"Harper?" I shift in my seat trying to lean forward with the legs of the chair hitting the floor. "Harper!" I whisper louder. "You can't just leave me here. Unlock me!"

"I'll be right back." She climbs the stairs and turns around before reaching the door, holding her hands in front of her, pressing downward in the air. "I'm sorry," she whispers, shutting the basement door behind her, locking it.

"What the...what?!"

Chapter 5
Harper 1993

My mother never uses the doorbell or knocks. She walks right in like the place is still hers. Well, technically it is still hers, but *boundaries* are something she doesn't understand. My personal space is invalid. She's talking about the party we are having Saturday.

There's a man handcuffed in my basement.

She's telling me about the food she wants to serve.

There is a MAN handcuffed in my basement.

She's pacing the living room, asking me if this person and that person are okay to invite.

There is a FUCKING MAN HANDCUFFED IN MY BASEMENT!

"Are you all right, Harper? You look a little flush." My mom stares at me, pursing her lips and tipping her head to the side.

"I'm fine," I say. Other than the really cute guy I've known for only two days and almost kissed just now who's handcuffed to a chair in my basement against his will while my mother yammers on about appetizers. I'm totally fine.

Totally fine.

"We want to have the party tents surrounding the gazebo. Let's go look at the backyard." She reaches for my hand, pulling me towards the door.

"Give me just a second, let me get something." I loosen from her and gesture towards my room.

"Harper, it will only take a second. Come. Let's have a look-see real quick. I need to call the caterer back on the head count." She grabs my hand again, pulling once more towards the door which I leave wide open with a quick glance back at the locked basement door.

Shit.

We discuss tents, headcounts and music in the backyard. My mother wants my opinion on each and every detail, although I know she already has her mind made up. I would have agreed to circus clowns serving hot dogs on sticks to speed this along. My mother sees my impatience and releases me while she talks to Chad who seems to have appeared out of nowhere, about a bouncy house for Bryson.

Because this party is for me, right?

I hurry back to my apartment, door still open and basement door still locked. I open it to find Reagan still sitting in the chair. He looks *so mad* right now, with his jaw clenched and his gaze burning through me... and it's so hot for some reason.

"I'm so sorry," I say as I run down the stairs, letting out an apologetic laugh that I cover with my hands. "I'm so sorry, Reagan." I lean down towards the handcuffs behind his back and remove them. But he doesn't stand. He holds his hands in front of him, rubbing his wrists and glares. I can only repeat myself. "I'm so sorry."

"Was that your mother?" His question surprises me. He doesn't ask why I left him there or why I didn't unlock him. He rubs his wrists a few more times, and I nod my head still trying to gauge his pissed-offness.

He nods back and stands avoiding eye contact. "I should probably go," he says, meeting my gaze.

"I'm so sorry," I say again.

He walks up the stairs with me behind him and towards the front door to leave but he turns around to face me before opening the door. He forces a smile and I trail my focus from the middle of his shirt and up to his face, wanting him to stay. He's silent, staring at me.

"Do you have my jacket?"

I shake my head yes and hurry into my bedroom to get it, handing it to him, "I'm sorry." Our hands graze each other's in the exchange.

"It's okay, Harper. I've probably deserved to get locked in a basement for some time now." His smile is slight, and I let out a relieved laugh, touching his arm.

"Will you stay for a little bit? I'm so sorry. I wanna make it up to you. I was gonna watch this new show called X-files in a bit and order pizza. Do you like that show?"

Reagan's face lights up with a grin. He blinks fast a few times, and then his face falls to serious.

"I *fucking* love that show!"

Reagan is on the couch tugging the pizza box closer when I come in with two drinks, humming to the X-file theme song now blaring from the TV.

When I sit down, I notice a white faded scar on his arm I hadn't noticed before. It runs from his wrist all the way to his bicep in a pale white line. I don't say anything when our eyes meet, I just smile, taking my own slice of pizza from the box. I groan from how good it tastes. Reagan gives me a smirk, agreeing with his own groan a few seconds later.

He's the perfect TV companion. He knows to be quiet during the show and only talks during the commercials. When Chad watches with me he becomes a full on conspiracy nut, debunking every scene like he's an expert on paranormal activity.

"You like to read?" Reagan points to the bookshelf as I begin to clear the coffee table during a commercial. My bookshelf of shirtless book boyfriends, hot romances and scorned lovers on full display.

"*Yes*, I like to read."

He gives me a humored arch of his brow and gets up, pulling out a few of the books from the shelf. I hear him laugh when I walk towards the kitchen which makes me smile. I like his laugh. It's husky and endearing. I walk back in the room to see him still standing at the book shelf.

"Is this guy for real?" He chuckles while squinting at one of the covers with a tall, blonde man, his hair flowing back, shirt open, chest heaving out while pressing his lips to the bare shoulder of a dark haired maiden standing in front of him with her cleavage peeking out. The two are standing in a field. These covers always have them standing in a field.

"Oh, he's more than real!" I grab the book from his hand, giving it a memorable glance before putting it back on the shelf. He grabs another one and belly laughs. He continues to pull others from the shelf and laugh while I answer the phone and watch him, trying to stifle my own laughter.

I giggle into my "hello," but stop when I hear my mother on the other end of the line.

"Oh Harper, I didn't know you had a boy over earlier. I'm sorry for interrupting." Chad, the town gossip must have told her. "Who is he?"

I muffle my answer.

"Harper, he's not some random guy you met on the street is he? You need to be careful. Men these days are ...."

My mind trails off watching Reagan put my books back on the shelf before returning to sit on the couch while my mother gives me her usual advice about men. She's been married to my father for thirty years and didn't date anyone before him, but that's not even my issue. Her relationship advice is firmly rooted in the 1950's and my issue is the way she repressively uses the word *intercourse* over and over. The word, coming from her lips, makes pleasure sound painful and sterile. I fade back into her talking with the word intercourse being used and I cut her off.

"Mom, I need to let you go. I'll call you later."

"But sweetie..."

"Mom..."

"Okay Harper, you just be careful. Your father and I love you."

Before she can get herself wound up again, I end the call and take a seat on the couch. I want to ask what I missed because now I have no idea what's going on. Reagan fills me in during one of the commercials without me having to ask, and I am certain he *is* the perfect TV companion.

"My mom was asking all kinds of questions just now about you, and I don't even know the answers," I say while the credits roll on the TV.

"Well most serial killers, like myself, don't tend to give a lot of details."

His answer makes me smile.

"Well, you know what I do for a living, but what do you do?"

I curl my legs up towards me on the couch, grabbing a throw pillow for my hips to lean on. He looks hesitant to respond, like I've asked him something that takes thought, and I have to think for a minute about my question. Did I ask him what he did for a living or did I ask him to calculate the square footage of my living room?

"I work at a preschool three days a week." He says it in a way that sounds tender, like he's reflecting on innocence.

"Wow! I've never met a male preschool teacher before." I smack his shoulder, giving it a shove. He smiles at me and shakes his head, conceding with his hands raised.

"Bryson just started at one up the street, Tiny Tots?"

Reagan's eyebrows rise.

"YOU work there?"

He nods his head.

"I just started. I don't think I've seen Bryson there though. I mostly work with the three and four year olds right now."

The image in my mind of him working with little three and four year olds is setting my ovaries on *you must procreate with this man now*, mode. It also sets my mind at ease because I have no doubt I will be roped into another Q & A session with my mother about what Reagan does if he comes to the party Saturday. I excuse myself to the restroom, returning with the handcuffs in hand because I didn't get to teach him well, and I need the practice.

"I was wondering if you wanted to try this again?" I ask.

I sit down, holding the cuffs out like a peace offering with my wrists exposed. Reagan smirks, and without a second thought, he locks the handcuffs over my wrists in front of me. I hand him the bobby pin with my fingers and guide him on how to maneuver it in the keyhole.

Even though I'm trying to focus on the cuffs, I can't help watching how his tongue glimpses out onto his lip and how his cheeks fill and release. I watch his chest as he breathes and listen to the small noises curling in his throat as he tries to get the right angle. The cuffs finally unlatch.

"Try it on me now," he asks.

Gladly.

I lock them on his wrists and put the bobby pin in his fingers. He works the bobby pin towards the keyhole making defeated grunts.

Very *memorable* defeated grunts.

"I can't do it." But he keeps trying. I give him reassuring smiles when he looks up at me. I hold the cuffs steady for him while my thumb begins to graze over the white scar on his wrist. I roll my thumb further up his arm towards his bicep and back down until I realize his efforts to remove the cuffs have stopped, and he's staring at my fingers on his arm.

"What happened?" I ask.

He doesn't answer me right away, but I wait. Something about his pause is asking me to hold on.

"I shouldn't be telling you this." He takes a deep breath in.

"What is it?"

He rolls his eyes up to the ceiling and back down at his scar.

"I got in an accident a while back. It's kinda hard for me to talk about." He meets my gaze, and I nod my head in understanding.

"You don't have to tell me. I was just curious." I trail my hand down his arm one more time and hold his cuffed hands up, pressing my lips to his wrist where the scar begins, catching his gaze, smiling with apologies for the accident details I don't need to know.

"Harper..." he says as we lock eyes, and I feel my stomach stir, but his gaze falls to his waist where his pager is lighting up.

He sighs, lifting his wrists while the cuffs make a small clanking noise. I pick the lock which releases the cuffs, and hold them while he pulls his hands away, pressing his palms down, fingers spread out, on his jeans.

"Thanks for everything." He stands, nudging his head towards the pizza box and TV as I stand.

"Sorry for locking you in my basement." I apologize for the hundredth time which makes a surprised chuckle reverberate from his chest.

"It wasn't so bad. I mean, I got a free meal out of it."

I laugh. "True."

He grabs his jacket from the edge of the couch, walking towards the door. I wish he could stay longer. He stands with the door open and turns to face me, arms arched above in the doorway. "What time is your show Friday?"

I stare at his arms flexed, like he's holding the molding of the door in place.

"Seven. Oh, but wait a second." I grab a card from a glass table near the door. "You'll need this. It's a guest card. You can't get in without it."

"Do you have more than one? In case I want to bring a friend?"

If he brings a date I will soon be known as the magician who lost her shit on stage. "You bringing a date?"

He smirks and shakes his head no. "Just a friend, Houdini."

His arms fall to his sides with my card in one hand. "I'll see you Friday, then?" he asks.

I nod as we begin sharing a stare that's making my belly ache. I don't want to say goodnight. I want him to stay. He studies my face for a moment longer like he wants to kiss me, but he's holding back.

"Goodnight, Harper." He meets my eyes, reaching his hand to my neck, pulling me in and kisses my cheek, but then pulls away.

"Night."

He walks down the path towards the street, turning to wave once he gets to the end and I wave back, closing the door. I lean on the back of the door, sliding to the ground, holding the cuffs in my hand, exhaling with a huge grin on my face.

We have this new thing called America Online now. I can type a note on the computer, called an e-mail, and send it to a friend electronically within seconds, but mine has been down. It's kind of a problem since my email is listed on the new business cards I just had printed and have been handing out to everyone. I have my fellow magician, Mike, here to help me. He's a computer wizard among other things and promises to get my email working.

Mike sits in the desk chair hunched over, the sound of keyboard keys clacking while I check my snail mail (as they call it) at the counter behind him.

"Who's SnowDontFall@aol.com?" he asks, turning at his waist in the chair to look at me behind him.

My eyes widen when I step closer, staring at the screen to see the subject as "Serial Killer held in basement."

Holy crap!

"It's no one," I say, pushing him off the chair as I take a seat and open the e-mail.

Just wanted to see if this gets to you, Houdini. Because you've supposedly been dead for years. - Reagan.

I chuckle.

"What's so funny?" Mike asks.

I shrug his question off saying, "it's nothing" while I continue to smile and hit reply. Within seconds of replying a small Instant Message screen appears from SnowDontFall.

SnowDontFall: Hi.

HoudiniHarper: Hi.

SnowDontFall: Busy?

HoudiniHarper: Kinda. I have someone over fixing my computer.

SnowDontFall: I hope they don't ask about the basement.

HoudiniHarper: Funny.

SnowDontFall: Wanna chat later? When you uncuff your friend?

HoudiniHarper: Such a funny guy. Yes. I'll be done at 9.

SnowDontFall: OK. :)

"Who was that?" Mike asks.

I completely forgot he was still here. I wipe the stupid grin off my face and tell him about the other night.

"You could have called me, you know. I would have gotten you."

"Mike, *you* were my date. Remember how you didn't show up?"

"Oh, yeah." He recoils with an apologetic grimace.

How he forgot he stood me up is beyond me. He still hasn't said Happy Birthday either, even with his apology in the form of a new modem he brought with him today. He hovers over the side of the computer as I close the message screen.

"Sign out and turn off the computer one more time."

I sign out and shut the computer down, rolling back in my chair on the hardwood floors towards the kitchen from my desk as he bends down underneath it to grab the CPU. He brings it to the table in the kitchen like he's carrying an explosive about to detonate.

"You ready for Friday?" He glances up for my answer and then down at the open CPU with a furrowed brow, using a tiny screwdriver like an open-heart surgeon as he unscrews the modem. I fully expect to be called nurse and asked for a scalpel from the way his eyes are shifting to me and back down to his surgery in progress.

"I'm as ready as I'll ever be," I say.

"I'm pretty excited to have you as my assistant." He's beaming as he says this.

I'm going to be his assistant on a trick where I'm the girl who gets sawed in half. I think he's more excited about what I'll be wearing. All his other assistants refused to wear it after the first time. The outfit? Let's just say it involves booty shorts and fishnet stockings.

Yep.

Mike has the kindest heart, but he's also a total guy which means he loves a pretty face and a nice ass. Mine to be more specific, even though I have zero interest in him. He's the first person I met at magic school when I quit college to be a magician. He made a point to say hi to me the first day during one of the lessons, and we've been close ever since. Of course, he would like to be closer.

When surgery has been declared a success, he puts my computer back together and tests it to make sure everything is working. We decide to run through our routine a few times and head to the basement. The trip to the basement this time though, is nothing like it was before with me handcuffing Reagan to a chair...and locking him inside.

God that was funny.

It's almost nine o'clock and I'm antsy for Mike to leave. He can tell too because I'm trying to rush him along in his monologue, and he's taking his sweet ass time releasing me from the box he just sawed. He finally lets me loose and gathers his things in a backpack he brought. I resist the urge to help him pack faster. He walks upstairs, taking each step slower than the last, as I follow a little too close behind. He looks back, grinning at my impatience.

"You want a piggyback ride?"

I guess I am following him a little too close.

When we get to my front door, he opens it but lingers in the doorway. I already know what he is going to say. He wants to ask me out *again*. I can tell from the way he's looking down with a shy smile and then back at me. I hate being the rejecter who has a heart. It makes every part of me feel like an asshole saying no thank you to his advances. An honest asshole.

"We should go out again. Catch a movie. I can make up for the birthday dinner I botched." He reaches his hand towards my cheek giving it a gentle caress, tilting his head in towards mine to kiss me. I flinch away, trying to be subtle and his lips press to my cheek by default. He pulls his hand away, standing back, dejected. *I hate this.*

"I'm sorry," I say.

I try to smooth over my abrupt rejection to his kiss, again. "I don't want to ruin our friendship. We have to work together and it's good right now. You and me? We're good together...like this." I say, gesturing to him and me.

He smiles, casting his eyes down towards the ground and back up at me. He probably wants to take back the kindness he offered in modem form right about now.

"I'll see you at six tomorrow?" I ask.

He nods. "I'll see you tomorrow, Harp."

I shut the door and notice the time. It's already well after nine. I turn on my computer and wait a solid ten minutes for my new modem to connect to one of the five numbers I have to choose from. All taking their precious time connecting until one succeeds. The sweet words, "Welcome! You've Got Mail!" greet me while I check to see if Reagan is online. I find his name and my heart flutters. Before I can send a message to him, he's already on my screen.

SnowDontFall: Hi. Free?

HoudiniHarper: Yes.

SnowDontFall: I was thinking about you today.

HoudiniHarper: Um?

SnowDontFall: I got locked out of my apartment and I thought if you were there with me, you'd probably know how to pick the lock.

HoudiniHarper: I do actually.

SnowDontFall: I knew it!

HoudiniHarper: What does your screen name mean?

SnowDontFall: It's sort of a joke my friends say.

HoudiniHarper: ?

SnowDontFall: Snow (my last name) don't fall (in love). I don't fall in love. I sound like an asshole right now.

HoudiniHarper: Why don't you? Fall in love?

SnowDontFall: Just never have.

HoudiniHarper: That sounds sad.

SnowDontFall: It's not as sad as it sounds.

HoudiniHarper: Never been in love? Really?

SnowDontFall: Well, I mean, there are a lot of things I've done that feel like love...

HoudiniHarper: Classy, Reagan.

SnowDontFall: Honest, Harper.

HoudiniHarper: Too honest.

SnowDontFall: There's no such thing.

HoudiniHarper: Spoken like a true guy.

SnowDontFall: What are you wearing? (Is that true guy enough for you?)

HoudiniHarper: I wish you could see my eyes rolling.

SnowDontFall: Me too.

ERROR: CONNECTION TO SERVER LOST

My new modem is an asshole.

Chapter 6

Reagan 1993

We've been chatting off and on for five hours when I finally say goodnight. I need to have something that resembles a coherent thought when I get to work later. Even if I do only work with toddlers who love my sleepy, babbling voice.

The toddlers were all amped today, which meant there was no downtime for me. Tired or not, I had to pretend to be alert. The only thing that kept me fueled were my thoughts rolling back over my conversations with Harper. She asked about my family, and I tried to be vague. It's usually not a problem to give short answers or deflect, but I don't want to with her. For the first time in a long time, I want to be honest with a woman.

We related to each other in being the black sheep because of our life choices. I didn't tell her why my last trip to jail made my family want to disown me. It's probably the only thing I'll keep to myself right now until the time is right, if it ever is; but I did share, maybe overshare, about my love life to which she found endless amusement. I could almost hear her laughter through the screen. She's the only girl I know who finds my sexcapades hilarious. Most find it despicable. She's had a few boyfriends, but her experiences are nothing like mine. She's the real deal. The guys in her past who broke her heart make me jealous for the time they had with her.

The last few kids are waiting to be picked up as I walk past the front playroom towards the time clock to punch out. I peek through the window of the playroom where I see a familiar little blonde. I enter and take a seat in the middle of the floor, holding a foam basketball. I'm like a magnet for the kids when I do this.

Bryson sees me and gives me a shy recognizing grin. I toss the ball into a basketball net near him and he retrieves it, jumping up to make his own shot. He throws it to me and I throw it into the net once more, making him clap and try for himself again. We do this a few times until the door opens with Harper peering in to see Bryson in a full mini Michael Jordan leap.

"Bry?" His face lights up, and he drops the ball to run to her, squeezing her tight. She sees me and I stand to greet her.

"Hi."

God, she looks good.

"Hey," she says, like every secret I've shared with her is written all over my face.

"You taking Bryson today?" I ask. I focus on the way her lips curl as she nods, looking over at Bryson and back at me. Any fatigue I had has vanished at the sight of her.

"You look beautiful today." I shouldn't have said that, but she does.

She flushes and says, "Thanks."

"Can we go now?" Bryson asks. He adjusts his backpack over his shoulders like it's restricting his movements. Harper brushes her hand over the top of his head when she nods, grabbing hold of his hand. We stand there, silent while the few kids left scream and circle around us as I hold the ball out of reach above my head.

"You gonna be online later?" she asks.

"I can be." I smirk, arching my brow which makes her chuckle.

Bryson tugs her hand. "I wanna go," he says, and she nods again, almost feverish this time.

"I'll talk to you later then," she says with a wink, and I hold my breath when she opens the door and looks back over her shoulder before it closes.

God, those eyes.

I watch out of the playroom window, waving at him, but I'm really staring at her.

"You can put your tongue back in your mouth now, Romeo," says one of the aides.

Romeo? That's a new one. I haven't heard that before. It surprises me, so I mentally add it to the list of names I've been called.

"She's not your type," says another aide.

Not my type? She couldn't be more my type if the sweet baby Jesus himself asked me what I wanted.

Jealous bitches.

Gus is on the computer when I get home, so like the asshole I am, I lift the house phone receiver from my room which disconnects his connection to the internet. I can hear him swearing from my bedroom as I change into pajama pants.

Gus calls from the couch with the TV remote in his hands when I walk into the room and over to the desk, pulling my shirt on. “You’re playing with her heart, Reagan.”

“I’m not playing with her.”

Gus smacks the remote a few times in his hands trying to get it to work. “What do you call it then?” He puts the remote down on his leg, gripping it and focusing his full attention on me. “You think when this is all over she’s just going to be fine with never seeing you again?” He slaps the remote on his pant leg as he talks.

I walk to the edge of the couch with my hands planted on the sides of my waist. “It’s my job to get close to her, isn’t it?”

He looks away, dismissing my answer and begins to aim the remote at the TV again, pressing the power button. “Not with the chat I just saw from last night it isn’t.”

I take a seat next to him on the couch, watching him and the remote battle for dominance. The TV illuminates to a commercial. Satisfied, he sets the remote on the couch between us and gives me the stare of a disapproving father. I humor him with a wide eyed stare back, shrugging my shoulders.

“What do I do, Gus?”

He narrows his eyes. “Tell her you have a girlfriend or you just got out of a bad relationship. Tell her your wife won’t be happy. Tell her you’re gay! But please, don’t mess around with this poor girl’s heart. You’ll break her. You’ll shatter her.” He pauses, letting his words sink in. “Distance yourself, Reagan. Stop chatting. No going over to her place. No getting handcuffed to a chair.” He turns his head towards the TV like it's settled. We're done.

God, this big brother shit sucks, but even with it happening, I can't stop. I don't want to distance myself. *Did I say we were done?* Gus turns in to face me, leaning his arm over his leg, and I know he's far from done.

"There's no happy ending here if you continue. There isn't a white picket fence with kids running around in front or a sunset you two run off into," he continues. "You're gonna break her heart."

That's the last thing I want to do. For the first time in a long time, I'm hopeful. I don't want to think about how this can't work.

Like the good listener I am, I wait until Gus leaves for work before I log on. Harper sent me an email with just a picture. I smile when the picture downloads and reveals...handcuffs. I go into chat rooms to pass the time until she logs on. One in particular is about time travel. Only one guy has it right, and he's the guy everyone hates. *Go figure.* I almost want to send him a message to say he's right.

HoudiniHarper: Miss me?

SnowDontFall: More than you know.

HoudiniHarper: You still coming to my show tomorrow?

SnowDontFall: Wouldn't miss it.

We chat again for a solid five hours. It's like time stands still until I talk to her, but when I do, the time slips through an hourglass on warp speed.

SnowDontFall: You ever had a one night stand?

HoudiniHarper: Yes, but it didn't go so well. You ever?

SnowDontFall: Um...quite a few. I'm not proud. Well, I take that back. I'm kinda proud of some of it.

HoudiniHarper: Classy Reagan.

SnowDontFall: Sorry, Just being honest. What didn't go well with yours?

HoudiniHarper: Lots of things. Mostly me. The last one sorta changed my way of handling one night stands. I met this guy at a party. Super hot guy. Sweet, funny. He said all the right things.

SnowDontFall: Like me? :)

HoudiniHarper: Yes, exactly like you. Anyway...we went back to my place. I had the most amazing sex of my life with him. Fell asleep in his arms, the whole deal. I woke up and he was gone so I called him. No call back. Thought I would see him again at a party or two. Nothing. Called again. No call back. I felt really desperate and just horrible. Like I completely betrayed myself by letting him in (literally). I heard from him three weeks later and we went to dinner. I was so happy to see him and after dinner he told me he was getting back together with his ex. We could still be friends though. Yeah. No thanks. I felt stupid. This isn't the first time a one nighter has turned out like this.

SnowDontFall: Damn. I'm sorry Harper. I wouldn't do that do you, except for the amazing sex part. ;)

HoudiniHarper: Thanks, I think? :) It's my own fault. I've told myself I'm going to wait until I get to know someone first before just giving myself away like that again. I'm just not good at casual. I get hurt too easy.

SnowDontFall: I could come over right now and hold you if you want. You know, take the sting out of that last guys fail.

HoudiniHarper: Are you being funny?

SnowDontFall: I'm just offering my services.

HoudiniHarper: I dare you to try.

SnowDontFall: I'm on my way.

HoudiniHarper: Don't tease me.

SnowDontFall: :)

I'm so not teasing her. I would come over if she gave me the word, but it's late. I have work. She has work. I hate saying goodbye to her. I feel an ache in my gut that's been absent for years. When she signs off, I send her an email with just a picture...bobby pins. I laugh at myself when I hit send and log off, shutting the computer down. I pass out in less than ten minutes, my mind swirling in thoughts of only one person.

Friday.

Finally.

Harper's performance is in an old theatre. The main hall has bright red carpet flooding down the aisles with gold colored trim taking over every inch of the vintage architecture. I take a seat in the third row from the front, reserving the seat next to me with my jacket for Gus. He arrives just as the lights lower and rise twice, indicating the show is about to begin.

I sit through performance after performance, waiting, hoping for the next one to be Harper. There are some talented performances, but stage presence? *Shit.* A brief intermission breaks until the lights dim again with the next act being introduced. A man in a black tux with tails and a top hat enters the stage. Just his presence alone makes the audience hush.

"Thank you for coming this evening. We hope you are enjoying the show. We have one of our favorites with us tonight assisting another fine performer. Please give a warm round of applause to our very own Houdini Harper." Loud applause follows with whistles and cheers. The announcer waits with a polite smile until the crowd mellows for him to continue. "And our very own...Magic Mike."

You have got to be shitting me.

I turn to look at Gus who is snickering, and I join him, but both of us stop when the curtain opens and Harper appears on stage. I see her and feel my breath escape with the intentions of never returning.

She's so beautiful. My God.

She stands center stage wearing combat boots, fishnets, black bootie shorts and a red bustier covered in a long red tail jacket with sequins dispersed throughout. Her strawberry blonde hair is flowing down in soft waves with her dark painted eyelids cast down and red lips sparkling. She raises them, brown eyes glittering with her arms reaching to the sky while she shifts her weight onto one hip as Magic Mike enters the stage.

He looks nothing like anyone from that movie Magic Mike by the way. Let's just be clear about that, *no one*. He's tall and lanky with feathered brown hair sticking out of the bottom of a black top hat. He's in a full black tux with tails and has the gold chain of a pocket watch dangling from his vest. He's not a bad looking guy, but he's no Magic Mike representative. Sorry ladies and gentlemen.

Mike takes Harper's white gloved hand and escorts her to the coffin shaped box where she climbs in and lays down, being sealed in with only her head, hands and feet showing. She smiles big as Mike details what's going to happen.

"So, Houdini Harper...what did you say your father did for a living?" Mike asks.

"He's a magician, like me," she says, but I'm pretty sure he's a lawyer.

"How interesting," Mike says. "What's his favorite trick?"

"He saws people in half, like you." Harper winks at the crowd.

"Any brothers and sisters?"

"Only a half-brother and two half-sisters," she says, which makes the crowd roar.

Mike begins to saw while Harper keeps her face stained with a smile. *A beautiful smile*. When the two halves of the box are exposed, the audience cheers almost as loud as when the box is put back together and Harper steps out one long leg at a time... in one piece.

Fucking breathtaking.

They both nod to each other in a *job well done* way and acknowledge the crowd, bowing hand in hand. Harper's smile falls when she sees the two empty seats in the front row for her parents. She recovers, although I can see how disheartened she is. Her eyes flow over the room and stop short where every hint of disappointment fades into a full blown smile when her eyes meet mine.

Gus takes my car to work while I stand outside the theatre as the performers and audience members come out to meet. I see Harper being surrounded by fans, taking photo after photo.

The crowds disperse one by one until it's just a few standing nearby when she registers I'm there. She grins, talking to the person in front of her while glancing over towards me every few seconds. She waves her hand for me to come closer, and I lean in giving her a side-hug with a small peck on the cheek when I reach her.

"This is for you." I hand her a single yellow rose.

Why yellow? Why not red? One: yellow is her favorite color, and two: Gus wouldn't let me buy her a red one. In fact, he didn't want me to buy her one at all which made for a fun display at the counter in 7-Eleven. Me saying I wanted to congratulate her on her performance with a rose, just one, and him giving me the disapproving Gus face while I made the purchase anyway. I could tell the lady behind us thought Gus was a total dick for telling me not to buy a flower for a girl.

Harper takes the flower and holds it in her hand. "Thank you, Reagan," she says, while holding three bouquets in her other arm. The fan in front of her looks eager to regain Harper's attention.

"Do think you could take our picture together?" the fan asks me. Harper raises her eyebrow my way.

"Of course," I say. "I'm Reagan." I put my hand out to the fan.

"I'm Allison. Ally. My friends call me Ally."

"Nice to meet you Ally," I say.

She lets out a nervous giggle, and I release her hand. Harper sets the bouquets on the ground in front of her but holds onto the single yellow one I gave her. I steady myself in front of the two of them while Ally hands me a Polaroid camera.

Holy shit.

Harper is smiling big with her arm outstretched over Ally's shoulder. I take the picture, wishing I could take one just for myself with Harper, and hand the camera back to Ally.

"Oh my god. Thank you. Thank you Harper. Oh..." Ally says, smitten with Harper.

"You two want a photo?" Ally asks Harper and me. She must think I'm an after show admirer. I am, but in a whole different way. We both look at each other giving a shrug with nervous laughs.

"Huddle close," she says, disregarding our indecision. We stand close. I reach around Harper's waist and she turns in towards my chest, resting her hands and arms on my shoulder. We lock eyes for a moment.

I'm actually speechless.

"Ready?" Ally says, interrupting us. We look straight ahead and smile. The camera makes a high-pitched sound followed by a snapping flash. Harper holds the pose with me still holding her as Ally comes close, handing Harper the photo developing by the second. Harper looks at it and hands it to me. She releases from me to hug Ally.

"Thank you, Harper," Ally says.

Harper wraps her arms around her. "It was a pleasure to meet you, Ally," Harper whispers. A tiny squeal escapes from Ally as she turns to leave and walk towards the parking lot.

"You were so good!" I say.

Harper wasn't shy with any of the others who told her the same thing a hundred times before me, but she is with me saying it.

"Thanks," she says, flushing light pink in her cheeks.

"You wanna grab a bite, or do you have plans?" I ask, noticing a few other performers walking towards us.

She shakes her head saying, "I don't have plans," as they walk closer to her. They circle around and Harper introduces me, but the only one I remember is Mike...Magic Mike or MM as I have to think of him, otherwise I can't control my laughter.

"You wanna go with us and celebrate?" asks the guy who pulled a rabbit out of a hat in the most melodramatic way.

"I'm gonna hang back with Reagan," she says, and I have to admit, I'm flattered. They all hug her and say goodnight while MM looks at me and back at Harper who gives him a wide-eyed *go away already* kind of stare.

"It's a nice night. You mind walking?" I ask.

She likes the idea, and we drop a few things off at her car but she keeps my rose in her hands.

"Where should we go?" she asks as she shuts the car door and locks it. I love that she locks it.

"There's a place I've heard about up the street. I met this one magician chick once in a parking lot of the restaurant nearby."

"Chick, huh?" She smirks, buttoning up the front of the jacket she grabbed from her car, leaving the top few unbuttoned.

"We don't have to go, if you have a better idea."

I can see the wheels turning in her head.

I like the wheels turning in her head.

"I like your idea," she says. She's still wearing the costume from her performance, and I can't help but stare every few seconds. Her cleavage is right there begging to be looked at. *RIGHT THERE!* She catches me and give me a playful squint, shaking her head.

We walk the short distance to the restaurant with the streetlights casting fuzzy hues in small beams every few seconds. She brings the rose to her nose, sniffing it, with her lips brewing to life in a smile as she looks at me.

"You know, I got a lot of flowers tonight but this one...is my favorite."

Her words make everything melt inside. I don't even know who I'm turning into right now. Where's that guy who doesn't give a shit? Mr.

Snow Don't Fall? No strings attached? I want every string attached...with her.

"You told me you liked yellow." I shrug with a small grin as she grins back. We walk in a comfortable silence that I've never experienced. We stop at a streetlight waiting for it to change so we can walk with a few other people waiting nearby, both of us exchanging glances. I love looking at her and seeing her eyes look back at me with the same fire.

When the light changes and we begin to walk, she places her hand in mine, entwining our fingers. Under any other circumstance, with any other women, this would be a sign that I need to get the hell out. But with her, I want nothing more than to stay in it.

I like this.

I grip her fingers, bringing them to my lips with a small kiss, and she lets out a small gasp, holding her breath and releasing. It's a reaction I savor. I hold her hand to my lips a second longer and bring it down between us as we walk. Her free hand slides into the fold of my arm and grips my bicep, holding tight.

God damn. I want to kiss her in the worst way right now.

We enter the restaurant where she's recognized by the hostess and the wait staff, one of which is Mary. Hail Mary, but for a whole other reason now. We take a seat in a booth, both of us on one side, hands still entwined but release to hold our menus. She looks up when the waiter comes and Harper asks for a coke.

"For you, *SIR*?" A male voice asks with disdain.

I know that voice, and I know I am so *fucked* right now when I look up and see Gus.

"Water." I swallow hard. "Thanks."

Chapter 7
Harper 1993

"You okay?" Reagan doesn't look up at me when I ask.

He nods, giving me a sideways glance and focuses back on the menu, gripping it tight. I focus back on mine but spy him out of the corner of my eye looking towards the waitresses and our waiter. His head bends down a little lower when our waiter returns with our drinks.

"You two ready to order?" he asks.

Reagan still has his nose in the menu, like some serious research is taking place.

"We need another minute," I say, and the waiter arches his brow at Reagan then turns to talk to another couple at a table across the way.

"Do you wanna go somewhere else?" I ask. I'm not sure if it's me or this place, but Reagan doesn't want to be here. He finally looks up, almost realizing how awkward he's being and shakes his head no, confused by my question.

"You're being weird. I mean, I don't know *you* weird, but this is weird. You. Right now." I continue studying my menu even though I already know it by heart from eating here so many times, and I try to decide if I want to order anything at all from how thick the air has become.

"I have to tell you something." Reagan sets his menu down, putting both hands on top. "I know our waiter."

"Wow, shocker, Reagan. I'm surprised you don't know all the waitresses too," I say.

He shrugs, and his face scrunches tight.

OK what? Why is he shrugging like that?

"You know them too? How?"

"Gus, our waiter? He's my... roommate." He says this like the meaning is obvious. Because the waiter is his roommate, of course. That's a perfectly good reason to be distracted and speechless all of a sudden. I have friends I'm close to who are waiters, cashiers, and servers, but I don't forget the basic functions of speaking when I'm with someone in their presence. I give Reagan a blank stare because this explains nothing about how weird he's being...unless....

"Are you two..." I tip my head to the side, nudging it forward.

"Are we?" He scans my face for clarity.

"You know..." I give my head a little shake side-to-side.

"I *don't* know." He searches my face further, and I arch my brow.

"Wait...NO, no we aren't TOGETHER together. He's just my roommate. Jesus, Harper."

"Hey, I don't know." I let out a nervous laugh giving my menu another glance. "How do you know the waitresses? Especially that one?" I point to a blonde with green eyes who's eying him like he's a delicious dessert. Reagan sees her and looks away quick.

"I kinda hooked up with her," he says.

He sinks a little in his seat like he is ashamed, and he should be. She's the worst waitress here. Even with her pretty Barbie doll face and nice ass,

Mike won't touch her, and that's saying a lot. Before we can delve further into his poor decision making in hookups, which we can't even blame on alcohol, Gus returns.

"You two ready to order?" he asks.

I turn to Reagan. "You know what you want?"

He nods, but answers with, "Ladies first."

What a guy.

"I think I'll have the turkey club with a side of you should join us, Gus, and I'll have an extra side of tell that waitress to stop staring or I'm going to make a scene. How about you, Reagan? What are you going to have?"

Cray Cray may have just made a visit. Just to warn you.

"I'll have what she's having." Reagan's scanning my face with a puzzled smirk while I force a smile at him and look back at Gus. Gus doesn't even know what to do right now. Write down our order, sit or walk away? I've shattered whatever plan he had going on in his head.

"I'll be right back," he mutters.

"You're mad?" Reagan asks.

"I'm not mad," I say. I'm not really sure what I am. Gus returns and sits down opposite of us with Reagan and him exchanging some sort of unspoken code. I watch them both. They can't decide who is going to speak first, and the decision is taking an absurdly long time to make.

Christ on a cracker, what kind of shit have I gotten myself into?

"Should I go? Or are you guys going to eye fuck each other all night?"

Wow, that really came out of my mouth, huh? Thanks brain. I have no idea what has gotten into me. I kinda wanna leave.

Gus and Reagan snap their heads to me and then resume their eye fuckery with each other.

What is happening?

"This one's got a mouth on her." Gus smirks, nudging his head towards me while his eyes stay fixed to Reagan.

"Yeah, she's feisty," Reagan says with a heavy sigh.

"Hello? Right here?" I say.

"You know this guy here is trouble right?" Gus says to me, and motions towards Reagan.

What does that even mean?

"He's a heart breaker. Just warning you," Gus continues.

Lovely.

"Can I ask you something, Gus?"

"Ask me anything," Gus says.

When I engage my focus on him, I notice he has the most beautiful brown eyes. I've never had a word to describe brown. It's always just been brown. *You have nice brown eyes.* I've heard it all my life. *I love your brown eyes.* Blue has all the best descriptions. Blue like Reagan's eyes. Blue like sapphires dipped in the ocean, or blue like an indigo summer sky, so warm and inviting, pulling me in. But brown? No dice. With Gus' eyes though, it comes to me. They're brown like copper mixed with the sweetest bits of honey. Kind and soft, even with the scowl that reappears when he looks at Reagan.

"How do you two know each other?" I ask.

They both stare at each other, and Gus presents the first grin, softening those brown eyes when he responds to me.

"We worked together. It's a long story."

Oh, ok then. Not.

"I've got time. You, Reagan? You got time?" I ask in a way that makes it clear to both men an answer of anything that isn't yes is the wrong one.

"We met a few years back when Reagan ran into some trouble with the law." When Gus speaks, Reagan winces, touching my leg under the table.

"I'll be right back," he says, heading towards the restrooms with career waitress Barbie following close behind. My inner Cray Cray notices, but Gus steals my focus when he speaks.

"I don't know if he told you, but he's got a bit of a past. He's trouble, Harper." He softens his tone. It's a lot like my father's when he is having a heart-to-heart with me.

"Not in a law breaking way, he's just complicated and I don't know you to say this or give you any advice, but I feel obligated. He'll break your heart."

I don't like this warning. It's the classic warning from every one of my romance novels. Stay away or you'll get burned. He's no good for you. He's from the wrong side of town. He's complicated. God, that's the most classic of them all. What's the one thing every girl or guy does in this scenario? Jump right in head first telling the person warning them *okay,* or a variation of *fuck off*...depending on the author. What do I do? I nod.

Classic.

Reagan returns a few minutes later with Barbie nowhere to be seen. He and Gus resume their telepathy.

"I'm...gonna go check on your order," Gus says, patting the table.

I'm not even hungry now. This is a sign something is wrong because I can eat through any emotion. Reagan glances at me and I try to read his expression, but it's mixed and I can't gauge if he is better or worse than before.

"He told me you're trouble. You're gonna break my heart." I search his face for a smile to match my jovial tone, but I don't find one. "Reagan?" He's staring at my lips, my hair and my eyes. He gives me a smile that looks like a mix between a grimace and polite rejection. "What is it?"

"I don't wanna break your heart, Harper. I'm afraid Gus is probably right. He's known me for years. It's nothing I would do intentionally, but it's probably going to happen." He takes my hand and holds it on the seat between us. "I'm into you... *really* into you." He locks his gaze to mine like he wants to burn his words into my memory. "But I break the things I care about. I hurt them in the worst way without thinking. I don't wanna do that to you."

"I don't know what to say," I say to his heartfelt unravelling as Barbie arrives with our turkey sandwiches. *Worst. Waitress. Ever.* She sets the plates down, and we don't acknowledge her with more than a quick nod, resuming our conversation.

"You don't have to say anything. I just needed you to know what I was thinking about."

I did want to know what he was thinking about five minutes ago, but now I'm at a loss for words. The whole ignorance is bliss saying? Understood...loud and clear.

"I kinda want to leave. Get some air," I say.

"Okay," he says, with a crack in his voice.

He clears his throat and scoots down the seat to let me out, looking down at the floor as I make my way towards him. I open my purse to get money and he puts his hand on mine, shaking his head no. I close my purse. I'm standing in front of him now, but he won't look up at me. I lean in towards his ear, putting my hands on the sides of his arms, and I kiss his cheek.

"You're coming with me, right?" I ask. He straightens his stance a bit and I continue. "To walk me to my car? I hear there's a serial killer on the loose."

He lets out a small croak of a laugh. "Okay." He nods.

On our walk back to my car Reagan's hands are in his pockets, mine are crossed and wrapped around my chest. We don't really say much other than commenting on the weather and how we can smell rain in the air.

I've dated guys who didn't remember my favorite color. Guys who couldn't be bothered to make sure I got somewhere safe, or who acted like I was just another pretty thing to look at. Hell, I even have friends and family who forget my own *fucking* birthday! But this guy, I want to know him so bad it hurts. I want to know what it's like to be kissed by him, touched and entwined even if it breaks me. The sudden urgency of these feelings is overpowering my thoughts.

We get closer to the theatre and the parking lot where I can see D.C. sitting all alone. I look over at Reagan who gives me a shy smile back, and I stop walking in front of the alcove of a hobby store which has closed for the day.

"Reagan?"

He stops walking, lifting his head towards the sky, but doesn't turn around until I say his name again. His breath is visible in the coolness of the night. He turns around, hands still in his pockets and gives me his shy smile again when I approach him.

"I want to know you. I don't care what Gus said. I want to know you even if you break my heart." I place both of my hands on the edges of his jaw as he looks down and back up at me, placing his hands on top of mine.

"I'm gonna break your heart, Harper."

"Break it."

I pull his face close to mine and press my lips to his, urging him off of the sidewalk and into the open alcove of the store front, away from street view. He grabs onto my neck with his thumbs caressing my cheeks as his lips curl over mine.

"God, I've wanted to do this since I first saw you," he breaks to say, and I smile into another kiss of his lips.

He's eager and warm to the touch. He feels so good against me. The rain begins to fall, shielding the vision of us from cars passing by. I shrug my jacket off, letting it drop to the ground, exposing my shoulders. His hands caress my neck as his lips skim after his fingers, marking my neck with tiny sucks, making every part of me ache. He pulls me into him from behind, letting me feel how excited he is, and I want more...more of this...more of him. I run my hands over the sides of his shirt and tug, trying to pull it up so I can feel his skin underneath, making him smirk.

"Slow down..." he whispers, placing his hands over mine and pushing his shirt down. "I wanna enjoy this."

No guy says that, and it only makes me want him more. I loosen my grip, running my fingers back through his hair, letting his mouth meld with mine. It's better than I imagined it would be, the way he tastes, the way he guides my head to mold with the touch of his lips. I don't want it to end.

"Harper..." He breaks again, breathless. "We should get you home," he pants, brushing the fingers of one hand over my temple while the other stays cupping my neck.

No.

I focus on his lips no longer pressed against mine. "Will you come with me?" I ask.

He sighs deep, and I can tell he wants to say yes. I want him to say yes.

Please say yes, Reagan.

"I can't. But I'll see you tomorrow... at your party."

I look down at his chest still heaving into mine. "Okay."

"Hey." He lifts my chin with his forefinger and thumb. "I promise I'll see you tomorrow okay? We'll do something special to celebrate...a belated Happy Birthday."

I'd believe any promise he told me right now, with his eyes regarding me sweet and tender.

"You gonna get my car towed again?" I ask with mild hesitation, and he laughs.

"Come on," he says, as he shields me with his jacket while we run to my car. I unlock it and sit admiring his wet frame, yet again. He leans in to give me a slow kiss.

"I'll see you tomorrow?" he asks.

I nod and he closes my door. I take a deep breath in, and I put my car in reverse with my headlights embracing his silhouette.

He's definitely going to break my heart.

My mother has outdone herself. She loves planning parties. She especially loves planning parties for people who don't want them, like me. When I was twelve, my mother threw me a Cabbage Patch themed birthday party. All totally fine, if it wasn't for the fact that I had already sprouted boobs and a menstrual cycle...*and I wasn't five*! Her timing has always been rich. I think she still wishes I was that little girl she could cradle in her arms instead of the rebellious wild child who does magic for a living.

The backyard is full of white tents and people I haven't seen since grade school or a guilt laden visit to church. You know those circus clowns with hot dogs on sticks I joked about? One is handing me a hot dog right now while I sit on the steps near the back door. That'll teach me to say what I don't want out loud. I'm pretty sure my mother missed my sarcasm.

"This seat taken?" Mike leans down and sits as I take a beer he's offering from his hands and twist off the cap. "This is quite a party your mom has going on for you." He smirks while we both sip our beers. I like Mike a lot even though I don't want to date him. We can sit in comfortable silence without feeling like the space needs to be filled, and I like that. We both look out onto the backyard, laughing every now and then at Bryson, who looks adorable, and the clowns, who look miserable.

"That guy you were with last night? What's his name? Reagan?" he asks.

I nod, taking a long sip of my beer, wondering where this is going.

"He didn't get an invite?" Mike's fake concern is written all over his face.

"Oh, he was invited."

Another sip.

"He stand you up?" He arches a brow as he waits for my response.

Big sip.

"Must be a thing with you men. I'm prime stand up material, I guess."

Really big sip.

"Harper, I'm sorry. You know I didn't mean to stand you up."

"I know, I know." And I do. Mike has a brother with special needs that he cares for when his mom works. Sometimes she has to take a longer shift and he covers. I don't follow up with anything other than a shrug of my shoulders, and we both fall silent...sipping...watching.

"You like this guy don't you?" he asks.

He wants me to say I don't like Reagan. I know that's what he's getting at with these questions, but I'm the rejecter with a heart, twisting that knife and saying sorry at the same time.

"I do," I say.

Mikes face drops from curious to a pout for a beat, and my bottle... is now empty.

"You've known him what? A week?"

I shake my head yes and he nods.

"Just be careful, Harper. That's all I'm gonna say. I don't wanna see you get hurt. A guy comes out of nowhere, sweeping your feelings off their feet...just go slow."

"Well, he's not here so, slow...doesn't really seem to be a problem right now."

"He'll show. A girl like you? He'd be crazy not to show up."

And that is why I always feel like an asshole for being honest about my feelings. Mike always knows just what to say.

"You want another?" he asks.

See?

He tips his empty bottle against mine, making a clinking sound. I sigh staring down into my empty bottle, and he wraps his arm around me, giving me a squeeze.

"Let's go, birthday girl."

We walk towards the tin barrels filled with beer and soda in the gazebo where my dad is standing and looks to be giving a clown a talking to. It would so happen to be a sad clown he's scolding...or not scolding. I can never tell with him. My father, Hal Adams, has perfected the poker face making it impossible to read his true emotions.

"Harper." His face bursts into a grin when he sees me. "How are you enjoying the party so far?" He leans down to grab a beer from the barrel, his hands ice cold when he reaches his free hand around my shoulder.

"It's pretty..."

"Your mother is nuts, isn't she?" he asks with a warm smile.

I love my dad. He knows how crazy my mom is, and I can always turn to him for that understanding. Even when I quit college, he went along with my mother but talked to me later, telling me he wished he had done what he loved rather than what he had to do for the family name.

"You should sneak off with your friends. I won't say anything," he whispers with a sly grin.

I love him, did I say that already?

The one person I want to sneak off with isn't here, so I settle for the one little guy I know can kill my blues. Bryson is the only kid in the bouncer when I join him, and I'm met with his loud squeals when I start to jump. We jump and fall for a solid thirty minutes until I'm drenched and need a drink. I take a seat on the low brick retaining wall that circles the backyard, catching my breath and drinking water with the night air breezing over my skin, cooling me, when I hear footsteps in the gravel behind me.

"You left this."

A yellow rose appears in front of me from behind, attached to the hand of the man I've missed since last night. I take the rose and jump up from the wall, turning around to hug Reagan tight. He holds my hips while my arms swing around his neck.

I may be squeezing him just *a* little *too* tight.

"Is everything okay?" He leans back to look at me, and I shake my head wanting to ask where he's been all day, but I don't.

He's gonna break your heart.

Don't get too attached.

He motions to the wall and we both sit. Bryson is in the distance watching one of the clowns make a balloon animal. My mother and my dad are busy in conversation with people from their church. Mike is talking to my brother, but keeps glancing over at me and Reagan every now and then.

"I missed you today," I say, against everything that told me not to.

"Sorry I wasn't online. Gus had the computer on lockdown today. I tried to call you, but you didn't answer. You didn't get my message?"

"I've been out here, setting up for this." I gesture to the yard.

"Harper, you know what I said last night?"

I blink with a subtle twitch of my head.

"It's been on my mind ever since I said it....about breaking your heart."

I'm glad I'm not the only one.

"It was a little dramatic," he says with a small curl of his lips.

I'll say.

"I'm not supposed to be dating anyone right now, or fraternizing as they say...while I'm recovering."

I angle myself closer into him. "You're recovering? You mean with drinking?"

He nods.

"Gus is more than my roommate, he's my...he's like my father figure right now, guiding me, watching me. He's trying to keep me on the right path."

I look over at my dad who's being coerced into the bouncer which makes me smirk. He'll do anything Bryson asks, even if it may mean he won't be able to get out of bed tomorrow.

"Is that why Gus was telling me what a heartbreaker you are?" I ask.

Reagan catches my eyes, his lips curling. "It's why he wants to protect you from me, Harper."

"Because you're complicated?" My sarcasm drips with each word.

"I *am* complicated!" He chuckles to himself, putting his hand to my cheek but removes it, taking in a deep breath and letting it out slow. "I'm sorry to be unloading all this on you. We just met, and now I'm telling you all this *shit* that's probably gonna make you lose my number because I'm all messed up."

"Some of the best people are all messed up. It's what we decide to do with those flaws that make us better people. Wait until you see mine," I say.

A smile reaches his eyes as he looks at me, hopeful and honest. I give him a small feather of a kiss, watching his eyes open slow and tender when I pull away.

"You wanna get out of here?" I ask.

"Yeah."

I glance back and see my dad gazing over at me. He salutes me with his beer and turns towards my mother to keep her occupied while I leave the party. Reagan takes my hand as we walk to his car. It's parked almost a block away.

"All these people are here for your party?" he asks, as we walk past car after car.

"It's embarrassing," I mutter.

"You're pretty lucky to have all these people in your life, you know. You sure we shouldn't stay? Won't they miss you?"

"My dad has it covered and most of my friends already left. Besides, you're the only one I wanted to see tonight."

PETE

Chapter 8

Reagan 1993

I'm lying on the hood of my car with Harper in my arms, staring out at the night sky, and it's the most peaceful moment I've ever felt in my life. It's sudden and perfect. I want to tell her so much about my life: why I'm here, what she means, what's going to happen in three months when this is over. *God, when I can't see her anymore.* I wince at the thought, and I'm glad she can't see my face.

"What are you thinking about?" She lifts her head from my chest, her arm lying across.

I don't dare answer this honestly do I?

Tell her all my secrets right now?

I want to. God I want to.

I settle for an old standby. "You."

She gives my answer a snide wrinkle of her nose and presses her head back down. It's not untrue. It's more of a summary of what I'm thinking about. "What are you thinking about?" I ask.

She props her arms on my chest and rests her head in her hands. "I was thinking you and I should go on an actual date. Like a movie or something. Oh, I'm having a game night next weekend. You like games?"

"What kind of games?" I ask, unable to hide my smile. There are a lot of games I know about, though I'm sure she won't mention any of them.

"We do a theme game night and this one is the eighties, so everyone is bringing their favorite game, movie, whatever. What was your favorite board game as a kid?"

I have no idea what board games I liked as a kid because mine were electronic. "Sorry?" I ask, hoping that having her repeat the question will give me time to think of something, but she hears it as a statement.

"Oh, that's a great game. I think I may have that one still."

Sorry. What the fuck is Sorry?

I make a mental note to Google it later, and then I realize there is no Google here. It's Netscape. You have no idea what that is do you? I'll spare you all the nerd details I learned from my roommate back home, but to put it simply, Netscape is like the generic version of every browser you've ever used today. It's like the safe browse on your work or college computer. I think some libraries still use it. Anyway...you get it now, and I will have to Netscape what the game Sorry is. Netscape it. *That does not have the same ring.*

"So, you'll come to game night then?" she asks.

I can't say no to her even if I wanted to. The way she's staring up at me all sweet, it's like kryptonite. I'm weak.

"I'll be there, I promise. But I'm not much for board games."

"You've never played them with magicians...crooked as *fuck* sleight of hand, magicians!" She leans up kissing my cheek, and I belly laugh.

She begins to shift her body back down, but I hold her in place, stilling her movement. Her eyes rise to mine and she adjusts, laying on top of me with her arms bent next to the sides of my head. Her fingers needle through my hair while my hands rest on her lower back, playing with the belt loops of her waistband.

"What movies are out that you want to see?" I whisper, and I know she likes my question from the glimmer in her eyes.

"Are you asking me out on a date?" she asks, while giving me a light kiss.

"It's what you wanted isn't it? An actual date?"

She nods, giving me another kiss.

"I'm not really thinking about movies right now." Her voice is soft and husky.

Neither am I.

I've never made out on top of a car. In a car? *Come on.* But on top? *Nope.* Her lips are sparking things inside I didn't even know could spark. The way she's pushing her hips into mine. Her hands run their way up my shirt, touching my chest and wrapping around my neck through the opening of my collar. She lifts her shirt so she can feel my skin against hers. I may combust. It's not something foreign to me, but with her it's brand new.

Headlights appear in the distance aiming in our direction. We both notice and she lifts off of me to a seated position, tugging her shirt that I may or may not have tried to free her of. The headlights get closer, and I realize the car is a police car. I freeze inside.

I cannot get arrested. It will blow everything.

"Are we in trouble?" Harper asks.

I shake my head no. "I don't think so. Just be polite, no matter what."

I've learned this the hard way: Be an asshole, say goodbye to the nice cop who was just checking this here part of the park to see if things were on the up and up.

Two cops approach with their flashlights shining right in our eyes, making us squint.

"You kids know what time it is?"

We both shake our heads no.

"The sign back there says this here park closes at dusk. Sure looks a lot later than dusk don't it?" The first officer speaking looks at his partner, returning to us with a shit eating grin.

"I think you two best be going now, don't you?"

We both nod, agreeing and begin to lift off the hood of the car.

The officers shine their flashlights on Harper and what she's wearing a little to long for my liking, but I remind myself, *I cannot get arrested.* Her white V-neck t-shirt is still askew from my tugging, which is making her bra and cleavage visible. The officers watch us gather the blanket from the hood, folding it down into a neat square. Harper stands by the passenger side door waiting for me to unlock it while I put the blanket in the trunk.

The footsteps in the gravel crunch behind me. The officer who has been doing all the talking shines his light at my license plate and then at me.

"You got your driver's license on ya?" he asks.

Shit.

I reach in my pocket for my wallet and pull it out, handing the officer my license. I glance at Harper who gives me a shrug, and I shrug back.

"Wait here," the officer says, and walks to the other one standing by the patrol car.

Both of them lean into each other whispering and studying my license. I wink at Harper to ease the tension, and she gives me an uneasy smile back. The officers are now sitting in their car, both their heads leaning in towards the center console with lights from the dashboard decorating their faces. A few minutes later, they both step out and walk towards us.

"You got anything on you I need to know about, Reagan?" the chatty officer asks.

I shake my head no.

"What about you, darlin'? You got anything on ya I should know about?"

Harper shakes her head no, and the officers search both of us. The silent officer checks Harper and steps away. The officer checking me is patting my legs like I've got some serious contraband hidden between them.

"You on parole, Reagan?"

I nod.

"You're pretty little friend here know about that?" he whispers as he turns me around with his face close to mine.

I nod and he smiles, but it's unsettling.

"You know you're across the county lines?" he whispers.

I shake my head no. I didn't know, I just drove, like an idiot.

"I'm gonna need you to turn around and place your hands on your head," he says.

I turn to see Harper who can't believe what's happening.

"You too pretty thing."

Handcuffs are placed on both of us as we stand next to each other in front of the police car in silence. The quiet officer stands next to Harper who is wiggling her arms, and I know exactly what she is doing which makes me smirk.

The quiet officer leans in to whisper at Harper. "My daughter loves your magic."

She looks up with a polite grin and says, "Thank you."

"Seems we got ourselves a real pickle here." Chatty returns. "You, my sweet pretty thing, are free to go, but you, Mr. County Lines...your parole officer is on the way. Says he would like to escort you himself. Your car can go home with this young lady or it can stay here, which I don't recommend."

I glance at Harper who stares at me for an answer. I didn't exactly tell her I was on parole. Me and my new honesty kick slid right past that one.

"She can take my car. I can get it from her later. Is...Is that okay, Harp?" I ask.

She shakes her head yes as the quiet officer gestures for her to turn around so he can remove her handcuffs. Harper moves her hands in front of her with the cuffs dangling open, which makes the officer chuckle.

"Sorry, I couldn't help myself," she says, handing the cuffs to him. Both officers step towards the driver's side of the cop car whispering and staring down at the handcuffs Harper just unlatched.

"Where are the keys?" she asks.

I nod my head down to my pocket. She places her hand in my front pocket, grabbing onto my keys while she kisses my lips like I'm being sent off to jail for the next six months.

"Whoa...okay little darlin'." The chatty officer intervenes. "We don't need to get him all riled up with that business." He lets out a nervous laugh.

I'd like to challenge that. I honestly would.

She grins with her hand still in my pocket as she pulls out my keys, eyeing the Beavis and Butthead key chain attached. "I'll see you soon?" she asks, but I'm too focused on her cleavage to notice the question.

"Reagan?" She giggles, and I look up.

"I'll see you soon?" she repeats.

"You'll see me soon."

But I don't see her soon. I don't see her for a week because I have been sent back home to contemplate my actions. *Fuck.*

2035

For most people who have been away on a vacation or a business trip, coming home is a breath of fresh air. It's your own bed, your own pillow. Everyone and everything right where you left it. But for me, it's different this time. My bed is cold, my pillow doesn't feel like mine and everyone and everything feels out of sync. Although, I wasn't lying when I said I would cry tears of joy when I saw my cellphone only had three bars of Wi-Fi. I totally broke down which made my roommate Dade look at me like I was having a nervous breakdown.

"Tell me again why you downloaded AOL Instant Messenger on my laptop? And why we are switching laptops?" Dade regards my request to swap computers with suspicion as I give him mine to use.

Dade is my roommate at my actual home, who also works as an IT pro at Best Buy. Yes, they still exist. You would think he's Bill fucking Gates from the way he talks about computers...and then there is politics. Don't even get him started on having a female for a president. He will literally lose his shit right in front of you.

"I need to use your computer to chat with someone, and I can't have it tracked like it would be on mine," I say.

"So I would be aiding and abetting you in criminal activity against *the man*?" he asks.

Anything involving helping me get away with something I shouldn't is right up Dade's alley. He doesn't care what it is ...as long as he can't get in trouble. I always do my best to make sure he doesn't.

"Yes, well kind of. I mean, you don't have to *know* I'm using your computer. Just, leave it out..."

Dade nods his head, grinning like I just laid out the perfect plans to rob a bank. Don't put it past us, we have dissected the idea of the perfect robbery but have never acted on it... of course.

"Who's the girl?" Dade asks while overdoing the placement of his laptop right in front of me on the table.

"The girl?" I ask.

"No guy like you is jumping on AOL to chat with someone without a vagina. WHO is the girl?" He doesn't mince words and knows me all too well.

"Her name is Harper. She's beautiful....and she's the case I've been suspended from working on."

"Shit, bro. You fell for the girl in the case? Is that? How does that? *Shit.*"

From his mouth to my thoughts. *Shit, indeed.*

"Are you going back? Is the case over now?" he asks, and catches a glimpse of the smuggled turtle pies in my bag and opens one, sniffing it before he stuffs it in his mouth, his eyes rolling back in ecstasy from the aroma.

"I'm going back. I just have to sit it out for another week."

"Does she know you're a *time traveler*?" His arms wave up and down like he's casting a magical spell.

"She doesn't know. I haven't told her."

"So what are you gonna say when she asks where you are?"

I've thought about this nonstop. What am I going to say? I still have no idea. Dade begins to talk with his mouthful. It's not only visually unappealing, but it's also making a mess on my floor.

"Tell her your Grandma got sick and you had to visit her, or tell her your probation officer made you leave the state and go back home to clear your head."

All fine answers I've thought about myself, but what if she wants to come see me? Then what? Dade grabs another turtle pie from my bag, and I stare at him like he is entering enemy territory, but he ignores me.

"Be vague about it I guess...if you think she's gonna wanna come check it out. Tell her you had to take care of some stuff. Girls hate and love a vague guy."

It's true. Girls do like the vague guy.

I pull up a picture of Harper on his computer. It's her in the magician's assistant costume. The one I saw her in at the performance the other night. He furrows his brow and twitches his head at what he is seeing.

"Dude. Is this an obituary?" he asks.

"It is if I don't save her."

I finish my download and login to see if there is any possibility I will see Harper online. It's crazy to think she would be, but I search her name and it comes up empty.

"Any luck?" Dade asks, sitting next to me at the table.

I shake my head no.

"Let me see it." He aims it away from me, hitting the keys like a mad scientist on his final discovery, then he turns the computer back towards me and says, "here, loverboy. I'm not sure if this will work because of the time difference, but see if you can find her now."

I search her name again and see her. *HoudiniHarper* with the word *Online* next to her name.

"Holy shit dude! What did you do?" I stand and hug Dade like he's just won me the lottery. "I could kiss you right now!" In my excitement and mid-hug, we both inch back when I say the *kiss you* part.

"Sorry...how'd you do this?" I ask, and he gives me a sly stare.

"You may think I just work at Best Buy, but I know stuff." He taps his forehead. "I know stuff about this between worlds shit you wouldn't believe."

He has no idea what I would believe, but I settle for nodding and accepting his answer.

SnowDontFall: Harper?

She doesn't reply. I don't know if it's the connection or if she is really pissed. I've been gone for over a week without contact, so I send her email after email telling her I'm sorry and I'll make it up to her. The whole time I wonder if she will even get them.

"We're going out tonight. You wanna go? It'll be a Tamera free night. I promise." Dade calls from the hall as he heads to his room.

Tamera is an ex I'd like to keep my existence in town from for as long as I can. She and I have a history that I'd rather not be reminded of if I can help it. But I know my time is limited. As much as I enjoy the crazy ex-lover, occasional friends with benefits services she can provide, I don't conjure up anything when I think about her like I do when I think of Harper. I send another message to her. Each one probably sounds more desperate than the last, and I close the laptop.

"You going with us?" Dade returns in a Hawaiian shirt and jeans.

"Not if you're wearing that." I gesture to his shirt and he looks down at himself. "This my friend, is my get lucky shirt, and it goes where I go tonight."

Holy Christ.

"Where are you going?" I should know this answer, but it's been two months since I've been here, and I'm still gaining my bearings.

"Dude, its Saturday. Tiki's Tavern! Remember?"

I hear nothing after the word Saturday because it's Saturday and I promised to be at game night.

"You still know that guy who can crack this?" I lift my left hand where a small incision shows. Dade looks at my hand, giving me a sly nod of his head like the mission impossible theme music is about to start.

Mago is a wiry five foot tall guy who works out of a comic book store in a small room hidden in the back. I follow Dade past the shelves of comics and figurines to the blue door all the way in the back. Dade knocks and is asked the password by a man on the other side.

Dade's face is stern as his brow furrows when he says, "Old gamers never die" and pounds three times on his chest. I know the seriousness of all this between these guys, so I don't dare laugh out loud. But on the inside? *I'm dying*. The door opens to a room filled with electronics and lit up diodes at every turn. Red and green blinking in sync on one side with blue and yellow on another.

"What dost thou request?" Mago asks, and I try to keep a straight face.

God this is hard.

Dade speaks for me. "We need your help slipping this for a few hours and getting him back to nineteen ninety-three."

Mago looks at me and down at my left hand, gesturing to let him see it. I place my hand on the desk he is sitting at while he inspects my incision where the monitoring chip sits underneath the skin. He grabs a small scanner and runs it over my scar.

He nods his head. "I can get you there but you have to do me one favor."

"Anything," I say. He shows me a picture of what he wants, and I agree to bring him back a rare He-Man figurine.

Holy fuck, this is my life right now.

I can't even believe it.

"Can you two wait outside?" He tips his head to the door while holding the scanner with my chip details on the screen.

Dade nods, and I follow him to the other side of the blue door.

"Is this guy legit?" I ask Dade in the hall.

"He's the Mago..." Dade infers.

The wizard. I get it.

Mago opens the door a few minutes later and gives us an address for me to go to. "The service that monitors your chip is going to be down for *maintenance* from midnight to six a.m." He winks. "You have to be back by five a.m. or everything is going to go to shit."

I nod.

"Good luck," he offers, with a praying motion of his hands and a bow.

Dade drives to the closed library where we enter through a door in the back. We pass the dark aisles of the library towards the periodicals in the fiction section where the elevator awaits. Dade holds the keycard given to him by Mago and the doors open.

"You ready for this? Five a.m. Don't be late," Dade says.

We share a mutual nod. I step inside the cab of the elevator and look at Dade who is holding his cell phone over his head like he's the actor John Cusack holding a BoomBox in the movie Say Anything. He begins to sing the song "In Your Eyes" by Peter Gabriel as I push 1993 on the elevator keypad, shaking my head at him and praying it works.

1993

The doors open seconds later and it's the same empty library, but no Dade. I walk the aisles the same way I did when I entered, opening the back door to see a yellow cab waiting.

"You Reagan?" A driver in a suit and cap asks.

I nod and he opens the back door. I take a seat in the cab, half wondering if I am in the right year when the driver turns and says, “What’s the password?”

I repeat, “Old gamers never die,” like Dade said at Mago’s, and the driver waits for the last part of the whole ritual. I beat my chest three times. He smiles like the ritual has been complete and looks out his side mirrors.

He begins to pull away from the curb. “Where to?”

I give him Harpers address but ask him to stop at the store.

After a quick stop, we make our way to Harper’s place. “I’ll be back at four-thirty to get you, but if you need me, page me.” The driver hands me his card.

It’s after midnight when I reach the stoop of her front door and knock, unsure if she is home or if she will even take me in. I hear footsteps and then silence. A chain unlatches as the door opens slowly to a crack and a visual of her tired eyes.

“Harper? I know it’s late. Don’t shut the door. Please. Harper! Harper!”

Okay she’s a little mad.

I talk through the door, begging for her to let me in. “Harper, please. Let me explain.”

I don’t hear any footsteps, so I know she’s still by the door. “Harper, just give me five minutes. If you don’t want to talk to me after that, I understand. I just...I need five minutes.”

I turn halfway around when I hear footsteps behind me. “I don’t think she wants to see you.” A voice calls and I recognize it as Chad’s. From the tone of his voice, I expect to see a shotgun resting in his hands, but when I turn to face him completely, I only meet a fierce stare.

"She was pretty upset when you didn't call or write saying where you were. That's not something I like to see my little sister doing over a guy she just met. You did leave her your car though. That was an odd gesture."

I give him an appeasing nod, taking in his words. I don't have an excuse, and I can't explain where I've been. My silence isn't helping.

"I think you need to leave," Chad says. He motions towards the street.

"I just need to talk to her. I just need to see her."

The door cracks open, chain still attached. "It's okay, Chad."

I turn to see Harper, still shielded partially by the door.

"Harper, you should let this one go." Chad isn't moving.

"It's okay, Chad," she repeats, closing and unlatching the door, opening it with a wave of her hands for me to come inside, so I enter. Chad stands outside the doorway, cutting his eyes to me and back to her.

"You sure about this?" he asks.

She begins to close the door. "I'm sure."

Once inside she locks the door and turns around, hands still gripping the handle from behind. Her eyes filling with tears. I step closer and she puts her hand up, silently asking me to stop while she wipes her eyes with the other.

"Harper, I'm sorry. I couldn't get back here."

"You couldn't call me? You couldn't email me?" She sobs, and my heart aches watching her.

"I couldn't. I'm sorry."

"Were you in jail? Is that it?"

I don't confirm this, but I don't deny it. *Why didn't I think of that as an excuse?* It was right there, and technically I was in jail, only it was house arrest...forty two years from here, but still! I reach for her again, and she lets me pull her into an embrace. She cries on my shoulder and I hold her, kissing her head.

"I'm sorry," I whisper. "So sorry." I pull back, cupping her face, wiping her tears with my thumbs.

"You really are a heartbreaker." She wants to laugh, but she only cries more. I sigh into a small chuckle at her and how sweet she looks even in tears. I want to say I love her in this moment, but she doesn't know how much I know about her and it's too soon for her ears to hear what my heart has known for months.

She takes my hand and walks me to her bedroom where we sit on the bed. Her room is lit by one small lamp near her bedside. I look around but don't really notice much in the dim light other than the floral pink bedspread and books on her nightstand.

"I have something for you." I unzip a small duffle bag I have with me, and she gives me a timid smile while watching me as I turn my back to her to pull a plastic bag out. I turn back around revealing the game Sorry with a pout on my face. She chuckles amongst her tears and takes the game from my hands. It's the first real smile I've seen on her face since I got here, and it bleeds my heart.

"It's still game night, isn't it?" I ask, and she nods still chuckling. I have something else for her, but I don't want to give it to her until I leave.

"I don't have a lot of time tonight, but I wanted to spend the time I do have with you," I say.

She sets the game down in her lap. "How much time do you have?"

I glance down at my watch. It's already 1:30 and I groan. "Three hours."

Chapter 9
Harper 1993

When I saw Reagan at the door I was relieved, I was excited, I was happy and I was *pissed.* No phone calls or emails for a week? And here he is, begging to see me? All sorts of *hell no* going through my mind. But his voice was so remorseful outside my door. He sounded so broken. So honest and raw that I couldn't hold the door closed to him. I wanted him close more than I wanted to push him away, and now he's here in my bed.

I wrap myself around him, hoping the time we have left will somehow suspend itself and slow down. I kiss him as many times as I can and as long as I can. I'd missed how close we felt just a week ago on the hood of his car, and I want to bring everything about that feeling back again.

"I've missed you," I whisper, resting my head on his shoulder and studying the stubble on his chin with my finger. I don't care if he returns my sentiments; I just want him to know.

"I've missed *you,*" he says.

He looks so at peace when he touches me. His fingers comb through the side of my hair and sweep it behind my ear. I wrap my arms around his waist and squeeze tight as his arm does the same around my shoulders.

"Will I be able to see you this week?" I ask.

His chest lifts and falls with a deep sigh in his exhale. "I won't be back for another week."

He kisses my forehead with a long press which makes my eyes close on contact. I want to ask where he will be, who he will be with, why we can't have contact, but I leave those questions in the air. Maybe we will get to them, maybe we won't. They seem too heavy and weighted for the moment we are in.

"I have something else for you." Reagan tilts his head and I lift from his chest. "I was going to wait until I was about to leave to give it to you. It's nothing exciting but I thought maybe it would help you while I'm not here."

He lifts both his arms, gesturing towards the side of the bed where his duffle bag is, and I move off of him. His shirt shifts at the waist letting the side of his torso show, revealing another scar like the one on his arm. I want to touch it, but I only watch his muscles contract until he shifts onto his back, urging me to lay on him again. He hands me a black and white composition notebook and I study the outside where the words *This is me, until I'm with you* are written in black marker.

"I want you to wait until I leave to look inside, okay?" He smiles.

I shake my head and lay it back down on his chest while his hand kneads my hair. He takes the notebook and sets it on top of the books on my nightstand. I rub the outside of his shirt where the scar is, moving my hands under his shirt to touch it.

"Will you tell me about this one day?" I ask.

His hand covers mine as he shakes his head yes. My fingers trace over the line of the scar. It looks like the result of something painful and deep from the length and width.

"Harper..." Reagan winces, gripping my hand.

"Am I hurting you?" I ask.

He shakes his head.

God, I want to know. What hurt him?

"I want to tell you so much." His hand releases its grip on mine to start a soft rub on the top. I tilt my head to see his face better. His eyes are on the verge of tears.

"What is it? Talk to me?" I ask, pressing my hand to the side of his face.

"We need more time," he says. His tone is foreboding and the words feel like they have more than a single meaning. Searching his face, I place a small kiss to his lips which brings about a small wretch from his throat. His hands brace the back of my neck, keeping me in their embrace against his lips.

What am I doing to him? What is he holding on to that he can't share?

"Harper..." he whispers. His eyes close tight in thought and open, blazing the most crystalline blue. "When I come back, I'll tell you everything."

I nod. It's the only response I can give. He looks gorgeous and broken all in the same moment. His arms wrap tight around me and I lay my head back down, feeling his heart race.

The alarm chimes on his watch, and we both groan.

"Ten more minutes," he says.

It's the most *excruciating* ten minutes. He pulls me tight and releases.

"I've never wanted to handcuff anyone to my bed so bad in my life," I say, making him laugh. He brings his hands to my neck, pushing my head forward and into his lips as he smiles.

"You can one day, I promise. I won't even try to escape." He curls his lips around mine again. I can still see the hurt in his eyes. I want to take it away. Our last ten minutes involves me kissing him like my life depends on it, and him letting me while he tries not to laugh.

"I gotta go, Harper," he whispers, and I hate those words. My eyes lower, resigning to what he needs to do. I lift off of him, rolling to my back, watching him sit on the side of the bed, slipping his shoes on. He stands to tuck his shirt in, and I want to ask him if I can keep it.

"Do you have a nickname you like?" he asks, adjusting his belt through his jean loops.

"Nickname? Everyone's always just called me a variation of Harper like Harp or Har, or my brother's favorite, Harpoon," I say.

"Like babe or..."

I wrinkle my nose and he laughs.

"Sugar?"

I wrinkle my nose again and he laughs deeper this time.

"Angel?"

I smile.

Angel.

I like the sound of it from him and how sweet it makes me feel inside. Reagan leans over me on the bed.

"Angel." His voice is smooth and soft like he has found the right spot, and my god, he has.

I wrap my legs around his waist, and my arms wrap around his neck, pulling him down on top of me into one last kiss. He chuckles, surprised, and I can tell he's feeling the same anxiousness over saying goodbye that I feel.

"I'll see you soon, Angel."

I hate and love *that* sentence. I blink with agreement. Lifting off the bed, he holds his hand out for me to take. I grab onto it and follow him to the door.

"Take care of my car?" he asks, while turning to face me in the open doorway.

I nod, unable to let go of his hand. His alarm sounds again telling him it's four-thirty, and we both groan in unison.

Tears are welling, and I don't want them to fall. I don't want his last memory of tonight to be me, crying in the doorway. His hand goes to the crook of my neck as his lips press to mine for one more lingering kiss.

"Angel." He smiles, and I smile back.

I love every word from his lips, but Angel is now my favorite. He pulls away, reluctant to let me go, and I watch him walk to the end of the walkway, get in a cab with a wave back...and then he's gone.

I watch out my peephole in the door to see if he is really gone, and after a few seconds, I resign to going back to bed. I lay back down with the scent of Reagan consuming my room. My pillows smell like him, my nightshirt smells like him and my bedsheets smell like him.

I am never washing any of these items ever. Ever.

I close my eyes, knowing that I'm not going to be sleeping much. I love how Reagan was a gentleman with me. He could have done so many things while lying in my bed, but he didn't. He let me lead what happened. I think back to one of our late night chat sessions where we talked about sex, our past partners and how I wanted to wait to get to know the next person I dated before jumping into something so intimate with them. I think about how Reagan was the complete opposite of the spectrum. He never waited. He was the type that asked a girl's name after the fact, if at all. But tonight, he wasn't like the guy he described himself to be at all. I wonder if I'm special or not enough for him all at the same time.

I finish inhaling his scent from my sheets...again, and I pick up the composition notebook on the nightstand, opening it to the first page. Unlike Mike and my brother's handwriting, which resembles doctor script in need of a decoder to figure out, Reagan's is neat and clear. It's masculine in its style with a gentle slant, and his words are written in black pen.

This is me, until I'm with you.

(Don't skip ahead to day 2 or 3...or 4 until that day is here. This is day 1. Read me first.)

Day 1

Harper,

Since we can't chat every night like we were, I wanted you to have something from me each night, as if I was talking to you in person.

So...here are some stories about me you might like.

When I was 7, I met the most amazing girl. I fell in love instantly. She would always make me smile when I was sad and never said no when I wanted to play. She was by my side when I had a broken arm from falling out of a treehouse, and she loved to eat the snacks I didn't like. I was lost without her. She was my best friend. Her name was Riley, my dog.

P.S. My middle name is Riley.

-Reagan Riley Snow

Do you think he would know if I skipped ahead to day two?

Really?

Dammit.

Closing the book, I begin to drift away, thinking about his lips as I sniff my pillow like an addict and pass out.

Reagan's car is parked in front of my house when I leave for practice with Mike in the morning. Reagan drives a black Mazda Rx-7, which my brother calls a douche mobile. But I think my brother's just jealous because he got stuck with my parents' old minivan. I unlock my car and take in the sleek design of Reagan's compared to mine. My car looks like scrap metal next to his. Maybe I should drive his car today instead. *Would he mind?* I haven't been inside it since I drove it home after Reagan and I encountered Barney fife and his silent partner.

But when I did drive it and park it on the curb in front of my house, I scoured that mother effer like a one man forensics team for any clues about Reagan I could find. I searched the glove box and found his registration with his address listed, and a few mix CDs which I played and played and played. His center console had a pack of condoms, an Altoids breath mint tin and eight sobriety coins. I wasn't sure whether to be softened by his commitment to getting better, or overwhelmed by the preparedness in his sexual prowess. The side pocket on the door had a check stub from Tiny Tots and a wrapper for a Hostess turtle pie.

His car was pretty immaculate which threw my whole investigation off. So what did I do with these limited breadcrumbs? I stalked the shit out of them, that's what I did. When I didn't hear from him the next day, I went by his house but there was no answer. I picked up Bryson from daycare each day and was told Reagan was off. No further details, just off. So I stalked his house some more, and today, I'm waiting until I see movement and then I'm going in.

Reagan lives in an apartment only a few miles from my house. It's a large complex, but his apartment faces the street. *Thank god.* It's making it easier to watch his door from my car, but it's making it really easy for me to feel like I'm being noticed just sitting here.

What the hell am I doing right now?

Gus appears in the doorway of the apartment, and I perk up from my lounging incognito position in the driver's seat. Gus has mail in his hands and unlocks the door, going inside.

Where is Reagan? I should go knock. Gus will know where Reagan is. No, I should not knock. I'll look desperate, and no one likes a desperate girl. I should wait for Reagan to just show up. Dammit. I should knock.

I wait about twenty minutes before I work up the courage to knock on the door. When I do knock, Gus answers, recognizing me on sight. He doesn't say anything at first, he just stares at me, and I stare back.

"I suppose you're looking for Reagan." He opens the door wide and motions for me to come inside.

"Yes." I take a longer stride than usual when entering the apartment. The TV is on at low volume, and the smell of pasta boiling is coming from the kitchen. The door closes behind me, and Gus walks towards the kitchen table.

"I've got something on the stove. Take a seat," he says.

I sit down and take a mental inventory of the simple way Gus and Reagan live. There's no clutter, no dishes in the sink like I would expect two men to have. No musty smell from a garbage pail that needs to be emptied. Their kitchen is clean. Too clean. The same goes for the living room. It doesn't have that lived in feel. I meet Gus' eyes with a cautious smile.

"I'm sorry to just come over unannounced. I did try to call." I point to the phone and answering machine on the counter near the plate Gus has just gotten out of the cupboard.

"I've been expecting you, Harper." A timer dings, and Gus begins straining spaghetti. "I'm sure you've already guessed, but Reagan isn't here."

I nod with disappointment spreading through the hollow of my belly. "Where is he?"

Gus gives me a knowing grin and shakes the strainer of pasta in the sink. He slides the noodles back in the pot he boiled them in, looking up at me. "You want some?" He dips his head towards the pasta.

"Sure." I am hungry, and maybe it will get Gus talking if I stay.

He grabs a second plate and slides noodles onto it, placing a small dollop of red sauce in the center. "Reagan has a set radius with his probation, and he was outside that at that park you two visited."

"I didn't know. It was all my idea to go there. It's not his fault!" I say.

Gus sets a plate down in front of me with a fork on the edge. "I know," he says, while he takes a seat opposite of me. "The thing is, Harper, he's not supposed to be dating, and he's certainly not supposed to be lying on the hood of a car with a girl outside county lines. I know you're a good kid. I can just tell these things. Hell, Reagan can't shut up about you."

This makes me smile, and Gus smiles back like he's remembering his own youthful romances. "But, like I said before, he's gonna break your heart-"

"What does that even mean?" I interrupt, pointing my fork with uneaten pasta on it towards him in an accusing way.

"It means this: He's not a long term choice. You seem like the long term kind of girl. If you continue, which I am sure against all my warnings you will," he smiles, "Reagan's going to leave like this for a longer span of time and may not return. You'll be hurt." He takes a huge bite from his fork and concentrates on his plate before looking back up at me again. "He's a good kid. Don't get me wrong. But he's temporary."

I don't understand. Is Reagan dying, moving or is he simply just the love them and leave them type? He doesn't seem that way with me. He seems genuine when we talk, when we kiss. It's a pull that I've never experienced in my life. Not that I have a lot to compare him to, but he seems far from temporary, so far from a bad choice. But I am sitting in Reagan's apartment alone with his roommate because he got himself arrested. And there is that thing about him being on parole.

Maybe I do need to rethink this.

"Can I leave him a note, for when he gets back?" I ask.

Gus sighs at my request like I haven't heard a word of his warning and says yes while getting up from the table with his plate to get more food. I take a piece of notepaper and a pen from my purse and write to Reagan.

"Can I leave this in his room?"

Gus sighs again and shoots me a stare like I'm asking to move in.

"Please?" I ask again.

"Second door on the left." He points down the hallway.

Reagan's room is minimal just like the rest of his place. The blinds are half drawn. The room only has a bed with a blue comforter, a desk with a chair pushed in and a dresser with a framed photo on top. The photo is of him leaning over a younger guy in a wheelchair with similar facial features. Same indigo eyes and blondish brown hair. Both of their smiles are identical with small dimples in the corners of their mouths. I smile back at the photo and I walk to the desk, brushing my hand over his laptop. My mind trails to our many conversations and I imagine him sitting in this very spot typing to me until three a.m.

I miss it. I miss him.

I sit on the edge of his bed taking in the space and whatever essence of Reagan is in it while I caress my hand over his pillow.

After a few minutes I stand, placing the note I wrote under his laptop so the edge sticks out where his name is written. Gus is in the hallway as I exit Reagan's room, closing the door.

"You're welcome to stay and finish your pasta." His invite is sincere and I should take him up on it, but I have practice to do for an upcoming show.

"Thanks, Gus." I touch his shoulder and slide my hand up and down for a second. "Thanks for letting me see Reagan, and for warning me."

I can tell from his deep sigh that he knows I'm not going to take one word of his warning, but he gives me an understanding nod back.

"You're welcome, Harper."

He walks me to the door and opens it wide. I turn towards him before taking another step down the small set of stairs leading to my car.

"Will he be back soon?"

Gus scans my face before answering and takes a deep breath in. "I don't know."

But I know he knows. With a gentle wave goodbye, I nod and say, "Okay."

I get home just after nine and take a shower. Contorting yourself in a box so people think you got sawed in half is some sweaty work. I walk into the bedroom and see the composition notebook Reagan had left on the nightstand. I'm going to discipline myself and just read today's entry. Just today's. No others.

This is me, until I'm with you.

Day 2

Harper,

When I was 5, I stopped talking. No reason, I just didn't feel like talking anymore. My mom and dad took me to doctor after doctor trying to figure out what was wrong with me. I had hearing tests done, but nothing was showing out of the ordinary. I went to a therapist who asked me if I was being abused, and even at 5 I thought that was an extreme conclusion. My parents were losing their minds until I decided I was done and started talking again.

No real point to this other than I thought you would think I was a nut bag and it would make you laugh.

P.S. My favorite color is blue because inside I'm still a 5 year old with a favorite color.

Day 3

(You skipped ahead didn't you? It's ok, I still like you.)

Harper,

On my 16th birthday, my dad took me to a Vegas brothel because he thought I was still a virgin, and it was a rite of passage when you were 16 (in his mind) to have sex. He had no idea I lost my virginity when I was 13 to my babysitter.

I can hear you thinking Classy Reagan as I write this.

Sorry, but that's the kind of story you get when you skip ahead.

Miss you.

P.S. I have a fear of spiders. Don't judge.

Day 4

I miss turtle pies. That's all.

Day 5

Harper,

When I was 17, I made pot brownies with a friend while my parents were at work. They were the best brownies I think I've ever made. We ate almost all of them and went to my room. When I was walking my friend out later, my mom came home and had a brownie in her hand, mid-chew, saying these were the best brownies she had ever tasted. I wasn't sure if she had ever used pot before, so I sat with her and watched reruns of the show Mash while she laughed hysterically at the TV. Every few minutes she would ask me if I could see all the colors moving on the screen. She was high as fuck. My dad came home and stood in the archway of the living room just staring at my mother and me, shaking his head while she laughed. My mom still asks me to this day to make those delicious brownies again.

P.S. I don't smoke weed anymore, but I still make the best brownies.

Day 6

Harper,

In 5th grade I got in a fight with a kid named Dade. His name was Dade first of all. What kind of name is that? We were fighting over our shoes. His lit up, mine didn't. We got sent to the principal's office for fighting on the playground. He gave me a black eye, and I knocked one of his front teeth out. We've been best friends ever since.

His last name is Thurston. Dade Allister Thurston II. What a completely douchie name, right?

P.S. I took one of your romance novels from your book shelf and read it in 2 days.

Day 7

Since I know you skipped ahead and read the rest of these in one sitting, my next story is going to have to wait until I see you again. Feel free to write your own back to me, if you want.

P.S. I miss kissing you.

PETE

Chapter 10

Reagan 2035

It's been two months since I saw my parents and even longer since they had any interest in seeing me. But today, we have to meet to go over paperwork regarding my recovery and travel. My parents footed the bill and want an update on how their money is being spent. An update in the form of me in front of them for their personal assessment. This rivals standing in front of a grumpy judge times ten.

The one plus side to this day is that I get to see my little brother Owen. I say little, but he could kick my ass in a second if he wanted and he's confined to a fucking wheelchair. Another plus side to this day is Dade. He's coming with me as a buffer because my parents love him. He's smart, funny and the son of the wealthy donor to my parents' charities. He will always have a seat at the table...that is until the money runs out.

Dade and I arrive at my parents for lunch just in time to see Owen getting out of his car and adjusting into his wheelchair in the circle driveway.

"Owen!" I shout as I get near.

"Well, well, well. Look who decided to come to lunch," he says with a huge smile. "I see you brought a date." Owen tips his head to Dade who is walking towards the car, staring into his phone with a smirk.

"Yep, that's right. I'm spoken for," Dade says. He wraps his arms around my shoulders and tries to plant a kiss on my cheek, but before his lips reach me, I give him a jab to the stomach.

"He's so abusive, Owen." Dade cowers in a huddled position behind me. "Help me," he whispers.

Owen laughs, and I reach for the handles on the back of his chair to roll him up the ramp and into the house. Everything about my parents' house is warm and bright, except for their faces when they see me. My mom walks into the entryway when we come inside and only focuses on Owen. But, he deserves the attention.

"Owen honey. How are you feeling?" my mother asks.

She brushes her hand over his shoulder, giving it a gentle pat and hugs Dade who is standing beside me. I get a nod and a forced hello from her like I am an uninvited guest who just showed up. My dad comes around the corner giving Dade a bear hug with a hearty chuckle in his hello and taps Owens' chair, but me? He won't even look at me.

"We thought we'd have lunch out on the terrace. It's such a beautiful day," my mother says.

We follow her to the back of the house. *It is a beautiful day.* We each take a seat at the iron patio table set with formal dining ware, and I notice an extra chair. I don't ask, but it bothers me. My mother and surprise guests always bother me.

My parents have their personal chef serve lunch starting with salad being placed in the center of the table as chilled plates are set down in front of each of us. My dad grabs the tongs and begins serving my mother and then Owen.

"So, Dade. How goes the tech world?" my dad asks.

Dade eyes me before answering, but he knows why he's here.

My buffer. My parent approved, fun loving, buffer.

"The tech world is good, Sir." My father regards Dade like he is the first born he never had, and as if Dade can do no wrong.

"You know, it would be better if you came to work for me."

My dad has been trying to get Dade to work for him for years, but Dade likes the simple nine to five of Best Buy. He clocks in, he clocks out. End of story. There are no business meetings or late night deadlines to make like there would be if he worked for my dad.

"Yeah, I don't see much of a future in time travel technology, Mr. Snow," Dade says with a grin.

My dad lets out a hearty belly laugh and reaches for my plate, without eye contact, handing it back with salad on it in the same manner. Owen and I exchange a glance.

"How's the case this time?" Owen stops the flow of my dad's laughter to direct the conversation towards me. I know what he's doing and it's obvious as my dad sits beside me but acts like I'm not speaking.

"The case is...good. Really good," I say, thinking about Harper during my response. I can't believe how much I miss her and wish I could see her. I wonder if she read my notebook and if she laughed when I thought she would, or if she is writing me her own stories. My mom studies me, but she frowns the whole time. More food is brought to the table but served by the chef to each of our plates, and I'm thankful because it means no more questions for a little while.

"He met a girl," Dade says, mid bite.

"A girl?" My mother's whole face lights up. The only thing that could make my mother come out of her *I'm very disappointed in you* coma is the thought that there is a girl, and maybe a grandchild in her future.

"Aren't you supposed to be? What do they call it?" My dad searches for the right word to conclude his thoughts while staring down at his potatoes au gratin. "Abstaining?"

"Yes," I reply. "Harper is the girl in my case." I take a sip of water, watching what I said sink in.

"So how does it work exactly? You meet a girl back then and you leave a few months later?" Owen asks.

With any other girl, the answer would be a simple yes without any thought. With Harper, my mind is trying to find some hidden cavern of possibility that proves she isn't temporary.

"Pretty much," I say. My standard, heartless go to of a reply makes my mother grimace.

So much for grandchildren twinkling in her eyes.

"That sounds very wrong, Reagan," my mother says, "and very unfair to this poor...Harper."

"It sounds like the perfect relationship." Owen interjects, breaking my mother's disapproving words up into a sliver of a smile that forms as she chuckles.

"It's just enough time for a girl to show how insane she really is," Dade adds.

My father chuckles, and my mother shuts him down with one arched brow. It's not enough time for me to show Harper all the things I want to show her or experience with her.

The table turns silent until my mother's eyes widen and she lets out a relieved sigh as the back door opens. "We didn't think you were going to make it. Please come. Come sit."

The question about the blank chair is over because Gus is now filling that space. He sits on the other side of me as my mother serves him salad and an extra dinner plate is brought in front of him. We give each other a nod while my father excuses himself.

"Long flight?" I ask with a smirk.

Gus gives me a small nod back and hands me something under the table in an envelope and whispers, "I didn't give this to you."

The envelope is blank and when I rip the seal from under the table, I see Harper's writing and my whole body tingles.

"Don't open it yet." Gus leans in. "I just didn't want to forget to give it to you. Thought it would ease some of this." He nudges his head towards my mom and my dad, who is taking a seat back at the table wearing his reading glasses and carrying his binder.

Shit.

The binder is the equivalent of a spanking, and I am about to get spanked... by my dad.

My mother clears the plate in front of my dad, stacking it with hers so he can set the binder down. It's thick and makes a thud on the table.

"Seems there was a little incident we need to discuss, Reagan."

Of course there is. There is always an incident to discuss.

"Would you like to tell me, or should I just announce it to the whole table?" He's asking me like I need to give him permission, but I know better.

"Say what you need to say, Dad." I give him the false permission he requested.

"I thought it was odd you were back so quickly until I got the notice from Mr. Ballzer. Seems you had a run in with the law?" My dad knows the answer.

I hate this game.

"Oh, Reagan. You haven't started drinking again have you?" My mother interjects and sets me back two years with her accusation.

Have I started drinking again? Have I started DRINKING, AGAIN?

"No, I haven't had a drop." I sigh. "I went out of the county lines. It was an accident."

The table is silent while my dad lowers his glasses, flipping through the pages. With each turn he sighs until he gets to one paper in particular and holds it closer to his face.

"Pretty damn tired of accidents with you," my Dad mutters under his breath.

"Dad." Owen snaps in, hearing the unspoken current of those words.

"What's that supposed to mean?" I ask, knowing full well what it's supposed to mean. Gus puts his hand on my shoulder as if to ease my urge to lose my shit.

Too late.

My dad stares at me without a word and I repeat. "What's that supposed to mean, Dad? I should pay forever for my mistake? That all this giving back to society shit isn't enough? I can't say sorry enough. I can't apologize enough to Owen. He's the one who's in a wheelchair because of me and even he's forgiven me! I know I fucked up, but it wasn't all my fault and you know it!"

"That's enough, Reagan." My mother interjects while my dad stares at me as I stand up from the table.

"You guys don't seem to get it. I would trade places in a second with Owen if I could. I feel guilty every fucking day about the accident, but it doesn't change a damn thing." I rake my hands through my hair, awaiting a response. My dad is stewing and my mother is tensing with each word from my mouth.

Silence.

Unbearable silence.

Dade stands, coming to my side of the table, placing his hand on my back. "Let's take a break, man."

I don't want to take a fucking break.

"C'mon. Let's take a walk. Get some air," Dade repeats. I nod and follow him away from the table to the front of the house.

"It's cool, man. I don't need a babysitter," I say, walking down the sidewalk, raising my arms and dismissing Dade from following.

I take a seat on the curb across from a park just a few blocks away from the house. Kids are playing and screaming across the way at the small park with their doting parents nearby. They have no idea what can change that love. How impermanent a parents' faith and trust in you can be if you screw up too many times or break their favorite child.

I shouldn't have come here.

I wish I was in Harper's bed with her arms wrapped around me. I feel so at peace with her.

I pat the breast pocket of my shirt and take out an empty mini bottle of scotch, sniffing the cap and staring at the label. It's the last drink I took before the accident. My little reminder of where I came from. The letter from Harper sits in the same pocket and I pull it out, ripping the remaining edge of the envelope open. I trail my fingers over the cursive spelling of my name on top before opening it.

Reagan,

I don't know where you are, but I hope you're safe. I'm sitting at your kitchen table with Gus eating spaghetti and in a few words? It's fucking strange as hell.

I hope this doesn't make you mad, but I went through your car when I drove it home the other night and found your sobriety chips. I want you to know, no matter what happens with us, I'm proud of you. It's a huge commitment to change your life like that. I hope you know this. You're a good person no matter what you've done in the past.

Anyway, I hope everything is all right.

Harper

Xoxo

P.S. I miss you.

This couldn't have come at a better time.

I put the bottle back in my pocket with the letter and lift from the curb. Walking back to the house, I'm overtaken with thoughts about what I will never be able to do with Harper. She'll never meet Owen or Dade, or my parents for that matter, not that they would be a priority. We'll never walk this street I'm on right now. I stop myself from going further with these thoughts when I see Gus walking towards me.

"You come to collect me?" I ask.

"I came to make sure you were all right. If I want to collect you, I have my ways." He points to my left hand where the monitoring chip sits just under my skin. He pats my back in that way he has done many times before. The way that says *let me help you*, without a single word. We begin the walk back towards the house.

"You ever fall for one of your cases or someone in one of these travels?" I ask.

Gus sighs, patting my back again. "Once," he muses. "She was a beautiful girl. A jazz singer in fact. She had this voice." He pauses. "It was like Nina Simone and Ella Fitzgerald fused in one perfect melody with her." He smiles, reflecting. His eyes are shining and full of life.

"How'd you two meet?"

"We met on a case...much like yours. I was supposed to help her brother though, not her. Her brother played bass in the band and had some unpleasant affiliations. But boy...the second I saw her...." He sighs and shakes his head with a chuckle. "I knew I was in trouble. Kinda like you and Harper. I see the same look in your eyes that I had in mine."

"What ended up happening? What did you do?"

"Oh, I racked my brain trying to see if there was a way I could stay or some way she could come with me. But, nothing could change our fate. It just doesn't work out how you wish it would sometimes."

"Did you tell her who you really were?"

"I did. I did." His voice trails. "But she didn't believe me. I didn't think she would. She called me her day dreamer." Gus laughs. "I was that. I...was...*that*."

"How did it end?"

Gus stares at me, then looks ahead to the house we have finally reached and back at me again. "Her brother was shot, and I didn't save him. The case came to an end and well.... I blame myself for getting distracted and losing sight of the goal. Cost me twenty more years of this job. Of course my beautiful jazz girl didn't want to see me in the days I had remaining, and it killed me. I don't think I've known love or loss like that since."

Guilt sweeps over me for letting Gus remember this. He looks wounded by the memory. "If you had it to do all over again, would you still get involved?" I ask.

"I'd like to say I wouldn't and make you think better of me, but..." He chuckles. "But I probably would do it all over again. Maybe with a little more attention paid to why I was there. Maybe save the day like I was supposed to in the first place."

I nod. "I want to do the right thing, Gus."

"I know you do, Reagan. I know." He pats my back and holds his arm over my shoulder as we walk to the car. Dade is leaning with his back against the passenger side door of the car when we get close.

"Your dad wanted me to give you this," Dade says.

He hands me a folder labeled with my full name. *Reagan Riley Snow*. Inside are release papers signed by my dad, allowing me to continue the case and rehabilitation on Barney Ballzer letterhead. My dad has included a check to cover the next two months of costs as well as a check made out to *Reagan Riley Snow*, for *incidentals*, but I never cash the ones made out to me. They're just another item in the long list of things my dad has to hold over my head, and I don't want them.

"You driving back with me or Gus?" Dade asks.

I hand the release letter over and check for payment to Gus, closing the folder. My parents open the front door for Owen who wheels himself out after warm kisses and hugs from the both of them. My dad's face changes from pleased to stern in a matter of seconds when he sees me, and he turns to go back inside. My mother watches Owen roll down the ramp and waves while looking at Dade and Gus, closing the door.

I could really use a drink right now.

"Am I meeting you tomorrow morning?" I ask Gus.

"Nine sharp," he replies, and I nod.

"I'll catch a ride with Dade if that's okay."

Gus shakes his head and gets into his car, starting the engine and waving before he reverses out of the driveway. Owen rolls towards Dade and me.

"Don't let him get to you, Reagan. He cares. They both do. They just need someone to blame. I know this wasn't your fault," Owen says, tapping on his inoperable legs.

I wish I could give him mine and take the full brunt of his fate as my own. I nod, not wanting to argue the point of my parents' misguided blame.

"You leaving tonight?" Owen asks.

"Tomorrow," I say.

"You really got a girl back there?" Owen asks like he is debating his dating options.

I smile.

"He had me load America Online on my laptop so he could talk to her!" Dade says. "AMERICA ONLINE! Who the fuck uses that?"

I can't control my laughter, and neither can Owen because it's true. I'm using a relic to talk to a girl from the 1990's, although I do enjoy every bit of the chat rooms. Not gonna lie.

"Well, if she captured your interest for more than a night, she must be something." Owen taps my arm, arching his brow.

He's right. She has captured my interest, maybe even more, and I can't wait until I can touch her again, until I hear her laugh.

"She's...." I stall before finishing my sentence because only one word describes how she makes me feel. "Magic."

Dade and I don't talk a lot on the drive home. I grab my notebook from the back seat and write a note to Harper. I'm not sure if I can bring myself to say out loud what I had planned for day seven in the notebook I gave her, so I write it, just in case my mouth fails me.

"Who's watching over your girl while you're away?" Dade asks.

He hates silence, and I'm surprised it took him as long as it has to say something. I look up from writing and set my pen in the page binding so I don't lose my place.

"I assume it's Gus. I mean, that's the protocol."

"Protocol? Wow...that word from you? No."

"What? It's what it's called."

"Pro...to...col." Dade sounds it out like a school teacher teaching a student a new word. "I think I need clarity."

Dade presses the call button and says "Gus" as ringing begins through the car speakers. I try to press the end call button illuminated on the screen in the dash and even say the word *End*, but it doesn't work.

"She only responds to my voice." Dade holds his arm up blocking my attempts.

She?

"Gus Jackson."

"Gus, its Dade."

I see Gus in my mind, and he is probably displaying the *what the fuck* Gus expression at this very moment.

"Hello Dade." The dreary response from Gus tells me I'm right. I lean back in my chair, lifting my foot on the dash and listen.

"I was just asking Reagan if he knew who was watching Harper while he was away, and he used the word *protocol*. You and I both know that's a really big word for him to use, and I just wanted clarity as to the *protocol* in these situations." Dade arches his brow with a slow nod of his head.

"Well, Dade. The pro...to...col is the probation officer in charge carries out the duties with the case while the parolee is detained." Gus couldn't be more unenthused in his response. I'm surprised he's humoring Dade at all.

"I see... and how is said case going?" Dade asks. His sudden formality in word choice makes me want to jump out of the car. I have to admit, I am a bit curious now though. How is the case going without me?

"Is Harper staying out of trouble?" Dade asks.

Very curious.

Gus sighs. "She's been hanging out with that magic guy."

"Magic Mike?" I ask, a little too eager while sitting up in my seat.

Dade stiffens and mouths, *Magic Mike? Who the fuck is Magic Mike?*

"He's a friend of *said case* who can't seem to stay away. Been at her house *all* week," Gus says. He knows this is not what I want to hear, which is probably the reason he's saying it.

"What have they been doing?" I ask.

Dade is still dazed at the name. "Who is Magic Mike?" Dade asks, and is ignored.

"She's been in a bikini in the pool when she gets home with him right beside her," Gus goads.

Did we not just have a heart-to-heart less than an hour ago? *What the fuck?* Dade is ignored again when asking the same question.

"He's been right beside her as in…kissing her, hugging her? What?"

Why is she hanging out with that guy? Why is she sending me notes that she misses me when she's spending all her free time with dickhead?

"Gus?" His lack of response makes me even more annoyed.

"Reagan?" He replies with a calm and cool voice. "Take a breath. I don't need you losing sight of the goal here. She's been hanging out with the magic guy and that's all I'm going to say."

Fuck, that's not the response I wanted at *all*. I can't breathe, and I feel heat rising to my head in waves. The last time this happened….

"Dude, are you alright?" Dade asks, and pulls the car over to the side of the road. "Gus, are you close?"

My window rolls down and I breathe in and out, but I'm not getting air. Opening my door, everything is spinning and a sick feeling hits my stomach as I fall.

Not again.

Chapter 11

Harper 1993

"Harper?"

I hear the muffled sounds of my name and feel a tap on my back from Mike. We're practicing breath holds in my backyard pool for an upcoming magic trick I want to do in a water torture chamber. I told Mike my idea, and he has been over every day this week to help me.

His hand taps my back again and I rise to the surface, arching my back to stand and see a grey suited man who's calling my name as he walks down the stone pathway entering the backyard.

"Harper Adams?" he asks, walking closer to the pool where Mike and I are standing in the shallow end.

"Yeah, that's me." I say, holding my nose to make my ears pop from being under water. I glance at Mike squinting as the suited man squats near the edge of the pool. He gives a guarded smile to us and extends his hand to me.

"I'm Barney. Barney Ballzer?"

I shake his hand as water drips onto the cuff of his shirt, and I release before more water spills. I have no idea who he is, and my face wrinkles in the confusion.

"I see I've caught you in the middle of something." He motions to the fins and goggles on the side of the pool deck. I follow his gaze, narrowing my eyes and look back at him. The sun is hitting his forehead like a spotlight.

"Yeah, I'm practicing holding my breath for a show coming up." I ease into a full explanation and pull back because this makes no sense to anyone but me and Mike. "I'm sorry. I don't mean to be rude but..." I cut my sentence short when Gus rounds the hedges and walks towards the pool. Barney follows my focus and stands to greet him.

"Gus?" I ask.

"Harper." He nods.

"What are you doing here?"

He doesn't answer, looking over towards Barney who tightens his lips in a thin line before speaking.

"Do you have a moment, Harper? We'd like to discuss something with you. Alone," Barney says.

I turn to Mike, who I can tell is judging this situation the same way I am.

"What's this about?" Mike asks in a protective way.

Barney and Gus both reply with polite grins towards Mike, like he isn't part of this conversation.

"We'd like to discuss it privately with Miss Adams," Gus says.

"Yeah, but what is this about?" Mike repeats. He isn't letting their ignoring the question go, and I'm glad because I'm a bit speechless.

"It's about Reagan," Gus says.

My heart lurches in my chest at the thought of why these two men are here.

What does this mean? Is Reagan hurt? Is he in trouble?

"Is that the guy who was here last week?" Mike asks, and I shush him.

I don't think Reagan was supposed to be here. I wade to the steps, feeling the coolness of the water reaching my dried stomach, and I walk up the steps while grabbing a towel from the edge before I step out of the pool, bringing the towel to my face to pat the water off. I hand one to Mike who follows behind me.

"Do you want to talk in my place? It's right over here," I ask Barney and Gus as I point to the open French doors leading to my apartment and wrap the towel around my waist.

Both men nod and follow me.

Mike stands back drying off on the deck and yells, "I'll catch you later, Harp."

I nod back, feeling a tinge of guilt leaving him so abrupt.

My nerves take over when I pass through the French doors and walk along the stone path to my apartment.

Why am I nervous? I haven't done anything. What is so serious about Reagan that they couldn't tell me by the pool with Mike present?

I roll through thought after thought until I turn the handle of my door and open it wide for the two men to walk in.

"Thank you," Gus and Barney repeat, one after the other.

"Have a seat. Do you want some water or..."

Both men shake their heads no.

I adjust the wrapped towel around my waist and sit on the chair adjacent to the couch. The air conditioning has kicked on, making visible goose bumps spread over my arms. “So, what’s wrong with Reagan?” I ask.

Gus scrubs his hands down his face with a forced grin while Barney leans forward, arching his elbows on his knees with his hands held up in a triangle in front of his mouth.

“Has Reagan told you anything about where he’s from?” Barney asks.

I nod. “We’ve talked about where he grew up and his childhood a little. Is that what you mean?”

Both men look at each other, and I wonder if I am saying the right thing.

“He hasn’t told you why he’s here...specifically, or...what happened to him?” Barney asks.

I shake my head no. “He’s mentioned an accident, but he didn’t go into detail,” I add.

I wish they would both just spit it out. *Why are they here?* I don’t want to play twenty questions. I want answers, and I want them now.

“Where is Reagan?” My curiosity is unraveling into bluntness in the face of their secrecy. “Is he hurt? Is he in trouble?”

“He’s in the hospital right now.” Gus says, and my hands go to my mouth.

Hospital? Hospital? Hospital?

“Is he okay? Can I see him?” I stand, but both men stay seated and unaffected by my reaction.

"He isn't here... he's back home." Barney answers, and I have no idea what they are getting at or why they are still so calm.

"Can I go to him? Where is he? I want to see him!"

"Harper, he's..." Gus pauses to look at Barney before continuing. "Sit," he says.

"I'd like to stand. Where is Reagan?" I ask, ready to grab my keys and go to him no matter where he is.

"You're gonna want to sit for this. Trust me." I gather from Gus' tone that I am about to be hit with some serious shit.

"There's no delicate way to say this..." Barney says. My mind is reeling with thoughts of Reagan being injured, lying on his death bed. Barney pulls a folded white paper from the inside of his jacket pocket with a pen, setting it on the coffee table.

"But, before we go further, I need you to sign this." He slides the paper towards me. I reach for it, unfolding the paper and read the letters *NDA* at the top.

"What is this?" I ask, reading my full name already filled in on the first line and the words *will be granted conditional access to information owned by, produced by or in the possession of the United States Government* following after.

"It's a non-disclosure agreement. It says you won't discuss anything we tell you with anyone," Barney says.

The document has other jargon similar to what I used to see on the many legal papers in files I would view at my dad's practice when I was younger. I follow the words to the end and I sign. I hand it back to Barney who nods and puts it inside his jacket pocket.

"I'm just going to come out and say it because there really is no other way." He pauses. "Reagan...is a time traveler." He pauses again with a frozen expression, as if to convey his words deeper. But I give him a blank stare back, and he continues. "He's currently sitting in the year 2035 and came here to help you." Barney is so matter-of-fact, like there is nothing out of the ordinary in his statement.

Um.

I let out a bark of a laugh, but neither Gus nor Barney flinch from their deadpan stare at me. "What?" is all I can get to come out of my mouth.

Barney repeats his words. "Reagan...is a time traveler. He's currently sitting in the year 2035 and came here to help you."

I still have no understanding of what he is telling me.

"He had a little incident that's going to delay his travel and...we want to bring you to him. He's in a pretty bad way right now."

"What bad way? What's wrong? What?" I can't decide which of the many questions to ask first. My mind is slicing and adding more, faster than I can pull the words to spit out. "Is this a joke?"

"I assure you, the federal government doesn't joke," Barney says with an uneasy grin that fades as fast as it appeared.

He reaches inside his jacket pocket and pulls out his wallet, showing me his government I.D.

Gus does the same. Both of them place their I.D.'s on the coffee table for me. I lean down to look at both of them, but I have no idea what I'm looking at.

Do I stare at the faces, the names?

Everything looks legit, but I wouldn't know if they were fake. They don't teach this in school for Christ's sake.

"If you need someone to validate those, I can give you a number to call." Barney says this like he has a work reference I can just call up and ask about their time travel identification's legitimacy.

"Okay, okay..." I hold my hands to my forehead, squeezing my eyes shut, trying to process what the *fuck* I'm hearing. "Are you both time travelers too?" I open my eyes to ask and receive nods in unison.

Of course they are.

"And Reagan was sent here to help me?" I ask, and again receive dueling nods. "Am I in danger? Why is he helping me?"

Gus gets up from the couch to take the I.D. from me and places his hand on my shoulder, urging me to sit.

"We can't tell you the specifics of the case but..."

"But I should just trust two men who came into my house with I.D.'s that say they time travel and want to take me with them?"

"Let me ask you something." Gus sits on the edge of the coffee table. His eyes are so trusting and honest as he regards me. "Would you like to see Reagan tonight? I know you don't believe what we are saying and hell, I wouldn't believe it myself if it wasn't my job, but I promise you, this is the truth."

I don't know why I am entertaining the idea of believing Gus, but I do. His voice is soft and soothing. "Go get dressed and we will talk more on the way."

I don't refuse. I don't ask another question or express any other doubts. I nod and get up from my chair, walking towards my bedroom. When I get to my door, I close it behind me and see the notebook Reagan gave me, sitting on the edge.

This is insane.

I take the shortest shower I have ever taken and sit on the bed in my towel with my wet hair dripping down my back. I grab the notebook sitting on my nightstand from Reagan and flip through the pages where he wrote me his sweet stories. I close it so the back is facing up in my lap. I study the pattern of black and white camouflage formations like a hidden message is in them somewhere. The barcode catches my eye and within a second, my breath hitches as I read the writing around the barcode. *©2035 Work Pro Inc. Wilton, CT 06897.*

2035?

My purse is sitting beside my dresser, and I hurry to pick it up and look inside for the Altoids breath mints tin I took from Reagan's car. I turn the tin over. *©2033 Callard & Bowser.*

Holy.

I recall the night at the bar where Reagan gave me change to do a magic trick, and I get my wallet out, unzipping the change holder and pulling out the quarters. Money always has a date on it. The faces of all five quarters I have are dawned with George Washington's profile and the word *Liberty* on the top, but I notice only one has a date on the bottom. *1989.* I flip the remaining four quarters over to where the usual eagle would be displayed to find pictures.

I squint at the small beveled writing. The first one reads *California* at the top with the caption *California John Muir, Yosemite Valley* and the date *2005* at the bottom. The next reads *Virginia* at the top with the caption *Shenandoah* and the date *2014* at the bottom. I'm hunched over like a prospector who just found gold, staring into these coins.

Alaska, The Great Land with the date *2008* is the next one. The final one is for the state of Tennessee. The image is of a small banner and text that reads *Musical Heritage* underneath a fiddle, trumpet, guitar and music score. The date is *2013.*

"Harper?" Gus' voice calls low and delicate from the other side of my door with a soft knock.

"One sec," I say, still staring at the quarters in my hand.

Is what they are saying true?

My chest is tingling from...excitement? Lifting from the bed, I get dressed in jeans and a t-shirt with my combat boots and flannel for a jacket. I place a black beanie over my towel dried hair and open my bedroom door.

"I'm ready," I say to Gus, who is standing in the hallway near my bedroom door. "Can I bring my purse or..."

Gus nods and motions for me to lead the way. We walk towards the living room together and I open my front door, holding it for Gus and Barney to exit before I lock it. I follow them down the path to the street where they stop walking in front of a black Lincoln Town Car with heavy tint on the windows. Gus opens the passenger door for me and I get in, taking a seat. He gives me a relaxed grin as the door closes. The back door opens, and Gus gets in while the driver side door opens with Barney taking a seat behind the wheel. I feel like I'm going to dinner with relatives I hardly know.

The car pulls away from the curb, and I stare out my window to see Mike standing with my mom on the lawn, deep in conversation. I can only imagine the conversation.

Mike telling her, "Yeah, these two men told her something was wrong with that one guy she's only known a little while, and she got in their car."

My mother responding with a gasp and yelling "Hal! come quick!"

"So, what's wrong with Reagan?" I ask, after a few long minutes of listening to news talk radio at low volume.

"He really didn't tell you anything about why he's here?" Barney asks, completely surprised that I don't already know the answer.

I shake my head no.

"Wow, the kid actually did something we told him." He smiles in the rearview back at Gus.

"First," Barney tilts his head towards me, "Reagan is going to be okay, but he had a bit of an episode after visiting his parents. He has what we call post-traumatic stress disorder from an accident a while back. It seems to rear its ugly head when he gets upset or visits his family."

"I know what that is. My father had it after Vietnam," I say.

Barney acknowledges me with a nod.

"Has Reagan told you about what happened with his brother?" Gus asks from the backseat, and I turn in my seat to respond.

"He told me he had an accident, and I saw the scars on his arm and stomach, but he didn't want to talk about it yet. I didn't want to push him. I saw a picture in his room. Is that his brother? In the wheelchair?"

Gus nods. "The accident is probably best to hear about from Reagan, but it's the reason he was put in jail."

I nod, wanting more details, but I also want to hear it first hand from Reagan. He's more than willing to share almost any story except this one, and as much as I want to know, I don't want to hear it from Gus or Barney.

"Can I ask...how you time travel? Is that a fair question? Am I allowed to ask?"

Gus and Barney smirk at me.

"Why don't we show you?" Barney says.

He turns into an empty library parking lot and parks the car in a spot close to the entrance. He turns off the car and Gus gets out, opening my door. I step onto the pavement and follow Barney who has already started walking towards the library entrance.

"We're going to the library?" I ask, as we get closer to the door.

Gus smiles and swipes his left hand over a security panel on the side of the closed automatic doors, which makes them open.

"Trust me, Harper. This is like no library you've ever seen in your life." He winks.

It looks identical to every library I've ever seen in my life, right down to the two old librarians at the front desk who probably comment on every book a patron checks out. Each of the two ladies grins at Gus who gives them a tip of his imaginary hat with a nod saying, "Ladies," as we pass by.

We walk into the fiction section of the library passing bookshelf after bookshelf, and I spy a few of my book boyfriends on the covers of paperbacks in swivel racks.

"Wow, I didn't know you could check out magazines." I say, as we come to a door near the periodical section.

"No one does," Barney says while sliding his left hand over a black security marker on the side of the door frame.

The door slides open and disappears into the side of the wall, revealing an elevator car. Dark wood paneling lines the walls, and it smells like fresh paint. The doors close, and I stand towards the back wall and watch Gus slide his hand over a black box with a red light that turns green. He punches the numbers 2035, holding his eye in front of a black screen. A red light scans over his eye, and the elevator begins to ascend.

"You nervous?" Gus asks.

Am I nervous? Oh I don't know. YES!

"I'm curious." I reply with an uneasy smile.

"Don't be nervous."

2035

The elevator dings and comes to a stop. The doors slide open to the exact library we just left. We walk past the same periodical section, the same swivel rack of my book boyfriends, and up the ramp past the fiction shelves and towards the exit. The information desk is occupied by two different older ladies that Gus acknowledges in the same manner as before, only he says, "Good day, Ladies," as we pass them.

The doors to the exit open to a similar parking lot, but the buildings surrounding the library are not the same as before. We are in the heart of a city with a magnificent orange and pink sunset painting the sky. A city that could be compared to an oven on my face from the blast of heat that just hit it.

"Where are we? What city is this?" I ask. "It's hot as hell!"

"Come." Gus chuckles as we follow Barney to a town car parked in the same spot we parked in before. I catch a glimpse of the front license plate, hoping to see the state listed, but it offers nothing other than *US Government, For Official Use Only* with numbers in the middle.

"Are we in hell? Why is it so hot?!"

"You're in Arizona. Phoenix," Gus says, laughing at my question as he opens the front passenger side door for me to get in.

It's even hotter in the car, and I may have just gotten a third degree burn from the metal on the seatbelt I just touched. Barney gets in the driver's side and starts the car, turning on the air which blows hot on my face like a hair dryer set to high heat.

I'm not enjoying the future at all right now.

Gus closes my door and gets in the back seat, closing his door. I look back at him and see the perspiration on his forehead while he takes his suit jacket off. I pull off my beanie and grab a hair tie to pull my hair into a messy bun. My skull is sweating to the point that the smell of my shampoo fills the air.

"The hospital's not far," Barney says.

He puts the car in reverse, heading towards the main road. The future looks like a normal cityscape. Nothing out of the ordinary. No flying cars. No people traveling by jetpack in the sky. It's a bit disappointing...

Says the girl who just time traveled forty-two years via a library elevator.

"We are in 2035?" I sound loud and confused while staring out the window as we drive onto the freeway, and I glance over to Barney.

He nods and points at a part of downtown that's visible as we near an overpass. We take the curve in the road to another freeway where Barney veers towards the next exit off ramp. *Hospital Next Right* a sign reads. My heart isn't sure whether to be excited or prepared for the worst.

The car pulls right and into a hospital parking lot. Barney finds a spot close to the entrance and parks. Gus gets out first, opening my door to a blast furnace of air that stuns me.

"Fuck!" I say, as I stand and the air hits me. I try to place what I'm smelling and it's like wet cement and twenty different plants fighting for survival in the heat, but mostly it's Gardenias and trash; musty air and flowers. The future friends. The future. "Sorry, Gus."

He smirks at me. "It's quite all right, Harper. I've said worse than that the few times I've come here."

Barney begins to walk ahead, and we follow towards the entrance into the coolness of the lobby, which feels like an icebox. I can't believe I'm actually putting my flannel and beanie *back on*. We stop at the visitor's desk where we are each given guest badges to wear. We take an elevator to the third floor and are greeted by a nurse who has been expecting us.

"Right this way," she says. We get to a closed door where she cautions us. "He's a little out of it."

"Harper, would you like to go in and see him first?" Gus asks.

I nod, unsure of what to expect. The door opens, and Reagan is lying in a bed which is half raised. His eyes are closed. I'm unable to hold back, and I press my lips to his forehead. His eyelids flutter when I touch the side of his face.

"I've missed you, Reagan."

I pull away, setting my purse in a nearby chair and adjust the sleeves on my flannel. He doesn't have any visible injuries. Nothing seems broken or different. The scar on his arm is exposed in the short sleeve gown he's wearing, and I study the way it aligns with the curve of his bicep.

It's the first time I've seen him asleep, and even though we are in a hospital, he's quite handsome at rest. I can't help but smile while watching him. Leaning in closer again, I brush my fingers through the top of his hair, studying his lips and closed lids. I'm not sure what more I'm supposed to do, although staring at Reagan is among one of the many things I don't mind doing.

A few twinkling lights that look like they are coming from a plane landing catch my eyes from the window. I walk over to check out the view. In a nicer temperature, the city would be quite beautiful. I hear Reagan clear his throat and turn to him. His eyes are open and staring straight at me. He looks as confused as I feel when I think about my night and getting here.

PETE

Chapter 12

Reagan 2035

"Harper?"

She isn't here right? She couldn't be standing by the window staring at me or walking towards me with a huge grin. It's not possible. Right?

"Harper?" I say her name again, almost waiting for the fade of her image to begin, but she's getting closer. Her hand is going to my face, and that grin...God, that beautiful smile is getting bigger and bigger the closer her lips get to mine.

"Hi," she whispers.

Her lips encase mine, and I give her everything I have in return. I pull her head closer and brace my hand around the back of her neck. I can feel her. I can *fucking* taste her. I lean my head back, admiring how beautiful she looks. Her name is ringing in my head.

"Harper...." I whisper, again and again, my voice raspy and low.

She smiles even more at my repeated words. She's here. She's really here.

"I've missed you, Reagan." She takes a seat on the bed close enough for me to lay my hand over her thigh.

"How *are* you here?" I ask. "I'm not dreaming am I?"

She laughs and shakes her head no. She's coy and smiling as she does this. I study her lips, her eyes, her adorable grunge style beanie paired with the flannel she has on. Her eyes trail to the scar on my arm; then to my neck, my lips and my eyes. It's a silent stare we've both found solace in on more than a few occasions.

"Sure wish we had something to talk about right now," she says.

My delayed reaction to her sarcasm makes her frown until I catch on and smile. I take her hand in mine, lacing my fingers with hers, rubbing my thumb over her knuckles.

"How was your trip here?" I ask, trying to sound humored while knowing how she got here, but not *who* brought her here.

"I don't have a lot to compare it to," she says. "It's not every day two men named Barney and Gus tell you the guy you're seeing is a time traveler and he needs to see you, so grab your things."

I nod, smirking at her. "What did they tell you?"

"They told me you were in the hospital and I could see you. When I asked where you were, they told me you were a time traveler." She giggles. "A time traveler! Just like that, all nonchalant." Her voice carries and she grins which puts me at ease. She isn't scared by this, and she seems to be entertained by the whole idea.

"I did have to sign a paper saying I wouldn't say anything, but honestly, who would believe I time traveled via a library elevator in the suburbs and landed in the same library smack dab in a city forty-two years later?"

"There are a few guys in the AOL chatrooms that would."

Harper giggles again at me, narrowing her gaze to mine for a second before softening her expression.

"Do you want to tell me what's going on? Are you all right?"

I exhale with a deep sigh. "I had a panic attack and fell. I get them when I see my family sometimes. I was having lunch with them, and my dad and I got into an argument. Well, I got into an argument I should say. They both just sat there."

"Was it about the accident?" she asks.

I don't know what she has been told, and I'm not sure I'm ready to tell her. I glance over at the composition notebook sitting on the nightstand, and Harper's eyes follow.

"I was writing about the accident in the car on my way back to my place. My roommate Dade was driving, and he called Gus from the car to ask about you. Gus told me you were hanging out with that Mike guy and...I started to freak out I guess." I feel stupid saying this out loud. *Who has a panic attack over a girl?*

"Me and Mike?" she asks, almost insulted as she leans back.

"He said Mike had been at your place all week and you were hanging out in your bikini in the pool at night."

"And you thought I was doing something with him? Like...DOING something? Just like that?" she asks.

I shake my head yes.

"I'm not interested in Mike. He's just a friend." She tightens her lips and softens them as she continues. "Mike isn't even my type. There's someone else I'm interested in anyways."

"Someone else?"

Harper nods as a huge grin takes over, but I can't seem to match it.

"YOU, stupid. God." She hits my shoulder.

I let out a relieved chuckle.

"Me?" Whatever this last panic attack was about has made me slow in the head.

Harper nods and brings her lips to mine again with a quick peck. If she could just stay and do that some more, I think I'd be healed in no time.

She shifts her body closer, leaning in with her arm arched over the side of my head against the back of the bed, supporting her weight. She caresses my cheek and runs her fingers around the nape of my neck, feathering the hairs like she did in her basement. My eyes close right on cue from how good it feels. She hovers over my lips.

"Time traveler..." she whispers with a giggle, and I open my eyes with a huge grin.

She's just about to lean in again and kiss me when my doctor walks in and steals my thunder. Harper sits up and with one look towards my doctor; I know she has gone into book boyfriend heaven.

I can admit when a man is handsome. I'm secure enough in myself to acknowledge a good looking guy when I see one. Doctor Evans is a handsome man, and his eyes are a hypnotic blue that makes people as tightly wound as my mother come undone. It's pretty fantastic to watch.

Harper hasn't stopped staring, and now he's smiling at her.

Great.

"Should I go?" Harper asks.

I look at Doctor Evans for an answer as he regards her with a warm grin. It's a grin that has made my beautiful girl's face flush.

"You can stay," he says.

God, she's melting from those three words alone.

"If it's okay with Reagan." He motions to me, and I shrug but realize we might be discussing the accident, so I grimace. Harper notices my change in demeanor.

"I'll go, it's fine. I'll just be right outside."

She kisses my cheek and gets up from the bed to stand, turning to leave. Doctor Evans gives her another warm smile that makes her cheeks flush even brighter in color, and she gives me a shy wave as she walks towards the door. If I didn't know he was happily married with five kids, I would be jealous.

"So, Reagan. Is that the mystery girl?" he asks, once the door to my room closes. "Mind if I sit?"

I nod.

"She is," I say, with an uncontrollable smile.

Doctor Evans checks my chart, setting it down to get a better look at me. He's been my doctor since the accident and helped my brother when he was here as well. He knows me like a therapist should.

"She's beautiful. How'd you two meet?" he asks.

"I met her on a case. Well, she *is* my case."

"Ah, I see. Love at first sight, huh?" he chuckles.

I nod with a sheepish grin.

"You know I met my wife on a case?"

My eyes widen at him.

"She was a patient actually." He arches his brow with a happy glimmer in his eye. "Most beautiful woman I ever saw." He sighs. "I didn't see it coming at all. But, sometimes love doesn't ask for permission, it just barges in like an unexpected freight train." He laughs, and I chuckle.

"The problem is...she isn't from here," I say, without having to explain. Doctor Evans gets that I'm talking about travel and the distance with time. He gives me an understanding nod.

"You love while you can and as much as you can, Reagan. Not when the timing is right." He pats my leg. "These things have a way of working out how they're supposed to no matter how hard we try to intervene. Trust me."

"I've never been much of a believer in love until I met Harper," I say.

Doctor Evans nods. "Neither was I until I met Em. You like this girl?" he asks.

I shake my head yes.

"Let's see if the powers that be will let her stay for a day or two," he says. "Show her your life here. Show her who you are and where you came from. Might do you some good to balance the bad memories you have of this place with some good ones."

"It's not gonna feel good when it's over." I shrug.

"Don't think about the end, think about how much you want to share with her in the time you have together." Doctor Evans stands, grabbing hold of my chart.

He's like the older, wiser brother I wish I had. "You look good, Reagan." He peruses my chart, giving me a glance. "You ready to leave this place?"

"I might need bedrest with Harper as my private nurse," I say.

"That's my boy. You're already back to your old self." He grins. "I'm going to recommend some down time with this Harper in the form of a cryptic doctor's note." He winks at me and scribbles in my chart as he continues. "I do see noticeable improvement in your mood already with her very short visit so far."

My doctor is a romantic, and he looks like a *fucking* Greek god.

"I'll be back in just a bit with the discharge papers."

Harper enters as Doctor Evans stands to leave. Both give each other knowing smiles, only Harper's is shy, and her cheeks are flushing rosy pink again.

"I'm sorry, I forgot my purse," she says.

Doctor Evans puts out his hand to her. "I don't think we've officially met. I'm Doctor Evans." His smile is big and endearing when Harper takes his hand.

God, I love her shy side. It contradicts everything I have seen of her confident stage persona.

"I'm Harper," she says, batting her eyelashes.

Adorable.

"He's all yours," Doctor Evans says, and Harper meets my adoring gaze.

"You like my doctor?" I ask as she comes closer. The bed dips as she takes a seat close to me like before.

"He looks like a romance novel come to life in a doctor's lab coat. Those eyes are so beautiful. It's like he was staring into my soul," she says, and I smirk.

"Are you trying to make me jealous?"

"You? Oh no, you're *my* romance novel in the flesh. All mine!"

She brings her hands to my cheeks, cupping my face. I can't help but smile at her.

"And a time traveler no less." She gives me a wry grin. "Oh, I have a little surprise for you."

She lifts from the bed to grab her purse, sitting back down and placing it on her lap as she digs inside. She pulls out a Hostess turtle pie and it makes me belly laugh.

"Harper, is it too soon for me to say I love you?" I ask. The sound of her laugh flutters over me in tingling waves, but I do love her. I wish I could tell her just how much.

"I brought something else for you too." She pulls out the composition notebook I gave her and hands it to me. "I didn't wait to read all your stories. I'm sorry. I missed you. I just couldn't wait to read your words."

"I kinda knew you would read them all. Did I make you laugh?"

She grins, and it's every bit of what I hoped her answer would be. "I loved the brownies story. God, your poor mother!"

"Oh don't feel bad for her." I brush my hand over her cheek, making her eyes close and open in response to my touch. "Are you giving this back to me because you want more?"

She glances at the notebook and back at me with a reserved smile.

"I'm giving this back to you because..." She hesitates. "I wrote some stories and...and I wanted you to finish day seven. That's today, you know?"

I tighten inside over day seven because day seven is what I wrote about in my notebook while in the car. I gloss over her curiosity of it and ask, "Can I read it?" Outstretching my hand for the notebook.

She presses her hand on top of it, shaking her head no with a mischievous grin.

"No?"

"I want you to read it when I'm not with you like you did to me, and I want to know about day seven, or I'm not giving it to you."

"Oh is that right?" I smile at her challenge. "You know, I have ways of making you give it up." I shake my head yes while she shakes her head no and grab her in my arms, tickling her. She laughs loud and screams, "No!" while trying to fight my hands off of her sides.

"Harper, give me the notebook!" I laugh while continuing my assault. I pull her closer onto my lap, still needling my fingers into her sides as she howls and pants from laughing.

She reaches her arms around my neck as I slow my fingers from tickling her. She holds the notebook in her hands behind my neck, and she kisses me. Her beanie is now lopsided and I pull it off, releasing the wavy mess of her hair and adjust it back onto her head.

"I'll give you the notebook, but promise me I get to read more stories...and day seven?" she asks.

I can't resist her. I can't. I nod, and she winks at me. She begins to lift off of me, but I hold her steady.

"I'm not done." I squeeze her tight in my arms.

"Not done what?" She smirks. I adjust my arms around her, loosening my grip, studying her eyes. There's so much truth in them, so much vulnerability yet she lets me in, lets me hold her like this. I think I could survive on the way she looks at me alone. I'm in so deep for her. Fuck.

"I want to tell you something about this day seven you are so curious about."

"Okay." She matches my furrowed brow.

"I want to tell you what happened with this." I point to my arm and the side of my body. "But it's hard for me to talk about, so I wrote it out in the notebook over there. I want to be there when you read it okay?"

Harper nods in understanding, and my lips curl. My hands curve around her jaw as I close my eyes and kiss her. She's unlike anyone I've ever been with, so open and trusting of me when she has every reason to run.

A cough interrupts us. A cough attached to Gus. One of the many reasons that could make her run. Harper shifts off of my lap and towards the bedside chair as Gus walks towards me.

"You two get reacquainted?" he asks, motioning to me and Harper. His sarcastic tone doesn't go unnoticed by either of us. Harper's doe eyes glance down and back up at me. I crave the way she looks at me when we're apart.

I can tell Gus likes Harper and the effect she has on me. He's told me on more than one occasion that she brings out my honest side. The fact that he's brought her here tells me he isn't so against us being together like he was at first.

Gus stands at the edge of my bed, his hands in his pockets. "We should talk." He has his *all about business* face on.

"I can go," Harper says, beginning to stand and gather her purse.

"No, Harper, you should stay," Gus says, and he gestures for her to sit, and she does. Barney comes into the room with a smile directed at Harper but he has a frown saved for me.

"Seems this young lady has worked some magic on the good Doctor Evans. He's insisting she stay for an extra day or two until you are back to normal. It's not an order I've ever seen before," Barney says, and I feel a jolt of a tingling sensation take over my whole body. Harper sits up straight in her chair, gripping the arms tight.

"I get to stay?" she asks.

Barney eyes her, still frowning, but softens to a grin when he sees her trying to hide a smile. Even Gus smirks at her. I love how transforming her whole demeanor is on others. Her face is showing the excitement I'm trying desperately to hide. Barney's head turns back to me, morphing his face into his usual *unhappy to see me* stare.

"This goes against every rule in the handbook, Reagan. Every god damn rule we've set in place to keep you out of trouble and on track. You can thank your brother for getting Harper here and forcing the powers that be to agree to her coming all this way."

I really want to smother my brother with every ounce of brotherly love I can muster right now. "Is Owen here?" I ask.

Barney shakes his head no, which sends a wave of disappointment to my heart.

"I've got your discharge paperwork here." He sets it down on the side table next to the bed. "You have one day, and then you both go back. One day," he repeats.

One day. I have one day to show Harper my life here. It sinks in fast and spreads wild throughout my body. This is something I never thought I would get. My mind is racing with what to show her first. Do I take her to see my brother? Show her my place? Take her somewhere she's never been? Do we go out or stay in?

Gus tries to maintain his authoritative stare, but I can tell he's having trouble from the smile on my face and Harper's.

"Is there a way to tell my parents? So they don't worry?" Harper asks.

Barney regards her request with a conceding nod.

"We can have someone get in touch with them," he says.

"There's just one thing," Gus says. He walks closer to Harper. "We need to give you a chip, like Reagan's. Just a precaution. We don't need a rogue case killing our kindness in this situation." Gus continues. "It's a small incision that goes right here." He touches her left hand, trailing his index finger in between my thumb and forefinger.

"Will it hurt?" Harper asks, looking over to me.

I shake my head no.

"It doesn't hurt. But it does feel strange at first." Gus assures her, and she nods.

"You good with this?" Gus holds up a tiny chip the size of a pinky nail encased in a small bag. This little chip he is holding has every detail of Harper's life on it.

Harper nods.

Doctor Evans walks in with a nurse beside him who is wheeling in a small tray. Harper is set into the trance that Doctor Evans seems to cast on every woman.

"You ready to become computerized?" Doctor Evans smiles at Harper as he wheels a rolling stool closer to the chair she's sitting in.

She nods her head, following with a nervous giggle. The nurse pushes the silver tray towards Doctor Evans.

"Can I see your left hand?" he asks.

Harper gives him her hand with a shy grin. I don't know if he's helping or hurting by smiling even bigger at her. Either way, he's distracting her from the incision and chip being implanted.

"This is all kind of weird, huh?" he says, while working with her hand.

Harper shakes her head yes with another small giggle.

"You're all set," he says, taking off his gloves and setting them on the tray. The nurse grins and rolls the cart out.

"It's going to itch a bit, Harper, but that's normal. Try not to scratch it and let me know if you have any problems, okay?" I'm not sure from Harper's face if she is registering anything he is saying. She's giving him the same blank stare she gives me when she goes somewhere in her head.

"Okay?" Doctor Evans smiles, studying her face.

"Harper?" He smiles bigger.

"Yes." She flushes. "Yes, sorry." She stammers, which only makes Doctor Evans chuckle. He's gotta know what he does to women. It's like an obscure super power. He pats her leg and stands.

Gus takes out a small handheld scanner. "Can I see your hand, Harper?" he asks.

She holds out her hand, and he runs the scanner over her incision. The scanner beeps, and Gus gives a pleasing nod at the screen. "Great. Everything's good." He winks at Harper, releasing her hand.

"You call me if you need anything, Reagan." Doctor Evans eyes me.

"I will. Thanks. Thanks, Doctor Evans."

"Don't mention it. Be safe and remember what we talked about." He nudges his head towards Harper. I give him an understanding nod back.

I sign the discharge papers, handing them back to Barney. I can feel Harper's eyes on me ready to pounce as soon as Barney and Gus leave.

"You two stick together, and I want you back at the office Monday at nine, sharp. If I don't see you then, you won't want to see me after. Understood?" Barney asks.

Harper and I both nod at Barney's demand. Gus pats Harper's leg, giving her a wink and shakes his fingers at me.

"Be good, Reagan," Gus warns.

Barney and Gus walk towards the door, and as soon as they do, Harper rushes me in the bed with a squeal, wrapping herself on top of me.

"One day!" she squeals, making me laugh.

"One day, Angel." My words soften her grip around me as she lays her head on my chest. "I need to change clothes if we are going to do this. I have so much I want to show you." I kiss her temple.

"I'm gonna go use the restroom. You change," she says.

I watch her walk to the bathroom, closing the door behind her. My clothes are folded in a bag, hanging on the edge of the bed. I pull out my shirt, the empty bottle and the letter from Harper still tucked inside the breast pocket. I stare at the bottle for a few moments, holding it in my palm and place it back into my shirt pocket. I pull off the gown, leaving me in my boxers when I feel

Harper's delicate hands wrap around me as a small kiss hits me between my shoulder blades.

Chapter 13

Harper 2035

"You didn't expect me to stay in there the whole time while you changed did you?" I ask, while studying a portion of a Japanese dragon tattoo that's resting on Reagan's shoulder blade.

He turns to face me with a smirk, holding his arms around my waist while my hands trace the outline of the dragon which wraps around his shoulder and over his pec. The colorful scales flow over his chest and end before his hip. It's a huge masterpiece of a tattoo. It's also hot as hell, and I marvel at how I've never seen it before. *How have I never seen it before?*

"I love this." I say, tracing my hand over the scales on his chest.

He looks down and puts his hand over mine.

"I've never seen you shirtless." I continue in awe, glancing up at Reagan but returning my gaze to his tattoo.

"I keep it hidden for work. Some people are weird about a tatted up guy hanging out with their children."

"Well, I am going to demand you be shirtless for the whole day I'm here." I say, making Reagan laugh. I rub my hands over his arms and follow up to his shoulders and neck.

"I should probably get dressed." He tilts his head towards the clothes on the bed.

"I don't like that idea." I smile into a kiss that trails onto his neck and the portion of the tattoo showing near his collarbone. He lets out a small moan that only urges me to continue. He pulls me tight against him.

"Harper..." he says breathless, and I know it's a warning to stop but also permission to keep going.

He removes the beanie from my head, rushing his fingers through my hair and kisses me. The attraction between us is as strong as ever. He's all I've been thinking about, and we're finally together. I urge him backwards towards the bed, and he smiles, letting me guide him until his legs hit the bedside. He lowers to a seated position on the edge, pulling at my legs to wrap around his waist, and I kneel over the top of him. Someone could walk in right now, and I guarantee they wouldn't say a word as they walked right back out.

"Angel," he whispers.

It sets me on fire when I hear him call me that.

"I want you so bad right now, Reagan. I've missed you so much."

He groans, tugging at my hips, gripping my ass and pushing me into him. I repeat how much I want him, and he groans again into my mouth with his tongue licking and dominating, claiming it as his.

"Harper."

I press on his shoulders so we fall back onto the bed, and I lift his hands above his head and hold him down by his biceps. He's strong and tone. His eyes are closed, letting me move my mouth around every part of him. The thrill of possibly being caught hinges in the back of my mind as I roam his body with tiny licks and sucks of his skin.

His hips buck into mine as I run my tongue along the tip of his earlobe and whisper, "I want you."

He braces my back underneath my shirt and up to my neck. His warm skin touching mine. I want all of him touching me. He starts to giggle when I trail my hands over his sides. His smile, those dimples, all for me.

"We gotta stop..." He groans, but keeps rocking his hips into mine. "We gotta..."

"You first." I begin to tug on the band of his boxers.

His hand grabs mine, his smile playful but stern at the same time.

"Harper, we gotta stop. As much as I want to keep going...we gotta stop."

I'm listening to him, acknowledging his words, but I'm not stopping. I push harder on his waistband, making him laugh and grip my hand tighter, bringing it up to his lips. He kisses it and sits up with me still wrapped around him. He lets go of my hand, cupping my face for a long, lingering lock to my lips that tells me we are stopping...for now.

"I'm not done, Reagan." I mimic him from earlier and wrap my arms around him tight. He laughs, kissing me again.

"We'll never be done, Harper."

The tone of his words takes me by surprise. It's more than what's happening in the moment. I give a heavy sigh and lift off of him. A grin stays planted on his face while he pulls his jeans on. He's beyond gorgeous right now. Tan, fit, tatted up. I may jump him in the car to wherever we are going.

"You're looking at me like I'm edible," he says, while pulling his arms through the sleeves of his shirt.

"No comment," I say with a smirk.

He chuckles, arching his brow and leans over me with his shirt unbuttoned. I can't help putting my hands on his chest and up to his neck, pulling him down to my mouth.

"I can't wait to hear you comment later." Reagan smirks back. He leans back up, buttoning his shirt, and I notice the imprint of a bottle in his breast pocket.

"Is that a bottle?" I ask, pointing to his pocket.

"It's a reminder. It's empty. Don't worry. It's been empty for two years." Before he can continue, the door to the room opens.

"I may be scarred for life from what I walked into earlier."

We both turn to see a tall man call from the doorway. Reagan smiles at him and shakes his hand as he comes closer.

"Dade, this is..."

"Harper." He interrupts, shrugging off Reagan and pointing to my visitor's badge. I shake his hand, and he smiles at me. He's tall, handsome and lean. Blonde hair, wide eyed with glasses. Reagan's best friend as I recall from the story in the notebook.

"You two ready to go?" he asks, and I stare at Reagan.

"He's my ride back to our place," Reagan says, slipping on his shoes. He places a slender black rectangle the size of a credit card into his pocket. The rectangle is giving off a faint glow.

"What's that?" I ask.

Reagan grabs it out of his pocket and holds it up to me. "It's an iPhone," he says as a matter-of - fact, bending and straightening it.

"What's an iPhone?" I have no idea what he is saying.

"Oh, this is gonna be fun." Dade says, with a mischievous grin.

The inside of Dade's car is lit with all sorts of screens. In some ways it resembles the cars from back home, but the LCD style screens covering the dash make for a stunning visual. Lights and numbers in green and white hues. I sit in the front seat with Reagan in the back while Dade tells me about his car's features.

"This button makes the car drive on its own. This button right here calls a service that will help you if you get lost. This button shows you facts about the places in front of you like that building over there. Look." He taps an icon in the shape of a cityscape on the screen in the center of the dash. When he releases, an LED screen appears in mid-air on the front window pane with details about the hospital in front of us. The emergency room wait time appears with the ranking of the hospital, the date it was built and a staff directory tab that Dade clicks, which brings up an *about* page for each of the members. He taps the same button again, and the LED screen disappears.

"This button pulls up a map of any address you type in. This one is so you can link up your computer from work or home, your phone, the security system in your house or even the lights. This one shows you traffic, which streets to avoid, which ones to take. This one picks music from over twenty thousand channels to listen to, and this one..."

Holy crap my brain is overloading. I almost want to ask which button calms him the *fuck* down.

"Dude, she doesn't need to know all this. Even I don't care, and I drive this car all the time."

I smile at Reagan for interjecting. He has his iPhone out, and he's pressing his thumbs over a mini keypad on the screen.

"What is that...what you're doing?" I ask, eyeing him in the backseat as he smiles up at me, still moving his thumbs.

"Texting," he says, holding his phone up so I can see the words on the screen. "It's like chatting, only you can do it with your phone and talk to people."

"Why don't you just call them?"

"Oh sweet, Harper," Dade replies. "You're adorable."

"What?" I smile because Dade is humored by me, but...

What? Really.

"If I called you all the time instead of chatting online, wouldn't you be annoyed with me?" Reagan asks. "Like, if I just wanted to ask you where you wanted to meet, or how your day was, or what you needed from the store."

I nod, but honestly, he could call me to ask me what color the sky was, and I wouldn't mind. He could call me ten times a day to ask, and I still wouldn't mind.

"You can play games, pay bills, chat, and call. Use Facebook, twitter...."

"What's Facebook?"

"HA!" Dade yells. "She's like my Grandma. *Holy shit*! I love it! Seriously, Harper. You're innocence is beguiling, and I wanna put you in my pocket!"

I do not want in Dade's pocket...just for the record. He's cool and all, but no.

"Facebook..." Reagan begins. The car stops at a light, and Reagan notices. "Here, come here. Come back here. I'll show you. Come." He opens his car door.

I open mine and get into the back with him. The seat belt takes hold of me as soon as the car starts moving again, and it startles me.

"Look." Reagan opens a screen and pulls up an image of him and others with news in small boxes as he scrolls. Pictures of Dade and others with their comments underneath.

"Scoot closer and we'll take a selfie together." Reagan says, and I study him. "A selfie," he repeats. "A picture of us together."

"You're going in my pocket, Harper," Dade says.

No, I'm not.

I huddle close to Reagan, and he puts his arm around me while holding his phone out in front of him as a picture displays on the screen of us together in a live feed.

"Smile, Angel."

I give a bashful grin as Reagan smiles at me and faces the camera. The flash goes off and he says "One more."

He kisses my cheek and takes another picture.

"Now watch."

I watch him, but I have no idea what he's doing. Within a few seconds the pictures of us together are on the page he showed me earlier with an added caption. *My Angel and me.* A few seconds later, his phone begins to ding.

"What's that mean?" I ask.

Before Dade can open his mouth like I see him about to, I say, "No," while looking at him in the rearview mirror as he stares at me laughing.

He mouths, *my pocket,* and I giggle.

"It means someone liked the picture or said something about it." Reagan shows me, and I see comments from girls. "Oh, lucky girl," "Wow, so pretty," "Who the fuck is this?"

"Just ignore that one. Old flame," Reagan says.

Old flames. I want to know more about these old flames of his. "Can I see?" I hold out my hand to look at his phone. "How do I see the picture bigger?" Reagan clicks on the picture, and it fills the screen. "Can I look at your photos?"

"Of course." He shows me how to scroll through them by swiping the screen with my finger.

"You have a lot of female friends," I say.

Reagan smirks.

"I wouldn't call them friends." Dade interjects, much to Reagan's dismay. Reagan takes the phone from my hands and swipes through the pictures.

"This girl, nuts. This one, horrible mood swings. This was my ex who had a thing for a friend of mine, and I caught them together. I should delete her as a friend." He pulls his phone tight towards him and swipes through buttons.

"You can delete friends?" I ask.

Dade is roaring in laughter.

ROARING.

"Friends are what you call people on Facebook when you add them so they can see your pictures and stuff. You know, like your buddy list on AOL?"

I nod. "Who has time for all this?"

"We have time to chat. We make time. You'll love it, Harper. In a few years, you'll be an addict just like everyone else. You won't be able to live without it."

I ease into Reagan, resting my head on his shoulder as he places his arm around me and taps on his phone with the other hand. I watch him press buttons with his thumb and view screen after screen. It's exhausting.

"You ready to see my place?" Reagan leans in to ask. His eyes are eager.

I shake my head yes and he kisses my forehead.

"I'm so glad you're here." He tightens his arm around me and squeezes.

"Me too."

When we reach the door to his apartment, there's a white paper folded and hanging in the crease of the door with Reagan's name on it. The writing is feminine and cursive. Reagan takes the note, dropping his hand in mine and studies it while Dade touches the back of his hand over the handle of the door, unlocking it.

"I hope you're ready. Reagan doesn't usually invite girls over to our place," Dade says.

Reagan gives me a conceding shrug, but doesn't respond with much more.

Interesting.

"It's probably a good thing they don't know where he lives!" Dade's voice echoes as we enter the space. I smile at him and give a small giggle.

"So, this is my place." Reagan lifts his arms, palms open. "Kitchen's over there." He points to the left. "Dade's room is over there." He points to a door just off the living room that's open with Dade standing near a desk inside. "My room is...down there." He points to a small hallway.

"And where am I sleeping?" I ask, full of sarcasm.

Reagan smirks, taking me in his arms. His lips press to mine.

"Who said we're sleeping?" he whispers, sending a chill racing from my heart to my throat.

"Show me this room of no sleep?" I ask.

Reagan loosens his hold and takes my hand, leading me down the dark hallway. He opens the door to his room, turning on a small lamp just inside.

"This looks exactly like your room at home...with Gus...in ..." I don't even know what to call his other place.

"My place in nineteen ninety-three? It sounds weird doesn't it?" he asks. And yes, it does.

I nod, looking around at the desk with a laptop and a few framed pictures nearby. I release my hand from his and pick up one of the picture frames.

"Is this your brother?" I ask, holding up the same photo from his room in 1993.

He nods, watching me. I study the photo of the two of them and how genuine and happy they are together. My thoughts drift to Barney saying Owen was the reason I was allowed to stay.

"I want to meet him."

"I want you to meet him too. He's amazing." Reagan reaches around me and pulls me into his chest from behind, his lips caressing my neck. "We can go see him tomorrow if you want."

I nod, still staring at the photo and set it back down. "What else do you want to do while you're here?" Reagan asks, and I have no idea.

"What can we do?" I ask, turning to face him, his arms wrapping around my back in a loose hold. My hands rest on his chest as I continue. "What do you do here? Show me your world. I want to meet your friends and see how you live."

"You want to meet my friends?" Reagan asks, humored, and I shake my head yes. "We can do that." He feathers my lips with a kiss and a smirk.

"What?"

"Nothing. I'm just...I can't believe you're here!" He exhales deep while studying my face. I lower my gaze to the white paper from the door hanging out of his pocket and tap on it.

"What's this?" I ask. His eyes shift down to the paper.

"It's nothing. It's ..." he says with a hesitant sigh. "It's from my ex, Tamera. We were supposed to meet up and she came by, I wasn't here...." He seems embarrassed by the honesty of his own words.

"Oh." I'm not sure what to say. My body tenses, and I can tell he feels it. His eyes narrow and release back to a curious stare.

"Harper, she's an ex. I promise. We decided to remain friends. Does that bother you?"

"It shouldn't really bother me. But, I don't really know this other life you have."

"I'll tell you anything you want about this life." He tilts his head to the side. "I have a past. We've talked about it, but as long as I can, I want you to be a part of my future."

His words hit me hard, especially the word *Future*. We have no future. As limited as my knowledge is about time travel, there is no way for us to be together. It really is temporary, just like Gus said.

Can I do temporary? How is he okay with this?

"We don't really have a future do we?" I ease back, away from him, taking a seat on the bed. "I mean, we can't really be together in the long term scheme of things." I glance at him and focus my gaze towards the pictures on his desk.

Reagan takes a seat next to me, brushing his fingers over my temple and down my cheek, and I turn to see how sweet his eyes are as they regard me. So tender and full of a longing desire to make this hurt less.

"I've stayed up many nights trying to figure out a way, and I don't know how a future works for us, but I do know I want to spend whatever time I can with you, Harper. Is it wrong to want that? Is it wrong to want a few moments of happiness with you?"

"It's not wrong. I'm just not good with temporary things. Remember my one night stand I told you about?" I search Reagan's eyes, and he shakes his head yes. "I had a really hard time with that one, and it was just one fucking night." My nerves force me to chuckle. "I'm just worried I'll get attached and then never see you again."

"I know." He angles himself, leaning in to me. "I can't promise you a traditional future, but I can promise you some really wonderful memories that might ease the pain later."

"The inevitable pain. The inevitable heartbreak." I chuckle again.

Reagan chuckles in the same nervous way.

"Harper…" He cups my cheeks, turning my head towards him. "I promise to make you smile. A lot!" He grins. "I promise."

"You already do make me smile a lot. That's the problem."

"Well, the way I see it, we can talk about how hard this is going to be when it's over, or we can just enjoy it while it's happening."

I can't help but want to agree. I rationalize that the pain may not be so bad. I'm strong enough. I can do this. I'll be fine. Enjoy the moment. Look at him. God, look at his beautiful sweet face staring back at me. "Have you done this before?" I ask.

Reagan shakes his head no.

"Snow don't fall, remember?" He smirks, and I mirror him.

My eyes cast down, unable to reconcile the mix of emotions I'm feeling with actual spoken words.

"If you want to leave, it's okay. I'll understand, but I don't want you to go."

"I don't want to leave, Reagan. I don't want to get hurt though. I guess I can't really win that one."

"Do you want me to make you a bed on the couch? Do you want to have more space between us? Would that help?" He's trying to be accommodating, but he has no idea how much I want to have less space between us.

"The couch?" I laugh. "Unless you're joining me, no. I don't want to sleep on the couch."

He laughs. "Well, it's settled then. You'll have to sleep with me here and endure quite possibly the most awesome night of your life." His hands slap on his legs as he gives me a look of finality.

"Classy Reagan is back, I see."

"Oh, he never left." He leans in to kiss me, and I let him. I let him take me the way I've been waiting for since we met.

This is going to hurt so much when it's over.

Chapter 14

Reagan 2035

She's half asleep as we lay in my bed naked and spooned together. Her body so close and warm against mine. I've never been with a woman I wanted as much as Harper. I've never felt what I'm feeling now lying next to her. My heart is expanding with so many feelings. I can hardly contain them all, but I don't want to scare her. She's already nervous about the future and what we can't have.

Her chest raises and falls in time with my slow breathing. She turns to face me with a coy smile. I'm so taken back by how beautiful she is right now. We smile at each other, but I can tell hers is full of more. She's thinking, and I want her to talk to me without having to push.

"You okay, Angel?" I run my hands through her strawberry blonde locks and curl my hand around the back of her head, holding it there as I search her eyes for confirmation.

She nods.

"Penny for those thoughts?"

"Do you think I could read your notebook for day seven now?" she whispers, and I can't help but smirk. She wants to know more about me even with our talk about the future being unknown.

"Of course." Although I'm not sure I'm ready to reveal what happened in the accident, I know it's time. She should hear what happened before she meets Owen. Before she meets my friends and hears second hand what happened by mistake.

I lean up from the bed, grabbing my duffle bag from the floor and pull it on top of my lap. I wrap the comforter around my waist and Harper follows, wrapping another sheet around her chest. She leans over my shoulders and kisses the side of my cheek from behind, then takes a seat next to me. I rustle through the bag and find my notebook. Staring at the cover and back at Harper, I open it and turn to the beginning.

"This is really hard for me," I say, and Harper nods in understanding. "Can I hold you while you read it?"

She nods again.

I push back towards the headboard, sitting against it. I cover my legs with the comforter and pat them for her to come sit. She wedges between my legs with the sheet wrapped around her body. Opening the notebook, she turns to the page I have marked and tilts her head up towards me.

"I want you to read it to me," she says.

I look at her, stunned by the request. It's not a story I've ever told out loud. I've written it many times and burned the paper it's written on in a ritual to forgive myself, but never out loud.

"Harper, I don't know if I can do it." I'm unsure I can keep myself composed long enough to finish.

"Try?" she asks.

With her brown eyes adoring me as much as I adore them, I nod, reaching my arms around her and taking the notebook so it's centered, laying across our laps. I open it wide, taking a deep breath in. Exhaling, Harper turns her head to kiss my shoulder, melting me as I begin.

"I remember like it was yesterday. I was celebrating turning thirty with my family at a restaurant. Everyone was calling me over the hill, trying to spur me on with insults, but none of it fazed me. I was the happiest I'd ever been." I stop for a moment, remembering how I really was at the perfect place in my life.

"My mother hugged me outside in the parking lot, telling me how proud she was that I had turned my life around. She squeezed me tighter than usual that day. My dad, who never really shared his feelings, gave me a hug for the first time since I can remember. He told me this was my year. *This* was my year."

Harper kisses my shoulder again, looking up at me with encouragement.

"I was at the wheel with my brother, Owen, in the passenger seat. We had just left the bar after celebrating with friends. My brother was telling me about his plans after graduation from college. How he couldn't wait to travel and see the world now that school was behind him. We talked about girls, and I gave him advice on love. He told me I didn't know the first thing about it. He was right." I chuckle, and Harper does too.

"We came to an intersection near my house. One I've been through a million times. Cars were crossing ahead of us, but our light was green. Our light was green."

I turn away for a second to catch my breath, stolen by those words that haunt me every night. How I could have slowed down, how I could have made the connection between the cross traffic and the conflicting light color. Harper wraps her hands around mine as I grip the notebook and continue.

"I saw my brother laughing one minute, and the next his eyes were wide with fear as he screamed, "look out," in the most panicked cry. There was a loud clash of metal, and then silence. My ears were ringing from how quiet it was. I reached over to see if Owen was okay, and he winced saying he was all right. I looked around to see what had happened, when I saw a car flipped over with a young couple crawling out of a shattered front window."

"A car seat was in the back, and I unlatched my belt. I asked Owen if he was okay one more time. I was halfway out of the car about to run to the flipped car. Owen shook his head yes, telling me to go. I ran to the flipped car where the young couple was huddled close to the back door. A little girl was strapped in her car seat, hanging upside down and unconscious. The man was leaning down, frantically trying to open the door but it wasn't opening. All the doors were stuck."

"Fuck, Harper," I mutter, setting the notebook down flat.

"It's okay...read." She assures me with soft eyes and a gentle nudge of her head towards mine. My chest is tightening more and more with each word.

"The smell of gasoline was so strong. The man and I shared this stare as the smell began to get stronger, like we knew what was going to happen. The woman kept yelling, "My baby, my baby!" Words I still hear in my sleep. The man hurried to the front of the car where the window was shattered, trying to climb back in towards the back of the car, but he couldn't get in the same way he got out. He was too big. I grabbed his shoulder, pulling him back and yelling, "I'll go. I'm smaller." He reared from the window as I moved inside."

"The little girl was still unconscious as I unstrapped her and let her fall on me. I tried to open the back door, but it wouldn't budge. The smell of gas was getting stronger and stronger. I rolled the manual window down in the back until it wouldn't go any further, but it wasn't enough space. The little girl was too big to fit through it. I tugged on the window edge, trying to break it open further. The man saw me and pulled as well until the window gave way, shattering to an opening big enough to pass the little girl through. I handed her to the man, scraping my arms against the cut glass. The couple stood back in tears, clutching the girl in their arms."

"The window space was too small for me to climb through, so I went back towards the front window. Glass shards were pricking and sticking me as I hurried. When I pulled myself out from the car, a piece of glass dug into my skin and cut my arm from my bicep to my wrist, slicing it with the precision of a filet knife. The couple thanked me and ushered me away from the car, which ignited seconds later with a thunderous boom, knocking me to the ground."

"I stood back up, not even thinking about my own injuries or the amount of blood I'd lost and rushed over to my car where Owen was still sitting in the passenger seat. When I reached him, his face was so pale. I asked him what was wrong, and he just stared at me and said, "I can't feel my legs."

Harper holds my shaking hands steady, turning to me as I feel the anguish of seeing my brother's face all over again. It's a punch to my gut that never goes away no matter how many times I relive this day in my mind. It never lessens.

Harper takes the notebook from my hands and sets it to the side as she turns around to me, straddling my lap. Her hands clasp onto my wet face while her eyes study mine, as if offering me strength with each blink.

"It's okay," she whispers, searching my eyes. She wraps her arms around my neck, pushing her chest flush with mine, holding me tight, letting me convulse and shake out my regret. I sob into her hair, holding her head and bracing her back. I've never let out my emotions from that day. This is two years of sadness and mourning for a day I can't change, now being released into this beautiful girl's embrace.

"I'm sorry," I whimper, loosening my grip to see Harper's eyes tearing as well. My fingers wipe her cheeks as she does the same to mine.

"Sorry? No, baby. No," she whispers.

Her acceptance only makes me sob more. I hold her tight, feeling the waves of my own sadness take hold again and again. She rubs my back, letting me unleash my sorrow without pressure to stop or explain.

"I want to read the rest to you," I murmur. Harper meets my gaze and nods as I bring the notebook into my hands. She turns to let me cradle her on my lap. I turn to the page we left off on, wanting her to have the full story.

"The hospital waiting room was silent. My mom and dad were huddled close. My mom was in tears, and my dad had his arms around her. I sat right next to them, but I couldn't have been farther away in their minds. My arm was stitched and bandaged as well as my side. I didn't even know I was injured as bad as I was until the EMT told me. We sat waiting for any news on my brother, which didn't come for hours."

"The surgeon came out calling the name, "Snow," and we all stood. The words he uttered next made me feel like concrete had been poured over every breath I tried to take in. "He has no movement from the waist down," and "could be permanent". My mother wailed at the words. She lashed out at me as soon as she gained her senses, saying I did this. She beat on my chest as I tried to hug her and pull her anger towards me into an embrace. I told her, "no, the light was green." But it didn't help anything. The news a short time later that I was intoxicated only made matters worse."

"My brother stayed in the hospital for weeks, unable to move his legs. I was charged with a DUI and reduced from a felony to a misdemeanor because my dad convinced my mother not to press charges for my brother's injuries. The couple with the daughter didn't press any charges because I saved their little girl's life. They had no animosity towards me. Not like my own parents did...and still do."

"An investigation into the accident revealed a faulty sensor on the traffic lights that made both sides of traffic green, but it didn't change anything for my parents. It was like this information didn't exist. The reduced charge was conditional. I would serve ninety days in jail, enter rehab for drinking and be put on probation while serving the rest of my sentence on what they called a repentance sentence, which means traveling back in time to give back to society."

The page is blank after this, and I close the notebook, letting it fall out of my hands and to the floor. I'm disgusted with myself, my choices and how Harper can be looking at me like my faults are few. She touches both sides of my face, and I can't look at her while she slides her thumbs over my cheeks.

"Hey," she whispers, nudging my head to face her. My eyes connect with her sympathetic gaze. Her lips press to mine and linger. I'm filled with so many emotions.

"What do you need? Tell me what I can do to make it hurt less." Her words fill my heart with gratitude. She wants to help me.

"Just hold me," I say, tender and soft into another kiss. We lower to a laying position in the bed and she molds herself to me, hooking her leg around my waist. Her hands are holding my jaw as my arms wrap around her, pulling her tight as we fall asleep.

Harper stirs in my arms. I'm already awake before the sun, thinking about the accident while I watch her sleep. Her eyes meet mine and hold there. It's as if she's reading my thoughts, wanting to be inside them. She doesn't say a word as she rocks her hips into mine, taking my mouth in hers, slow and controlled. My thoughts of the accident drift as her touch brings peace over me. I'm overcome.

She steadies my pace and I calm to her, rocking slow the way she wants it. She's as beautiful as she was the first day I saw her in the case file, the first day I saw her in person, and now she is hovering over me, letting me inside her. The sounds of her panting and muffled moans consume me, possessing me in an uncontrollable state.

"Don't come yet," she whispers.

Words that make my body tense with the pleasure of their sound from her lips. I smile into a kiss, trying to hold back until she tenses around me and releases, whispering, "Okay, now. For me...now Reagan."

I grip her hips, holding them with my hurried thrusts in and out. It's never felt this good, this intense.

"Come for me, baby," she pants.

I let out a moan with my release into her, pumping faster and faster to a slow, steady rock back and forth. Her hands are bracing my jaw, and our hips are moving slower as I cup her face, pulling her close.

"Harper," I whisper, gazing up into her eyes. "You're so perfect." I smile, making her smile back.

I don't want to leave my bedroom for the rest of her stay. I want to keep her here with me like this as long as I can. It's the first time I've ever brought a girl here, the first time I've ever wanted to and the first time I've ever wanted one to say I love you without being prompted.

Harper lays down over me with her head resting on my chest away from view. My hands circle across her back. The morning peeks through the blinds, bathing her naked body in a pale light. I press my lips to her hair, feeling her let out a faint moan. She smiles on my chest. She turns so I can see her face. Her fingers trace my tattoo, soft and gentle. I want to bottle every part of this. We fall asleep again, quiet and content.

I awake to find myself alone with the sheet half off my body. I wonder for a split second if I was dreaming, but then I smell food and hear Dade telling Harper he wants to put her in his pocket again, which makes me laugh. I put on pajama pants and open my door to head towards the kitchen.

Dade is in rare form. He's wearing an apron and a chef hat, which I had no idea we owned. Harper is sitting on a bar stool cradling her head in her arched arms, giggling as he jokes with her. She's wearing one of my t-shirts, which I will never wash again. Her hair is tousled and falling over her shoulders.

I round her unnoticed, surprising her with a kiss on the cheek saying, "Good Morning," as I walk into the kitchen to get a drink.

She startles and gives me a sweet smile while taking in my attire, or lack thereof. I love the way she's looking at me. Like I'm a dessert she wants to devour. I'm more than happy to be that. I catch her as I open the refrigerator and smirk.

"We're thinking of meeting Owen for lunch," Dade says, like he is now the tour guide for Harper's visit.

"Oh?" I look at Harper, who is smirking at me while Dade is burning his fingers on a skillet with a crepe cooking inside. I take a seat next to Harper, handing her a glass, motioning if she wants orange juice, and she nods.

"I really want to meet your brother while I'm here," she says. She steals a sweet and playful kiss while Dade isn't looking. I want to go back in the bedroom...now.

"We can see him," I say.

Dade puts out two plates with crepes topped with whip cream and filled with mixed berries and cream cheese. I had no idea he could cook. He never cooks. In fact, he hates cooking and only dates girls who can so he can get free meals. I narrow my eyes to his, and he gives me a squinty eyed nod of his head.

I think he's trying to impress my girl.

"Wow, Dade! These look incredible!" she gushes, and receives a smug Dade face that I know well. He is so proud of himself.

"Holy shit, Dade! These *ARE* good!" I say mid-bite.

He puffs out his chest and nods with confidence, as if there isn't any other nod he could possibly give. Dade was born with a confident nod. I swear he came right out of the womb that way.

"I got the recipe from your mom when you were off pouting the other day. She told me to ask you about your brownies," he says. He was there with me for the brownies. Harper snorts into a giggle. It's adorable, and I rub her leg with a smile back.

"I texted Owen, and he wants us to meet him around noon. You good with that?" Dade glances up from his phone to confirm, and I agree.

"Can I just say how amazing it is to see a girl actually eat?" he says to Harper.

Harper stops chewing and gives Dade a blank stare. "Girls don't eat around here?" she asks, like the future holds a new set of rules for females.

"Not the ones we know. They order salad and then don't eat it," he says, as a knock on the door catches his ear.

Harper shrugs and takes another bite.

"My shirt looks mighty fine on you," I say, pouring more orange juice in her glass.

She gives me a bashful smile back.

I turn my body towards her. She follows my lead, turning in towards me, placing her finger in the whip cream still on my plate. Her finger goes to my lips, and I lick it off, making her giggle while bringing my hand to the back of her neck and pushing her head closer for a kiss.

"Looks like you've got something on your face," a female voice calls.

It's coming from the entryway to the kitchen. Harper and I pull back, faces still brushed with smiles, and then I see Tamera, my ex. Dade is standing next to her, shaking his head and mouthing, "I tried to stop her," and leaves the room.

"I saw your post. Is this you're *Angel*?" She comes closer with her hand extended to Harper and hands me a large, soft white envelope with Harper's name on it in Gus' handwriting. Tamera's voice is full of resentment, and her fake smile even more so. Harper shakes Tamera's hand, but looks at me for an introduction.

"This is Harper. Harper, this is Tamera. My *ex*." I make sure the emphasis doesn't go unnoticed.

Harper gives a timid nod back. Her lids lower to her plate where she stirs the remains of her crepe in circles.

"Why are you here?" I ask, cocking my head and then shaking it.

"We had plans, remember? You never called. I thought maybe something was wrong. You didn't answer my texts or calls, but then I saw your post." She stares at Harper, who hasn't looked up from her plate.

On any other day, I would probably humor Tamera, but today she is an unwelcomed visitor I want to leave. She leans on the counter, exposing the cleavage falling out of her tank top a little more. Harper notices with wide eyes, but focuses back down at her plate.

Tamera is a beautiful blonde. Perfect bombshell figure, but as with most in this category from my experience...she's bat shit crazy. A fun fuck, but that's the end of the fun.

"I'm all good," I say, pressing my hand on Harper's leg, but she tenses this time.

"I'm gonna go shower," Harper murmurs with a quick glance to me and away. She gets up to leave, walking towards the hallway, and I do what I do best to get a woman I don't want around to leave me alone. I call out to the woman I do.

"Harper, wait. I'll shower with you." I lock eyes with Tamera as I say this, knowing it will get to her and make her want to leave. I grab both of the plates from the counter and walk past her to the sink to set them down, but Tamera grabs my arm before I reach the sink.

"Is she what you're into now?" she hisses. "You like little girls now?"

I jerk my arm from her grasp and continue towards the sink to rinse my dishes before heading to the shower. "She's not a little girl, and yes, that's what I'm into now. Very into." I square my eyes with Tamera's. She studies me, stepping closer so her chest is flush with mine.

"Can she do the things I can? Can she make you scream like me?" She juts her chin out, proud, like getting me to climax is a special skill.

"She already has," I smirk.

Tamera smirks back. She likes this game. She tilts her head to the side leaning in closer, pressing her lips to mine but I don't return the affection. Her long nails twist the hairs on the back of my neck.

"You sure? After all we've been through...you keep running back to me. You can't tell me we're really over. You still want me." She grabs between my legs, where I would usually be completely hard for her at this point, but I'm not. The surprise of this is written all over her face as she gives me a closed lip smile.

"Bye, Tamera. I have a shower to get to." I grab her hand off of me, leaving the kitchen, and I hear the front door slam as I walk down the hallway.

Chapter 15

Harper 2035

Remember the waitress who was staring at Reagan in the restaurant? The one that brought out my inner cray cray? Well, the cray cray is back.

I'm sitting on the bed, the smell of Reagan and me together still in the air, and I recognize what's happening. I'm jealous of his ex. The one he says he doesn't even care about, but she's here acting all possessive, and I don't do well in these situations. My instinct is to go all cat fight style on Tamera, but I'm keeping cray cray in check which is a full-time job in itself. I exhale a deep breath, lifting from the bed to go into the bathroom attached to Reagan's room.

The bathroom is small and simple just like mine at home, until I step in the shower. There are no knobs, just a screen centered in the tile. I tap it, and it illuminates in blue with simulated bubbles flowing down across the screen.

"Hello, please select your shower temperature," commands a soothing female voice with a British accent. The screen changes to a keypad, but I have no idea what to select. "Please select your shower temperature," the voice repeats.

After a few more seconds, the shower turns on and the voice returns. "Previous settings used."

I stare at the screen. The current temp outside displays as a hundred and twenty degrees. and I assume it's broken. The shower begins to spray, and I relax with my eyes closed, leaning to the side of the tile wall.

"Harper?" Reagan calls from the doorway.

"Yep." I'm distracted in my own thoughts, which makes my voice come across curt.

"Can I join you?"

I reply with the same curt tone in my voice as I say "yes." He gets in, standing behind me. Placing his hands on my shoulders, nudging me to turn around. I'm having the worst time trying to look him in the eyes. His arms wrap around me at my waist. His chest drips with water that makes his skin and tattoo sparkle.

"I'm sorry about that." He nudges his head towards the door.

"It's okay," I say with no conviction, making Reagan laugh.

"It's not." He smiles, cupping my face and tilting it up for me to look at him. "What is it? Talk to me?"

I look away and back towards him, not wanting to sound jealous. "She's so beautiful, Reagan. She looks nothing like me. Her hair, her boobs. Her body is unbelievable. Why would you want me when you could have that?" I stare into the center of his chest and down at my body.

"Tamera...is like a beautifully wrapped Christmas present, only the box that's wrapped... is empty inside." He smiles. "You..." He takes my chin between his thumb and forefinger. "Are a beautifully wrapped Christmas present with everything I ever wanted inside the box. She can't compare to you, Harper, on any level."

I smile with a shaky laugh but still feel like Reagan is just saying anything he can so I won't be mad. "You don't mean that. You don't really know me."

How could he, we've been together a little over a month.

"I know a lot about you, Harper. You're my case, remember?" His eyes are bright and glimmering at me. I am his case. I've asked him nothing about this.

"What does that mean? I'm your case?"

"I was sent to nineteen ninety-three as the last of my repentance sentence from my sentencing. I'm here to help you. I know more than you think."

"What are you helping me with? Have you been successful?"

Reagan carries a reserved smile. "I still can't tell you everything about it…but, it's going well."

"Because we slept together?" I ask, feeling a bit like a conquest.

Reagan shakes his head to my question. It's thrown him off guard.

"Falling in love with you wasn't a part of the plan." He smirks, his eyes are full of honesty, and I dwell on his words.

Love? Falling in love? With me?

"What do you know about me?" I ask.

Reagan scans my face, choosing his words with a deep breath in and out. "You were adopted when you were a baby after your birth mother gave you away. You hate the day you were born because of this. You've always felt a sense of loss on your birthday, and everyone around you seems to keep this feeling going by forgetting this day, almost every year. You never celebrate with anyone on the actual day...except this year, with me."

I don't have words and he continues.

"You went to school to become a lawyer like your dad. Almost graduated and quit because you saw a 20/20 special on Houdini and magicians."

I smile because hearing it out loud makes me sound crazy.

"You're passionate about what you love, Harper. I've seen you with Bryson, how you care for him. How you help others learning the magic craft. You're so full of life and adventure when you are on stage. I love watching you. I love being around you and seeing how you engulf yourself in the fantasy world with David Copperfield." He laughs which makes me laugh.

"Your fascination with romance novels and love. You're a beautiful romantic soul, and I love those things about you. I even read one of your books just so I could be close to you for fuck's sake!"

This makes me belly laugh. *I still can't figure out which one he took.*

"I know you, and knowing you like I do now is something I never expected."

He kisses me as the water to the shower turns off and the British female voice says, "Good day," making me giggle.

"She's a character, huh?" Reagan points to the screen. "Do you want me to turn it back on, or are you done?"

I want to stay in this shower with him forever. It's warm and he's saying everything I want to hear.

"I'm not done," I say, like we both did when he was in the hospital.

Reagan steps us both back towards the wall next to the screen and presses a button that turns the water on with a mild beep. He presses another and the song, Nuthin' but a "G" Thang begins to play. He turns his face away and back to me with the biggest smile, and I giggle as he begins to sing along while he rubs up against me.

I'm being seduced to the sounds of Snoop Dog and Dr. Dre, and I can't think of anywhere I would rather be right now. The bass is booming in my heart. He raps all the way to the bridge of the song where I stop him with my lips melding onto his. I wrap myself around him, enjoying every kiss as we lower to the floor of the shower.

"Gus sent this to you," Reagan says, handing me the soft white package envelope. He stands by his dresser with a towel wrapped around his waist, and I sit on the bed in his t-shirt and nothing else.

Put back on my underwear that's travelled forty-two years ahead? No thanks.

I'm not excited about the commando aspect with tight jeans, but I concede to my fate. I grab scissors from the desk and cut open the envelope.

I pull out a business card from Gus, my favorite tank top, underwear, a bra and shorts.

"He must like you," Reagan says, walking past me to his nightstand. "He's never brought me clothes." He gives me a peck on the cheek moving past me again. I'm stunned, but not because Gus brought me clothes, even though it is kinda weird that he went through my dresser to get them. I'm more surprised that he decided to bring me my purple striped underwear.

Jesus.

These are my sad underwear. Sad as in, they don't go near boys because they're reserved for that time of the month.

Commando isn't looking like a bad choice right now.

"You guys ready?" Dade calls from the other side of the door.

"Give us ten minutes," Reagan yells back.

"Ten minutes? You do know I'm a girl right?" I ask.

"Oh, I know you're a girl alright." Reagan leans over me on the bed and nudges me down onto the comforter.

"Make that twenty minutes," Reagan yells.

"Aw c'mon." Dade groans down the hall saying, "They're having kinky time travel sex. It's gonna be a few, Owen."

"Oh my...God," I say with a giggle.

"No, I'm Reagan," he says, leaning in for a kiss.

Dade drives us to a fifties style diner not far from their place. I hold Reagan's hand tight as we enter when the sensory overload sets in. Red booths, black and white checkered floors, with the front of a 1950's Buick Roadmaster jetting out of the bar. A perfect replica of fashion from the time comes towards us in the form of a snappy waitress wearing roller skates.

"You kids gonna sit or stare?" she asks, while smacking gum in her mouth.

"Stare, beautiful, stare." Dade outstretches his arm with his hand reaching for the waitress' but she is not having it. She rolls her eyes and nudges her head to a corner booth and we take a seat. Dade sits solo across from Reagan and I while the song Earth Angel by The Temptations begins to play from the jukebox.

"What do you wanna hear next?" Dade hunches towards the mini jukebox on our table, twisting the turn dial at the top, flipping through song selections. He stops searching to look at me, and I shrug. His attention turns back to the song choices. "I got it. If they come to get drink orders, I want a vanilla milkshake." He taps the table a few times before getting up to head towards the back of the place.

"You see anything you like?" Reagan asks, engrossed in his menu.

I wait for my silence to get noticed before saying anything.

"You see anything you..." He turns his head, speechless with a huge toothy smile, and I smirk.

"Yes, I do." I'm feeling flirtatious as hell right now.

Etta James kicks in with *At Last*, and the room closes in like our booth is the only one that's lit. My stomach is fluttering with each blink from him.

"You wanna dance?" His hand outstretches for mine.

I look around feeling exposed and shy. "Dance?" I shake my head.

He's beaming. *God, he wants to dance? Which one of my books did he just step out of?*

"Come on."

I take his hand, and he guides me to a huge jukebox in the back where a space is clear, and he pulls me into him. I put my arms around his neck as we lock eyes. It's as if there is a spotlight on us and its followed us to this make-shift dance floor. We sway as Etta belts out the last part of the chorus. The instrumental ending fades the song out and Reagan dips me, lifting me back up to a slow, lingering kiss.

Holy hell. He owns me right now. So, so owns me.

The whole room cheers and claps as the feeling of heat floods over my face. Reagan? Reagan loves this. He is a ham for the attention. He mimics a bow while holding my hand as we walk back to our table and take a seat. I bat my lashes, moving my lips closer to his, and together we make this booth a modern day lover's lane...at least until the waitress rolls up smacking her gum.

"You two lovebirds know what you want? To eat that is?" She smiles when she regards us, tapping her pencil on the notepad in her hands.

We order drinks, not forgetting Dade's, and she rolls off yelling our order out loud. Reagan and I smirk and go back to our menus. I've read the burger section five times and couldn't tell you a single thing that's listed.

"Damn she's loud."

We both turn to see Owen at the edge of the table.

"Dude, Owen!" Reagan slaps his hand in Owen's.

Owen steadies his wheelchair and maneuvers onto the seat across from us, scooting to the far end, leaving space for Dade. He reaches his hand over the table to me.

"You must be Harper." His smile is warm as he takes my hand. He points to himself. "I'm Owen...the better looking brother." He winks at me.

I like him already.

"It's so wonderful to meet you, Owen," I say.

Dade returns with the waitress who is carrying our drinks, and he takes his shake from her tray before sitting and greeting Owen.

"So what's the plan for you guys today? Just hanging out? Gonna see the city?" Owen asks, nudging his head towards me and Reagan.

"Do people do stuff here? It's so hot? How can you stand it?" I ask, getting laughs from each of the men at the table.

"Reagan tells me you do magic?" Owen asks, eyes glowing.

I nod and pull out a deck of cards from my purse. A magician always has a few tricks hidden, but even a table napkin, loose change and a salt shaker can work. I use all of them.

"Do you have a quarter?" I hold my hand out, and Owen digs in his pocket pulling out a few and placing them in the center of my palm.

"Watch out for her, she's got sticky fingers," Reagan says with a wink, and I elbow him in the side.

"Wait, wait, wait!" Dade leans over to the mini jukebox and selects a song. "Okay, okay. Begin Houdini Harper."

I give him a condescending smirk that grows into a full blown smile when This Magic Moment by The Drifters begins to fill the restaurant. I really like Dade. The guy is such a charmer.

I place the quarter on the table and cover it with the salt shaker. Then I cover the salt shaker with the napkin, wrapping it tight. "Watch this quarter go through the table."

"That's impossible," Dade says, like the nonbeliever I knew he would be. Owen smiles and shakes his head. Both he and Reagan have the same smile plastered on their face. So incredible to see in double.

"Watch." I tap the wrapped salt shaker over the quarter and move my hand back towards my chest, but the quarter is still there. I fake a grimace and do it again. "This trick usually works. Let me concentrate."

Reagan knows this trick, but he pretends like he doesn't. I bring the wrapped salt shaker in my hand back over the quarter but instead, I squeeze the napkin tight, pressing it down on the table flat. The salt shaker is gone.

"Holy shit!" Dade is a believer now. Owen and Reagan clap. "How'd you do that?"

I shrug at Dade, who wants to see the napkin and the salt shaker that I placed back on the table without notice.

"Show us another one." Owen wants more. They always do, and I can't resist.

"Dade, can we trade spots?" I ask, and he nods. Reagan lets me out, and I take a seat next to Owen. Both Reagan and Dade have their phones out now across from me, taking pictures.

"Can you hand me the pepper?" I point to the edge of the table, and Owen reaches for it. I drop it on purpose when he hands it to me.

"I'm so sorry," I say, as he looks under the table while Dade helps get it. Reagan smirks as he watches me because he knows. I've done this trick to him a few times. It never gets old.

Owen hands me the pepper. "Thanks, do you have a dollar I could borrow for this trick?" I ask Owen. He reaches for his wallet, pressing on his shirt pocket and jean pockets again. He turns to look at the seat on both sides to see if his wallet fell out, but stops searching when he looks up at me holding it.

"She's a pick pocket too. Just FYI," Reagan says.

Owen grins, and I hand it back to him so he can give me a dollar that I didn't really need.

"So this one... is a card trick. Pick any card." I fan the cards out for him. Owen selects a card from the shuffled deck, but Dade interrupts.

"I want to shuffle them when he picks it." I let him. Owen picks a card, peeks at the face of the card and places it back in the deck.

"You know which card you picked?" I ask.

Owen nods at me.

"You sure?" I smirk.

He nods again. I hand the cards to Dade to shuffle. He does this slow, like he's trying to be obnoxious.

"There's no way you're gonna guess his card," Dade says. He thinks he's being clever when he hands the cards back to me. Like his disorganized shuffling has somehow deterred my skill.

"You care to wager a bet on that, Dadey-O?" I shuffle the deck one more time.

"Dadey-O? Oh, it's on Harpie."

"One dollar if I can do it?" I ask. I shuffle the cards one more time, fanning them between my hands in a cascade, one portion of the stack to the other.

"Damn, that's a cheap wager," he says.

It's only cheap because I have no money with me. If I did, I would bet more than a dollar and slap the money on the table for the full effect of my over confidence. Dade nods at me with a smug grin, and I pull Owens card from the center.

"Whoa! Are you serious? Holy crap!" Dade shouts.

"Pony up disbeliever." I hold my hand out, palm up for him to pay me.

"Where the fuck is my..."

"Hmm. Weird. How did I get this?" I hold his wallet up as he turns to look at me.

Dade sneers and takes his wallet from my hands, opening it to give me a dollar.

"What else ya got, Clepto?" Dade wants more. I can give him more.

I pull out my handcuffs from my purse.

"Oh shit! Things are about the get spicy!" Dade hollers, making Owen and Reagan laugh. I giggle, motioning for Owen to put them on, but he shakes his head no.

"You know Reagan likes these. We should put them on him," Owen says, looking at Reagan who nudges me to come back over and sit by him. Dade gets up, and I move back over to my seat next to Reagan.

"I know all about his love of handcuffs. Trust me," I say, in a way that suggests more than I should share.

Dade almost chokes on his shake, and Owen begins to laugh which turns infectious for Reagan and me.

My mind trails off to last night, where I cuffed Reagan to the bed and made him tell me about the next episode of X-files because I was missing it. *I rewarded him. Don't worry.*

"Can I interrupt?" Tamera appears at the edge of the table next to Reagan, which turns the laughter into crickets. She's pushing out her chest and smiling, waiting to be offered a seat.

No one better offer her one.

"One sec." Reagan puts his index finger up, giving me a small kiss as he lifts out of the booth, grabbing Tamera by the elbow while he walks her outside.

"Did Reagan tell you about her?" Owen asks, and I nod.

"She came by this morning," I say, a bit unnerved at her reappearance in my day. I thought I had put her behind me. I'm here for one day and I've seen her twice in four hours.

My inner cray cray simmers.

"Yeah, she doesn't take rejection well," Owen continues.

Who does? God knows I'd be a head case if I was here and Reagan was flaunting his new love interest.

"How long ago did they break up?" I ask.

Dade and Owen exchange a glance.

"He didn't tell you everything?" Dade answers my question with a question.

This is never good.

I shake my head no.

"They broke off their engagement before he left for your case. I guess that's three months ago now?"

I've heard of the proverbial punch to the stomach, but I've never felt it like I am right now.

"I...didn't know they were engaged. He made it sound like she meant nothing." My head lowers, and the words on the menu before me blur. I don't like this feeling. I feel duped, deflated, lied to and sold a line of bullshit!

Cray cray?

"Harper, he wasn't *in* love with her," Owen says leaning in. "He just sort of went along with it for everyone else. He thought marrying her was the right thing to do."

What a giver.

Owen tries to console me by stretching his hands out to mine, and I try not to stiffen.

“You’re a million times cuter, Harpie.” Dade grins, digging his spoon into the bottom of his shake.

Harpie.

“She has boobs the size of my head! All...falling out of her shirt and shit! Really? I’m cuter?”

Dade and Owen laugh, and I laugh at myself out of frustration. But really? There’s no way I’m turning heads like she is. If we both crossed the street in wet t-shirts, I guarantee a car crash would happen from guys staring at her over me.

“You are worlds better though, and Reagan is different with you. He’s a man in love. We all see it, and I just met you. He’s never been like this before. The way he talks about you. Just give him a chance to explain.” Owen’s words soften me, but god dammit if I’m not still thinking about those giant boobs getting Reagan’s attention right now.

“Don’t be too hard on him,” Dade says. “He probably didn’t want to ruin the one day he has with you here by telling you about his hot mess of an ex.”

Hot mess. Not helpful.

“You guys order?” Reagan returns, sweating and pinching his shirt in the center, waving it back and forth against his chest.

I stare at my menu, which hasn’t changed since we got here. I should know what I want, but the more I think about it and simmer in my cray thoughts, the more I realize what I want isn’t on the menu. It's not edible. It's home. It's my home, my bed, my life. I'm surprised at the homesick feeling taking over.

"Our shouty waitress hasn't been back," Dade replies.

I can see all three of them out of my peripheral vision giving each other code with hand gestures, but I don't look up. I study the menu, feeling nauseated by the food choices now. There's no talking at the table, no jokes. When I do look up, each of them is on their phones texting and eying each other with every ping sound. Dade moves his thumbs, a ping hits Reagan's phone. Reagan moves his thumbs, a ping hits Owen's phone.

Reagan notices me staring at each of them and stares back at me, wide-eyed and caught. I widen my eyes with sarcasm back at him, and he gives me a tiny curl of his lips. The waitress returns, looking bored like we were the ones that kept her waiting, and takes our order starting with Dade.

Dade orders his burger with special requirements. "Lettuce on the side, half a tomato, pickle sliced, light mayo, double ketchup, bun lightly toasted, fries crispy but not too crispy."

It's a fucking burger for Christ's sake.

"You want a belly dancer on the side as well?" The waitress jokes, and I catch her eye with a smirk.

"Only if she's you, Peggy Sue." Dade takes her hand and winks. She gives him a loud smack of her gum and takes her hand back.

I will not do the girl thing out of anger and say I'm not hungry.

Owen orders a turkey burger with special requirements, but I don't feel as hostile because he's sweet and kind when he speaks. The waitress looks at me, and I point to Reagan.

"I haven't decided yet," I say.

I will not do the girl thing out of anger and say I'M NOT HUNGRY.

Reagan orders the biggest burger they have with everything. It's admirable and the waitress thanks him for not making her write a special order. Everyone looks at me, and I amaze myself with the words that come out of my mouth.

"I'm not hungry."

"Harper, you should eat," Reagan says.

I shake my head. "It's fine. I'm really not that hungry."

The waitress rips the page from her notebook, not sticking around to hear how I need to eat.

Reagan leans over and whispers, "Do you want to go talk?"

I shake my head no. *I should talk, but no.*

I adore this man, but it's taken him this long to recognize something is wrong?

I don't want to talk. I feel like I want to throw up, especially when I see Tamera walk by glancing back at our table. Dade, Owen and Reagan let out annoyed sighs at the sight of her, which gives me a small sense of satisfaction, and I smile on the inside. She takes a seat at a booth in the direct line of vision to ours, watching Reagan.

"I'll be right back. Will you excuse me?" I ask.

Reagan lifts from his seat, watching me like he wants to say something, but he doesn't know what to say and lets me out. I give him a polite smile, scooting out and walking towards the restrooms, past Tamera who stares at me and gets up to follow.

PETE

Chapter 16

Reagan 2035

I flag our waitress down and order Harper a burger because I know she's hungry, and I know now she's upset after I found out from Owen and Dade via text. I'm such a dick when it comes to women and gauging when they are mad. Of course she's mad. I just walked off with my ex and came back with no explanation.

"Just give her some space to breathe man." Dade's advice for every woman who gets mad is to let them breathe, like they're fine wine and can't be taken seriously without a twenty-five minute rest period after being exposed to the elements of our poor judgment.

"I didn't tell her about Tamera. I mean, I told her, but I didn't tell her everything."

"Well, she knows now. Way to go. Probably the one girl you'll ever come across who makes you a better man and you fuck it up." I take Owens words to mean so much more than a humorous vent. He's right. I've been open and honest with Harper, even told her about the accident which I've never shared with any girl, not even Tamera.

Our food arrives, but Harper hasn't come back to the table. It's been a solid twenty minutes.

"Should I go check on her?" I ask, and receive a sarcastic eye roll from Dade and a suggestive nudge of Owen's head.

Yes, I should go check on her. I get up to walk towards the restrooms where Tamera is sauntering back to her booth with a wicked grin.

"She's not in there, in case you're looking for her." She loves being able to talk to me about this, having some insight into my world right now.

"What did you say to her?"

I know Tamera, and I know she crushes delicate things that stand in her way. Beautiful things and innocent people that don't belong to her or have what she wants. She's a vindictive bitch, and I don't want her anywhere near me or Harper.

"Oh, I didn't have to say much. I reintroduced myself as your ex-fiancé since you failed to mention it. Loved the look on her face with that one."

I grab her by the shoulders, gripping tight enough for her to yelp. "Stay away from her. She's not your play toy."

She gives me a smirk as I address her, shrugging her shoulders to loosen my hold.

"If she wanted to be with you, she wouldn't have left. I'm still here though," she says.

I walk away, towards the restrooms and push open the ladies room door, "Harper?"

"There's no one in here," an older lady replies as she walks out.

I nod, looking for an exit towards the back and walk outside to stand in the rear parking lot. She's nowhere. She's gone.

Fuck.

I walk around to the front of the restaurant, squinting up the street and back the other way.

Where the hell could she have gone?

The entrance door dings and I stare at the couple exiting, grabbing the door open to go back inside.

"I have no idea where she is." My hands rake through my hair while I survey the place, taking a seat back with Dade and Owen.

"Shit. You lost a girl from nineteen ninety-three dude. In the hottest fucking town there is. She'll probably combust from the heat alone." Dade is not helping.

"You should call Gus," Owen suggests.

It's a call I don't want to make. I don't want to hear the speech from him. The, *I told you so* speech I know is a phone call away. But, he can track her by her chip and find her within seconds. It's the responsible thing to do. *This being responsible thing sucks.* I wrestle with making the call, taking a few bites of my burger in silence at the table and dial.

"Gus?" I plug my other ear while hunching over in the booth to hear better.

"You lose something?" I welcome his accusatory and flat tone.

"Gus, is Harper with you? Shit."

"She wants to leave, Reagan. She wants to go back home. What did you do?"

Fuck.

"Where are you? Don't send her back. Please. I can be wherever you are in a few minutes. Just don't let her leave. Please, Gus?"

He sighs. "You are a grown ass man. I knew this was a bad idea. I knew you would hurt her.

Why did I give you a chance? I know better. What did you do?"

I can see his angry eyes through the phone.

"I didn't *do* anything."

"Reagan?"

"I didn't tell her the whole story about Tamera."

"Shit, son."

"I know."

Gus sighs again, deep, the sounds of cars driving by fills the silence as background filler.

"Let me see what she wants to do. I'll text you."

"Okay...okay...Thank you, Gus. God, thank you."

A text from Gus comes through an hour later saying Harper is at the office, which means she is at the library up the street. It's an older smaller library that could be mistaken for a home, but the bright red tiled roof of the house next door and the neon sign out front blinking *Instant Wedding Chapel* with hearts flashing between the words make it hard to miss. Yep, the sanctity of marriage is still in full affect in 2035.

"You want me to go in with you?" Owen asks. He's driven me over since Dade had to get to work.

"I'm pretty sure I can handle this," I say. Owen doesn't unlock the doors when I try to get out. He wants to talk about Harper. I just want to go talk *to* Harper.

"What are you going to say?" Owen asks. He's always been the wiser one who counsels me on the right thing to do. Do I follow it? Sometimes.

"I don't have a plan."

"That's... a bad plan," he says, amused by my answer. "Why don't you tell her about Tamera, but the whole story?"

"I feel like a train wreck with all these stories I've been telling her."

"You told her about the accident?" Owen's posture stiffens and his eyes widen. He knows I haven't told anyone about it. "Wow, you really like this girl."

I can't help but smile.

"Tell her what happened, Reagan. She doesn't know."

He's right as usual.

"I'll be back in a few to get you. Just text me when you're ready."

I nod, getting out of the car. "Thanks, Owen."

He shrugs, shooing me with his hands.

The library is freezing cold when I enter. Two older ladies are at the front desk. Both smile when they see me. One points in the direction of the fiction section. I take the ramp down, passing paperbacks on swivel racks, wondering if Harper has checked out the books we have in this time period.

God help me if she discovers Twilight or Fifty Shades of Grey.

I spy her at a table. She's staring out the window with her hand curled to her lips when I approach.

"Hi."

She doesn't acknowledge me, but I take a seat next to her.

"Harper, can I explain to you about Tamera and then you can leave if you still want to?"

She nods, and I can tell she's been crying. *I'm such an asshole.* I reach my hand to her cheek, but she flinches her face away, refusing my touch.

"Tell me about your engagement?" she asks. Her voice is rough, and I sense the ache in her question. I should have been honest and just told her about Tamera.

"I asked Tamera to marry me six months ago. She was pregnant," I say.

"Pregnant? Are you...are you a father? Do you have..."

"No," I interrupt. "There's no child. Tamera..." I sigh. *I hate this part of my life.* "Tamera told me she was pregnant, and I thought the honorable thing to do was to ask her to marry me even though I wasn't in love with her. She was gonna have my child."

Harper softens, taking my hand in hers. "So, what happened? She lost the baby?"

"Not exactly." My body is beginning to tense, and I grip her hand tight. Best to start with what a terrible guy I was first. Just get it out of the way.

"I wasn't a good boyfriend. I'm not proud. You've heard me tell you stories about different girls, different days of the week. I was trying to be faithful, but Tamera and I met when we were both with other people, so we would go outside our relationship when things went bad out of habit. We would fight, make up, fight, and make up again. It was intense and *fucking* toxic. She's toxic."

"We got in a fight over wedding plans. She wanted to have this huge wedding, and honestly, I didn't give a fuck. I should have, but I didn't. She got mad that I wasn't into it and wanted to call everything off. I should have taken her up on it. It was the worst idea. Everyone warned me not to do it."

Harper gives me an understanding nod.

"Everyone sees things with that bird's eye view we don't see. Or, sometimes they're just birds that shit on you no matter what," Harper says with a small grin, making me laugh.

"Yeah, well...Tamera left telling me it was over. I didn't chase after her like I should have, and she didn't come back crying like she normally did, so I let it be. I figured we'd work things out or we'd do the best we could raising a baby apart."

"I saw her a few days later at a party acting like she always does. Flirting, wearing next to nothing, holding a beer. It set me off! She was fucking drinking with my baby in her belly! When I asked her about it, she told me she wasn't pregnant anymore."

"What? She lost it?"

"She aborted it."

"Oh..." Harper takes in a deep breath, stunned just like I was the second I heard my baby was gone.

"I was just getting used to the idea of being a dad and then boom. Fuck you, Reagan."

"Oh, Reagan. God...I'm so sorry. Why would she do that?"

"Because she's a fucking bitch! That's why."

"Shhhhh!" A lady at a table a few rows over whispers. Harper squeezes my hand, bringing my attention back to her.

"I'm sorry I didn't tell you. I don't know why I didn't just tell you when you met her this morning."

"I shouldn't have reacted all jealous without letting you explain. I'm sorry." Her hand brushes through the side of my hair, and I scoot my chair closer, pulling her legs into the empty space between mine.

"You reacted like you should have. I'm the dick!"

"Shhhh!" Same lady. I mouth the word *sorry,* but her furrowed brow doesn't fade.

Harper takes my chin into her hand.

"I'm sorry anyway. We have a lot to learn about each other. I'm not exactly an open book either."

"How so? You have an accident where you disabled your brother for life and an aborted baby story in your past too?" Harper chuckles at my sick humor. It solidifies why I love her even more.

"I told you my mother left me at a fire station when she had me at her prom, but I'm not supposed to be here. I mean, in all reality, I shouldn't even be alive."

"What do you mean?" I rub her hand in mine.

"My mom...well, my adopted mom told me I was left to die and almost did. For whatever reason, my real mom thought twice of sticking me in the garbage and took me to the fire station."

"Fuck. Harper, how did you find all this out?"

"When I was eighteen, I wanted to meet my real mom. She didn't want to meet, but she did write me a letter saying sorry and telling me I was a gift she couldn't keep. She told me about my birth and how afraid she was. I can't imagine being pregnant at seventeen, but I would never throw it away like garbage."

"You're far from garbage, Angel." My fingers trail down her cheek, and her lips curl for a second.

"Lots and lots of counseling over that," she adds, letting out a nervous laugh.

"This may sound shitty, but your real mom gave you a chance for a better life. Maybe not a better start, but if she couldn't take care of you..."

"I know. I've thought about it that way. It's just one of those things that's never found a quiet place to rest inside me."

"Did your adopted mom name you Harper?"

"I was wrapped in a letterman's jacket that said Harper in cursive. I guess it was my dad's name?"

"I'm so glad you're here. So fucking glad." I cup my hands, holding her jaw, kissing her with every ounce of love I feel for her. She's everything to me. The lady shushes us, but we ignore her. We're being as discreet as we can, but I can't hide how I feel. Nothing feels as good as Harper's touch, her warm lips embracing mine, the smell of her skin. Her past is coming out to help me with mine. She soothes me, quiets the demons of my past that stir even when I try to hide them.

"Wanna stay?" I pull away to ask, and she smirks with a breathy "yes" back. "Let's get out of here."

We walk towards the exit where Gus is standing by the information desk, talking to the older ladies behind it about yellow bells he just planted. I don't know how he keeps anything alive in this climate. He speaks with such ease and assurance. It's hard not to get interested in what he talks about. He also has a fondness for the ladies, and they love him.

"You two work whatever it was out?" he asks when we get close.

"Yes, I'm sorry for calling you and taking you away from your other obligations," Harper says.

Gus shakes his head, dismissing her apology.

"You don't need to apologize. It's this guy who needs to get his act together. He's getting there." He pulls me in for a hug, tapping on my back and whispers in my ear, "Don't fuck this up." He pulls back with a shit eating grin. "You kids be good, and I'll see you back here at nine in the morning, sharp!" Gus points to me.

Sharp. I got it.

Harper and I make our way outside and I realize two things. One, its fucking hot as balls out here and two, I don't have a car, so I pull my phone out and text Owen.

Reagan: So, I just forgot I don't have a car.

Owen: Is Harper with you?

Reagan: Is that a factor in getting a ride home?

Owen: It doesn't hurt.

Reagan: She's with me.

Owen: You worked it out then?
Reagan: We did.
Owen: Good. Hang tight. I'll be there in a few.
Reagan: Thanks O.
Owen: Don't fuck it up before I get there.
Reagan: No promises.

"So what are we gonna do? Should we go back inside?" Harper asks, squinting and looking up the street and back at me. There's a mirage of water rising up from it because of the heat. I look around, tapping on my phone to see what's around.

Nothing. Not a fucking thing.

Wait.

One thing does come up. I don't know if Harper will go for it. I'm probably crazy for thinking she will, but it's something I really want to do with her. Something I've never wanted more in my life at this moment. It's crazy, it's stupid, it's impulsive...it's me.

"Why are you smiling? What?" She jabs my shoulder.

"Marry me."

"What?" She steps back, processing my words. She follows my gaze to the chapel in front of us and back to her.

"Marry me," I repeat, getting down on one knee grabbing her hand in mine.

"Uh, no." She tugs her hand, but I won't let go.

"Please, Harper. I'm on one knee. I'm probably going to need a skin grapt from the flesh burning off of it right now. Marry me."

"You're insane!" She dismisses me, looking away and back again, her eyes wide.

Getting down on one knee was a really bad idea. It's hot as fuck.

"Yes, insane. Marry me." I don't care how many times I have to ask, I'm not stopping until she says yes.

"Reagan, we've known each other what? A month? And we're not even from the same time! No."

"Harper, I've wanted you all my life, I just didn't know where you were until now."

She's thinking...and smirking...and tearing.

"Marry me."

"This is *crazy*!"

I stand, still holding her hand in mine, placing it over my heart. "I love you, Harper."

She stamps her foot on the cement in a gentle protest, looking away and back at me.

"Marry me?" I ask again in a whisper with a pouting face, making her laugh. "I will take you over my shoulder if I have to, Harper. Marry me."

She belly laughs, still resisting, still turning away, but her head begins to nod in a subtle way at first, then nods rapidly as her arms swing around my neck. I kiss her, so full of happiness that she wants to do this.

Well, I convinced her she wants to do this, but still. *Fuck yes!*

Chapter 17

Harper 2035

"What would you have done if I told you I was a time traveler before all this? Before Gus and Barney told you?" Reagan asks as we lie naked in his bed, tangled in the only sheet remaining.

I gaze at the cheap gold band now holding a place on the ring finger of my left hand and think about what I would have done. I probably would have lost my shit, that's what I would have done, but I don't say that. I take his left hand and hold it in mine. The rings on our fingers align together.

"I probably would have lured you into my basement..." I say arching my brow with a mischievous grin.

"Mhmmm," he says, leaning closer and nuzzling my neck.

"...and maybe handcuffed you to a chair or pipe."

Reagan laughs at my plan as I continue. "I would have kept you down there. Fed you, brought you water, but I would have held you hostage as my personal fortune teller."

"Is that it?" Reagan pulls his head back, drawing his gaze to my lips and my eyes.

I nod.

"No sex outta this deal? Sounds very boring in that basement of yours."

"Oh I never said no sex." I run my hand down the side of his upper body, gripping his hip tight with my leg.

"What would you want to know? What would be your first question?" He touches the tip of my nose with his, urging my lips closer.

I narrow my eyes. While I take my time thinking, Reagan continues to nuzzle my neck. His scent and mine mixed together is still present on his skin. The tattoo on his chest and arm flexes while his hands roam the side of my body, distracting me from my thoughts. He's beautiful to look at, and I'm so taken back by how much he's told me, how he shared what he never shares with anyone.

My hot as hell time traveler and me just hanging out in bed after getting married. No big deal.

"You think of a question yet?" Reagan brings me back into the room and out of my head.

"Not if you keep doing that." I arch my neck up so he can reach the curve of my shoulder better. A question comes to mind, and it's ridiculous. But I say it anyway because I know Reagan will lose it, and I love making him laugh.

"Do David Copperfield and Claudia Schiffer get married?" I wait for his reaction because I already know what it's going to be. His lips stop and his hands still from moving up my body.

"What?" He lets out the full belly laugh I knew he would.

Yes.

I smirk.

"That's what you want to know? Out of everything you could ask me, right now?" He catches his breath, still chuckling.

"Yep."

"Holy shit, Harper." He cages his body over me, bringing me onto my back. His hands hold onto the side of my head and his pupils dilate. "You really don't have any questions about the future?" he whispers.

"I have questions, but what's the fun in knowing all the answers?"

"I don't know Harper Snow." His smirk turns into a full smile, loving the sound of my name and his mixed together.

I can't help wondering in the midst of our impulsive nuptials how all of this is going to play out when he has to leave. Does this change the inevitable heartbreak? Will I get to stay with him?

"Harper?" I focus back on him. "Where were you just now?"

Do I share my concerns? My fears about what I really want to ask about our future? I shrug with a shy smile, letting myself fall into the spell of his lips a little longer. Reagan rolls me so we are face to face, each hugging a pillow to our heads, long gazes between us.

"I can't believe we just got married! It's so easy. I didn't even need I.D.!"

"Yep, it really is that easy. Just a quick scan of the back of your hand. Boom. Chained for life." He laughs. "Try to get out of it? First born and a kidney," he says with a straight face, and I giggle.

"What are we gonna tell your parents? *My* parents? Oh my god! I've never done anything like this before." A wave of panic begins to set in as I think about my mother who is going to lose her mind when I tell her I got married to a guy she's never met. She's probably the one I'm worried about the most. Mike, Chad, my dad...they're guys, they will handle this different. At least I hope they will.

"What do you want to tell them? We don't have to tell anyone or we can tell everyone. I don't care. I'm wearing this ring until my finger turns green and falls off," Reagan says, studying his ring finger. I've never met a guy who was this into being married. Well, except for my book boyfriends who were all hopeless romantics, just like Reagan.

"I want to tell them. But, I want you with me when I do. Are you coming back with me tomorrow?" I ask. I don't think I can handle being apart from him now. I feel like I've grown these thick vines around him, and I don't want to be clipped away.

"I'm coming back. I still have a job to do."

"This job? Can you tell me about what you have to do?"

"I can't tell you." His eyes lower away from mine, almost pained. I want to ask more. I want to know what he's hiding.

"You do know I have ways of making you talk." I reach for the handcuffs dangling from the post of his headboard, getting him to smirk.

"You and those handcuffs are killing me. Look at my wrists!" He holds them up revealing a small red line marked across both.

"You shouldn't move when I tell you to stay still." I brace myself on top of him and push his arms over his head, feathering kisses over his neck and down his shoulder where the scales of the dragon are fanned out in shades of green and red.

"Mmmm...Harper."

"Mmmm...Reagan."

"You wanna do anything with the rest of your time here?" He lifts his head to watch me trail down his chest. "Or not." He lays his head back down. I crawl back up after teasing him, my head flush with his.

"What do you usually do on a Saturday night?" I ask.

"Before you?"

I nod.

"Before you I would have gone out with Dade and tried to hook up with some chick or just stayed home to sleep off Friday night's hook up."

"My classy husband." I smother him with quick kisses to his lips. I want to stay in this cocoon with him where nothing gets in to spoil what we have together.

His phone begins to buzz from the nightstand, and both of us turn to it. He reaches over to grab it, and I nip his arm with my teeth, making him jerk it back.

"You're trouble, you know that?" he asks with a smirk. He reaches again for his phone, but his face changes when he sees the caller.

"Shit," he mutters.

We've only been together a short time, but already I know this word from his lips is bad.

"Sorry, Angel. I gotta take this. I'm sorry." He begins to sit up, lifting me with him.

I roll to the side and watch him scramble for his boxers, answering the phone. He gets up from the bed and walks to the bathroom, closing the door. I wish I could have seen who was calling. I can't even hear him. He's not a quiet guy either.

I put his t-shirt on and grab my empty glass from the nightstand. *I still can't hear him.* I open the door to the hall and walk towards the kitchen, but on the way I look at the framed posters along the walls I passed by without noticing before.

One wall has three framed posters which I assume are Dade's just from what I've learned about him. The Godfather, Star Wars and something called Game of Thrones. The other wall has black and white framed posters of scenery. One has a lake with the mountains and clouds in the reflection of the water. Another is of an older home at the end of a pier. The last one catches my breath. It's of Reagan. He's shirtless against a black backdrop, wearing white jeans with his tattoo in full artistic display.

"Owen took these." Dade appears next to me.

"These are so good." I can't stop staring at Reagan's image.

"Yeah, he went to school to do photography for a living...before the accident."

"He can still do it, can't he?"

Dade nods. "I like the way you think, Harper. You wanna see more? We have a ton of them."

"Yeah, I do!"

Dade waves his hand for me to follow him into the living room and has me take a seat on the couch. I expect him to pull a photo album from the bookshelf, but he sits down next to me instead and taps on the coffee table with his fingers. The table comes alive with a screen in the glass top.

"Pretty cool, huh?" Dade eyes me.

I nod and giggle.

He swipes his finger over a folder as images scatter over the screen, and he moves the photos in mid-air. With each image, my breath is lost.

"Owen is really talented. Does he still take pictures?" I ask, watching Dade.

"He doesn't really take them anymore. He kinda lost his mojo after the accident."

I can only imagine what it's like to lose your motivation, but my god. He's so talented. Dade swipes the screen revealing more black and white shots of scenes that could be sold in an art gallery. Even the ones of Reagan are masterpieces. I point to one of him in a lake with just his torso above the water, dripping wet. His chin is down and tucked in with his eyes lifting to the camera.

Holy God almighty.

"Harper, can I ask you something?" Dade begins to drag the photos with his finger, placing them back in the folder.

"Of course," I say.

"Is that a wedding ring on your finger? Are you married?"

I don't answer right away. It's less than six hours old on my finger, and I haven't gotten used to the question or the word *married*.

"I'm..."

"Is Reagan messing with a married chick?" He looks at me, leaning back on the couch and raises his hand to his forehead. He scrubs it down his face and leans forward. "I mean, he's dated all kinds of women, but never a married one."

"He isn't messing with a married woman...well...I mean, he is but..."

"Oh, Harper. God! Are you in trouble? Is that why he's there to help you? Are you in an abusive relationship? Is he helping you get out it?"

"No, Dade, he's..."

"Jesus. That guy has the worst luck with women, I swear. No wonder he's all protective and attached. Just the other night I was telling him he needs to play it cool, and here he is messing with an abused married woman. Shit. No offense. I know you aren't to blame, but damn."

"Dade, he's..."

"His mom and dad are going to shit bricks when they find out about this. Does Owen know? Did he tell Owen about your abusive past?"

"Dade stop. Stop. Stop. Stop talking." I interrupt his horrible made for the Lifetime Network story about my fake life by squeezing my fingers over his mouth.

God, this guy has an imagination.

"I'm not in an abusive marriage. I'm married..."

"To me." Reagan calls from the doorframe of the hallway with a huge grin on his face. I smile back at him and turn my head to Dade, who looks like he just got told aliens are coming to dinner.

"You two?"

Reagan nods, taking a seat next to me on the couch.

"You two are..."

"Married." Reagan finishes Dade's sentence.

"Oh my god! Oh my god!"

"Is that a happy oh my god or a, *you're so fucked* oh my god?" Reagan asks.

"Dude...it's a holy shit! You're fucking married man!" Dade swings his arms around me and pulls Reagan into a hug. It's the most overly excited display of affection but totally fitting for Dade. He leans back and stares at us. Reagan takes my hand and kisses the ring.

"Owen knows?" Dade asks, and we both nod.

"He was there for it. You know that little chapel by the office?" Reagan asks.

"Yeah, they call it the walking dead's place." Dade laughs at his own joke.

"Well..." Reagan holds up our entwined hands. "That's where we did it."

"We should celebrate!" Dade shouts, and we both shake our heads no.

"Yeah, we should," he says, shaking his head. "We should go do something to celebrate like, I don't know. We need to do something. Wait, do you two have photos? Did they take photos? We need an official photo of you two. Holy shit. Married. We need to..." Dade gets up from the couch looking more excited by the minute. "I need to get my phone." He heads to his bedroom, but his phone rings first and he answers, shutting his door.

"Wow!" I exhale with a chuckle.

Reagan follows with the same relieved laugh with his bare chest expanding and tightening.

"I love the photo's Owen took of you," I say, pointing to the one in the hallway. "It's beautiful. I wish I could take it with me."

Reagan smiles and bats his eyes towards the ground at my compliment. "Owen's an amazing photographer. I wish he was still doing it," he says. I can tell he's thinking about the accident.

"Maybe we can have him take a few pictures of us before we leave. Maybe some artsy ones around the city will inspire him?" I ask.

"I love that idea, Harper." He lifts his head. "God, I love you." He places his hand around the back of my neck, pulling me in for a kiss. "I'll call him."

"Wait." My head tilts back a little. "Who called you just now?"

Reagan tilts his head back in the same way as me. "It was my dad." He sounds surprised by his own words. "He never calls me. Ever."

"What did he say? Was it bad?" I ask.

"Owen called him, and he wants to meet you."

"Really?" My excitement over meeting Reagan's dad throws him off even more. "Will I meet your mother too?" I ask.

Reagan smirks and studies my face before answering.

"You can, I mean, I'm sure she would like to meet you. I'm..." He hesitates. "It's just..."

"What?" I ask.

"It's just they haven't been interested in my life for years. I'm not sure what to think right now. I feel like they're going to try to talk us out of being together, like this is an intervention we're walking into."

"Do they know?" I ask, holding up my ring finger.

"Oh, they know. I'm pretty sure as soon as I scanned my hand for the justice of the peace, my dad got an alert message."

"Does this mean Gus knows too?"

"This means everyone knows, Harper." He puts his hand in mine.

He sounds regretful all of a sudden, which puts me off. *Is he regretting our impulsive decision?* Shit, that would be my luck. I can just see the headline now. Girl gets time traveler to marry her and he realizes his mistake in eloping only hours later when his family wants to meet her.

"Harper?"

"Harper?"

I fade from my tragic headline to see Reagan staring at me with an amused grin on his face. "Are you okay?"

"Yeah, I just wonder what this all means. I mean, with Gus. Are we going to be in trouble for this?" My conscience that has played a disappearing act since the diner has begun to make me nervous.

"You won't be in trouble, but I'll probably hear more than my fair share of shit tomorrow."

"Oh, Reagan. Did we mess up? Am I going to lose you? Is this what Gus meant by heartbreak? Is this it?" I ask, only to be given a kiss.

"You'll never lose me. I promise," he whispers.

Dade's door opens, and I pull away from Reagan. Dade has his phone and is taking pictures of us on the couch. Pictures I would like to burn, rip, delete, or whatever it is they do here. I stand, gesturing to see Dade's camera.

"God, I look like a mess. How do you get rid of these?" I say while scrolling through the photos he just took. Reagan pulls me into his side.

"You look beautiful, Harper. My beautiful bride." He gives a proud smile as Dade takes his phone back. Reagan's phone chimes, and he looks at it with an even bigger smile now. "I love this one," he says to Dade, who nods in agreement.

Reagan leans his phone over to show me, and it's a close up of Reagan and me kissing from just seconds ago. He does something to make it black and white which helps my distressed call of a look in a huge way. I curl into his side as he swipes icons on his phone and loads the picture on Facebook like he did with the others from the car. He captions it with, *happiest day of my life*.

PETE

Chapter 18

Reagan 2035

"A prenup?" I stare up at my dad from the table, confused by his request to have Harper sign the papers before me. He takes a seat next to me, scooting his chair closer.

"It's a post nuptial agreement, and it's not too late. You need to protect your future."

"Dad, she isn't even from here. She doesn't even know me like this." I ruffle the papers in my hands. I should have known the interest in my love life was about money. It's about my dad protecting himself from any financial damage as usual.

I sit back in the chair, staring at the papers in front of me. *A fucking post nuptial agreement*. Harper Liliana Adams is listed as my wife, and it reads like poetry next to mine. The thought makes me smile inside until my dad opens his mouth.

"You need to have her sign, Reagan."

"I don't even care about the money. Keep your money. It means nothing to me."

"Don't be stupid." My dad grabs the back of my neck with force, pulling tight on my collar. "You have her sign this or you'll never be allowed to see her again. Understood?" He holds his grip to my neck.

I resist him with a jerk of my shoulders, but he holds me steady, exactly where he wants me, like he always has since I was a child. I don't give him the satisfaction of my agreement, and he knows my defiant dismissal well. My mother comes into the archway of the dining room. Her eyes wide from what she has walked in on. My dad releases his hand from the back of my neck and straightens his stance. I shrug when he lets go, easing the tension from my neck and back.

"I was just showing Harper the upstairs suite we converted into an office." My mother glosses over the obvious and walks further into the dining room with her hands around the sides of Harper's shoulders. The suite she is referring to is my childhood bedroom. Owen's is right across from it, and it still looks like it did when he left for college, right down to the ribbons and trophies he won in high school for photography.

I force a smile at Harper who furrows her brow like she knows something is wrong. I stand and fold the postnup, placing it into the envelope with my name written on top. My dad watches my every move.

"You two want to stay for some coffee? I'm sure we can find something to nosh on." My mother's invitation makes me sick to my stomach.

Nosh on?

She hasn't invited me to stay for anything other than a tongue lashing. Food and drink are like the prefight hors d'oeuvres. I walk over to Harper and wrap my arm around the side of her waist. She doesn't hesitate to show affection back by sliding her body closer into mine.

"We should probably go. We're meeting Owen." Harper answers with a polite grin to my parents.

My mother's face lights up at the mention of Owen.

"Well that is a lovely idea, Harper, but it is getting quite late. Owen shouldn't be out at this time of night," My mother says. She has no idea how late Owen likes to roll. He clubs later than I do some nights.

"He wants to take some photos of us. I had no idea what a talented photographer he was until I saw some of the pictures he took." Harper gestures to the framed pictures hanging in the foyer.

"He hasn't taken many since..." My mother stops. "Since the accident." Her eyes lift to mine and I'm back to being a scolded five-year old all over again.

"His talent hasn't changed because his legs don't work. His motivation just took a detour. I think he's still got it in him," Harper says.

She takes my mother by surprise with this comment, and I love how brazen she is right now. "Reagan's a really great subject in the photos I saw earlier," Harper continues. She pats my chest and smiles, but I don't like the attention all of a sudden. I know my parents aren't thinking what a great subject I am.

"I think this one still has some growing up to do before he can be called a great subject." My dad scoffs, nudging his head towards me.

"I think you're wrong," Harper says.

"I'm never wrong dear Harper," My dad quips back, looking humored by Harper's challenge. I don't think he gets challenged much from women. In fact, I know he doesn't.

"Well, you are."

I could be wrong, but I think Harper's picking a fight right now.

"We should go, Angel," I whisper, trying to defuse what would probably be a spectacular light show of wit against my dad. I begin to step away, but Harper stiffens her stance, staring at my dad, who hasn't stopped his lock to her gaze.

"I think you may be a little misguided," he says.

"Misguided?" Harper goads.

"Harper? Let's go Angel. We don't need to do this," I say.

"No, I think I'd like to know how misguided I am."

"For starters, you don't know the first thing about this family," my dad says.

Harper takes a deep breath in and releases it slow with a forced grin. "Do I really need a lesson in your family history to know when one son is being chosen over the other? You have two sons who survived a horrible accident, and in the truest sense of the word, it was an accident. But, you only see one survivor. You only see the one who you think barely made it. I'll tell you something Mr. Snow, Reagan survived that accident too, and he barely makes it through being reminded of the memories each day, which come extremely close to the hell of having parents who can't forgive him."

My dad winces at her words.

My mother turns her head to him and back at Harper. "I think you two should go," she says.

"Yeah, I didn't think the truth would settle well." Harper turns, heading for the door, and I follow. She doesn't even wait for me to catch up. She hurries past the car and down the street.

"Reagan." My dad calls after me from the doorway, and I turn to see him holding the postnup envelope up. It's probably burning a hole in his hand after Harper's outburst.

"Fucking Christ, Dad." I walk back, snatch it from his hands and jog to catch up to Harper, who has already made it down to the end of the street.

"Harper?" I yell, and she stops walking but doesn't turn around. I'm out of breath when I reach her.

"I'm sorry." She turns around, letting her shoulders fall. I nod, waiting for my breath to slow. I pull her into my embrace and hold the back of her head as she sniffs against my shoulder. Her head tips back so she can see me.

"I'm sorry. I don't know what came over me. Your mom was talking to me upstairs, and I knew I was about to lose it, but I shouldn't have said what I said. I'm sorry."

"Don't be. What did she say to you?" I ask.

"She was showing me Owens room and kept going on about his trophies and showing me some of the pictures he took. He's so talented, Reagan."

I nod. "Baby, what did she say to you?"

"I asked her where your room was, and she pointed across the hall to the suite she remodeled. It kinda pissed me off. I mean, my parents redid my room, but they also redid my brother's. They didn't keep Chad's as some sort of shrine to him while he's still alive!" She lets out a nervous laugh.

I chuckle because it's true. It is a shrine.

"She also told me how Owen got me here."

My eyes widen.

"What did she say?"

"She told me he was negotiating a settlement from the city because of the traffic light malfunction, and he forfeited the last installment of money to bring me here. What does that mean? You can buy time travel?"

"Not exactly." I pause and take her hand, guiding her to a bench at the park just a few yards ahead. "You know the light and how I told you it was green on both sides of traffic?"

Harper nods.

"The city put in a new lighting system that would be perfectly timed so traffic would be reduced. Something about the grids being synced better depending on the flow of traffic and how many cars were on that street. I don't know. It was supposed to be foolproof. Which is funny, you know? I mean politicians' thinking something is foolproof, gloating about it in the media and then having it blow up in their faces? But anyway, the city came to us with a settlement in exchange for our silence to the media. Owen wasn't going to take it but my dad talked him into it."

"How much did they settle for?"

"Two point five million."

"Holy shit, Reagan."

"Yeah."

"Owen got his money in installments and the last one was supposed to be paid out. I'm guessing he told them to keep it if he could bring you here. He's pretty convincing. I don't really know, but money still talks no matter what year it is."

"Did you get money too? I mean, you were in the accident."

"I gave my settlement money to Owen. I didn't want it."

"Wow." She sighs.

"Did that piss you off when my mom told you how you got here?"

"No, I was really curious. But, I got pissed off when she told me I wasn't going to see a dime of that money. It caught me off guard. I didn't even know about the money, and I don't even care about it now that I do know."

"She said that?"

Harper nods.

"I'm sorry, Harper. It was a bad idea to bring you here. I shouldn't have."

"No, it was a good idea. I wanted to meet them, remember?"

I nod and smooth my hand over her cheek. "Careful what you wish for."

"They probably hate me right now. God, what a first impression. I insult your dad and run off."

"You told them the truth. Something they need to hear," I say. My lips encase hers as we sit on the bench in the low lit park. "You know I came here when I got in a fight with my dad the other day and read your letter?"

"My letter about where you were and how I was eating spaghetti with Gus?"

"Yeah." I chuckle. "It made everything better, Harper. It was just what I needed."

"Well, it's all true. No matter what you've done, you're a good person."

"Yeah, well I'm glad you see it."

"I'm not the only one." Harper gives me a quick peck on the lips and stands, slipping off the sandals I bought for her on the way to the house. She lets go of my hand to run towards the sandy playground equipment, taking a seat on a swing. "When's the last time you were on a swing, Reagan Snow?" She waves for me to come closer.

"Not since grade school," I call out, and walk closer to her, leaning my shoulder against the pole of the swing set. She swings back and forth with a huge grin on her face, and I can't help but return it with my own. She's so carefree with each passing. She jumps off, landing in the sand, laughing at herself.

"You should sit." She points to the swing.

"I'll break it," I say. She rolls her eyes and approaches me, grabbing my hand and leading me to the leather seat of the swing.

"Sit," she says, patting the seat.

I sit in the seat, which is way too small for me to be in, and Harper climbs on top, straddling my lap and takes hold of the chain links of the swing. We fall silent in a stare, rocking together. "You ever had a day with more shit jam packed in it before today?" She laughs, and I follow with a belly laugh.

"I can't say I have, other than the day I met you."

"You know I made a wish that day about being swept off my feet with romance, but I never expected it to be like this!"

I hear the sound of Owen's electric wheelchair and turn to see him snapping a picture, holding the camera lower to his chest and grinning.

"You two sure know how to make an exit," he says, lifting the camera to take another picture. Harper lifts off of me and walks to the sidewalk circling the playground where Owen is sitting.

"I feel horrible for what I said. God, it's hitting me by the second," she says.

"Don't feel bad. My parents need to get out of this mourning for the loss of my legs. I'm fine. Look at me." Owen does a 360 spin in his chair making Harper hoot.

"And mom was worried you shouldn't be out this late," I say, walking up to greet him and placing my hand on the small of Harper's back.

"She worries for all the wrong reasons," he says. "You two want to take a few photos? I have a cool idea for a photo near one of those lampposts. The lighting is perfect."

We stand by a lamppost with Owen directing us on which way to turn our heads and on how to stand so the light hits us just right. My arms are wrapped around Harper from behind. She turns to face me, and we both stare at each other in the same way we did the night I saw her after the magic show where her fan, Ally, took our picture.

"You should take your shirt off," she whispers, and I reward her with a huge grin.

"Oh what's that smile about? What are you saying to him Harper? Keep doing it." Owen clicks more photos, getting closer.

"I told him he should take his shirt off. I love his tattoo."

"Reagan? Your wife wants you to take your shirt off. Enjoy it while you can," Owen says.

I laugh and loosen my embrace with Harper to take my shirt off. Her hand goes to the scales on my dragon tattoo.

"You want one with just him, Harper? The light is perfect," Owen asks, and Harper nods, taking a step back to watch from the side of Owen's chair.

"Stop smiling," Owen directs.

I can't help it.

Owen snaps a few more of me and Harper joins. My phone begins to buzz in my pocket, and I pull it out to see Gus calling. I'm surprised it took him so long to call me. Harper sees Gus' name.

"It's okay, take it," she says. I debate ignoring it. "Take it, Reagan. Let's get it out of the way so we can enjoy the rest of our night."

She's right. I answer.

"You sure know how to make shit go south don't you, boy?" Gus says.

"Gus. I..."

"Yep, had to go and fuck this up. You know what this means right?"

"What? What does this mean?"

"It means you're going to be taken off Harper's case now, and I'm gonna have to help some other jackass get up to speed and hope he doesn't screw this up as royally as you have!"

"Shit, Gus, no!"

"You knew what you were doing, Reagan. You knew marrying her was the one way to keep her in your life. You're clever, I'll give you that. I can usually read you, but that one...that was good." He chuckles and stops abruptly. "You're off her case."

"No, I can't be taken off it! We've come this far!"

"Well, thank yourself for that. Why can't you ever just stick to the plan?"

"Gus, please. Don't take me off this."

"I should have stopped this sooner. It's my fault really."

"Gus, I love her. Please, I don't want to see someone else save her. I want it to be me. I need this. I need this closure. Please." There's silence on the other end. I look at my phone to make sure I'm still connected.

"Reagan, I think you are going to need to find your closure some other way. It's over."

"Shit..." I mutter.

"I'll see you and her at nine a.m. sharp. DON'T be late."

Gus hangs up, and I look over at Harper smiling with Owen, who is taking photos of them together. She's sitting on his lap with her arms around his neck in the most comfortable way, and it makes my heart hurt. *I'm gonna lose her.*

I walk back towards the two of them trying to put the call out of my mind.

"Is everything okay?" Harper smiles through her words as she glances up from the camera.

"Yeah, its fine."

"What did Gus say?"

"Nine a.m. sharp," I say.

Harper stands up and walks towards me, wrapping her arm around me. Every touch from her feels bittersweet.

"I'll send these to you," Owen says, and I nod. "So many good ones. You guys are like the perfect photogenic duo." He snaps a few of the sky.

I can see the old version of his photographer self, blossoming with each snap, and I have Harper to thank for that.

"You wanna come with us, catch a bite?" I ask, knowing Owen is going to refuse. He shakes his head no.

"I have to get to bed, my *mommy* said so," he says. I force a smile, and Harper notices but doesn't say anything.

"You parked at the house?" I ask him, and he nods. We start to walk, but Harper runs over to the bench where we were sitting to grab her sandals. Owen snaps another picture of her slipping them on.

"Here, you left this on the bench." She hands me the white envelope when she reaches us. "What is it anyway?" she asks.

Chapter 19

Harper 2035

"A post nuptial agreement? What the hell is that?" I ask, unable to move from the sidewalk as I look down at the papers in my hand.

Owen doesn't stick around for the answer. He backs up in his chair and turns it around, rolling down the street to the house.

"Do you think I'm going after you're money? Is that it? I didn't even know you had any money, Reagan." I back away from him as he reaches for me.

"No, I don't think you are. My dad wants me to have you sign it because I have family money invested in his business. It's to protect him really. I don't even care about it. I told him he could keep the money."

"What's this about the trust being released in its entirety only if the *trust beneficiary gets married*?" I look up at Reagan who is staring back at me with confusion.

"Where does it say that?" he asks, walking closer. I hold the paper out to him.

"Right here." I hand it to him with my finger under the paragraph. He takes the agreement, gripping it tight and sighs.

"Harper, I didn't know this was in here. I thought my parents were withholding my trust because of all my run-ins with the law. I had no idea they put this in here."

“Right, because it makes sense that you would fall in love and get married to me so quickly without another reason being there.”

“Harper, I married you because I love you. I do. I don’t care about the money. My dad can keep it. I don’t even want it. I haven’t used it all this time, what’s the difference.”

“I knew this was too good to be true.” I raise my hands in the air, staring at the sky full of stars. “You pursuing me and acting like the perfect guy just so you could get me to marry you.”

“No, it wasn’t like that. Harper, I’ve never lied to you. You’re the only girl I’ve never lied to. Think of all the times I could have asked someone to marry me, if I really wanted the money.”

“If you love me, why do I have to sign something just in case this doesn’t work out? We already know this isn’t going to work out! I’m from nineteen ninety-three for god sake! This is ridiculous. I’m not signing, Reagan.”

“I don’t want you to.”

“Good. Because I’m not. If we’re married for two more days or two years, I’m not going to sign some safety net so your dad doesn’t lose money on his son’s temporary wife! I’m not one of his investments with an agenda!”

“I know. Harper, there is more though. If you don’t sign it, we can never see each other again.”

“What?”

“My dad has to agree for me to travel, and he won’t agree anymore if you don’t sign.”

“Why does your dad have to agree? You’re not a child.”

"He helps fund the group that developed the technology for time travel. He has a lot of pull since he pimped me out as the first experimental prisoner to test it years ago."

I can't think clear. *How did everything get so complicated so fast?* When I made a wish to be swept off my feet, I should have added a part about a headache free romance. It feels like it was just yesterday Reagan and I were throwing flirty pickup lines at each other in a bar parking lot. Now I have to decide if I will sign off on assets if I divorce my time traveler husband, or I won't ever see him again!

"Harper?"

"I can't think, Reagan. This is all so complicated all of a sudden."

"I know." Reagan pulls me into a hug, and I tense as his arms squeeze me. A sudden rush of panic is hitting me at my choices right now. I should be focusing on my career, not this. *What am I doing?* It's hitting me hard. I ease back from him.

"You wanna get out of here? Forget about this for a little while? Go get something to eat?" he asks.

I want to go home. I don't belong here. This isn't my life.

"Harper?"

"Yeah, okay." I nod, taking Reagan's phone from his pocket without him noticing.

We sit next to each other on bar stools in front of a counter at a small twenty-four hour restaurant, saying very little. I'm a mix of tired and homesick again. Reagan notices my mood, and there's no buffer of Dade or Owen to hide it.

"I'll be right back." I gesture to the restroom sign to the right, and Reagan nods.

"Don't leave me again, Harper." He says this half joking, but I take its deeper meaning.

He's not wrong to read my silence this way. I want to leave. Not him, just whatever this feeling festering inside me is all about. Not even the best fries I've ever tasted can shake it.

"Reagan, no matter what, I love you." I kiss his cheek and head to the restroom.

I sit in the stall holding his phone with Gus' number in front of me and the word *call* on the screen. I'm about to work up the nerve to hit the call button when I hear what I think is Tamera's voice on her phone. Half believing my ears, I peek through the crack of the stall door, and there she is hunched over the sink staring into the mirror.

Well fuck me.

"I can see you looking at me." She stares right at me from the mirror, putting her phone back in her pocket. I unlock the stall door and step into her full line of vision.

"Why are you here?" I ask. "Are you following Reagan?" I begin to wash my hands even though I don't need to do it.

Tamera smiles and narrows her eyes to my left hand.

"Nice ring," she says.

All my uncertainty about where I am is morphing into cray cray's unstable hands. I give Tamera a mocking smile back.

"Did Reagan give you a promise ring?" she asks, with a sneering purse of her lips.

"He gave me a promise and a wedding ring," I say, searching the towel dispenser for a way to make it work. Tamera leans her hand over the center and the paper towels release.

"Mmm...he knocked you up too?" she asks.

Not that it's any of her business but, "No, I don't need to fake a pregnancy to get him to love me," I say back.

She smiles exposed in what I knew was a game from the second Reagan told me she was pregnant and aborted it.

"You're not as dumb as I thought," she says, standing close enough for me to smell the cherry scent of her lip gloss.

I sneer back at her and try to curb the urge to punch her in the face.

Simmer cray cray, simmer. But like any simmer, it either evaporates the water or turns into a boil. The next words decide its fate.

"I guess you kinda have to take what you can get though." She looks me over from head to toe. I'm in day old shorts and a tank top that smells from sweating all day, but I know my worth and cray cray has had it with the digs on my value tonight.

Within seconds, I'm pulling at her hair and both of us are grappling at each other. I don't even know how to fight. *What am I doing?* She hits the side of the bathroom wall near the door and we both fall when the door swings open.

Reagan is one of three men sitting on the bar stools at the counter, all of which are gapping at us. Tamera's shirt is pulled down so her bra is showing, and I am in mid-heave trying to pull myself up and back together. If there was mud, we could probably profit from how we look right now.

Reagan rushes over to help me. "You okay?"

He holds my arm as I pat my shirt down and nod my head.

"What the hell is going on in there?" he asks. I tip my head over to Tamera, and she smirks.

"Nothing, Reagan. Looks like you've got everything handled," she says.

What does that mean?

She walks towards the exit with every eye on her as she pulls on her mini skirt from behind.

"What did she say to you?" Reagan asks.

I sigh. "She didn't really say anything. I wanted to punch her from the moment I saw her."

"Harper, God what have I done to you?" He chuckles.

"Here." I hand him his phone. "I took this from you. I was going to call Gus," I say.

Reagan looks at me, wounded like I knew he would be.

"You were gonna call Gus?" He takes the phone from my hands and stares at it and back up at me.

"I think I want to go home."

"Harper, no. I'm sorry. I'm sorry about tonight. Please stay. I'll do anything. Don't go." He pleads, and it only makes my decision more difficult.

"I don't belong here, Reagan. I'm not myself. This isn't me." I point to the bathroom door still stuck open. "I'm picking fights. This isn't me."

"Don't go, Harper. Give me one more night."

"I can't." I'm breaking him and I can see it. "I think this was a mistake. I want to go home." I walk away from him, and he calls after me when I'm just outside the door. I don't know where I am or where to go. I lean up against the side wall of the restaurant and stare down at myself until Reagan comes and stands next to me.

"Harper?"

I can't make eye contact with him. I can't.

"If you want to go," he says, "I'll take you."

Gus is standing outside the library when we park. I get out of the car, not waiting for Reagan to get to it first and open my door. I greet Gus, who frowns to see me leaving. He scans his hand against the marker on the side of the sliding glass doors and we walk inside. Reagan puts his hand in mine.

We walk past the information booth and towards the ramp that leads down to the fiction section. We pass the paperback books on swivel stands, heading towards the periodicals. The same door I came through stares ominous and knowing back at me. Gus scans his hand again, and the doors open. We step inside, and Gus scans his eye letting the red beam cross over it. This is it. I'm going back home. The elevator ascends and stops minutes later. I let Reagan hold onto my hand as we follow Gus out.

1993

The library looks the same as the one we left, but the lights are lower. Outside, the town car Barney drove is waiting in the same parking spot.

"You can take it from here." Gus hands Reagan the keys and continues with, "Meet me at our place when you're done."

Reagan nods, taking the keys and unlocks the passenger side door for me to get in. I take a seat and watch Gus say something to Reagan. I can see the hurt in Reagan's face as he regards me and walks over to the driver's side door. I don't want to hurt him, but I can't help how I feel right now.

We drive in silence to my place and pull up in front. Reagan puts the car in park, turning off the engine, and we sit.

"I know what you're thinking," he says. He turns at his waist to face me, but I still can't make eye contact with him.

"You're thinking this is why they say don't get involved with the people in our cases. Gus warned me. I shouldn't have let it get this far. But I can't help how I feel," he says.

I know everything he is saying is true. I meet his gaze. His eyes look as pained as my heart feels, denying him the one thing he wants from me. I take a deep breath, and he cups my head in his hands, bringing his lips to mine. It takes me back to our first kiss and how every part of me wanted him to stay. Every part of me wanted him to feel as much as I felt for him.

"What can I do, Angel?" he whispers. "I'll do anything you want."

Chapter 20

Reagan 1993

"Harper?" I groan into her name because she's silent and beginning to show me how this is affecting her. I wipe her wet cheek knowing I should just enjoy this last moment with her. I should enjoy every second she gave to me. I should enjoy how she made me feel again, how she felt in my arms. But I'm greedy, I want more. I can't stand to let her go.

"I need to be alone. I'm sorry." She turns to open her door and begins to step out. I open mine and meet her at the edge of her walkway, putting my hand in hers. I walk her to her door, and she lets go of my hand to search her purse for her keys.

Gus said I would break her heart, but right now, I feel mine breaking instead. The heart that never loved is crumbling into pieces.

"Can I come in?" I ask, watching her turn the key in the lock. I want her to say yes, and she wants to. I can see it in her eyes. "Please?"

"I can't," she whispers.

I fight back tears at her words. How bittersweet it is to finally find love. To hold it right in front of me, only to have it restrained by bad timing. I don't offer any other words. No other begging. I nod in resistant agreement as she kisses my cheek and places her hand on the other. I follow the ring on her finger as she cracks open her door. She looks back at me, and I stand at her doorstep, paralyzed. She turns and walks in without another word and closes the door. I hit my fist on the side wall and hear something rattle inside the apartment. I wait, hoping she will come back out, but after a few minutes I walk to my car.

I sit at the wheel in front of her house feeling devastated, staring up into her window for some guidance as to what I do now, and I wonder if I will ever see her again. It's more than I can bear to think about. I close my eyes, sliding back in the seat and cry at what a mess I've made.

2035: Three Weeks Later

"You should probably eat something," I hear Owen say.

I squint as the image of Gus appears to be opening the curtains in my room. I haven't moved from my bed in five days.

"God, what died in here?" Dade enters my bedroom fanning his nose.

"I did," I reply. I don't move from lying on my stomach to acknowledge them further. Gus slides the window open but closes it when a burst of hot air floods into the room.

"You just gonna wallow in here and that's it?" Gus asks, and I groan.

"Just let me die in peace," I mutter while rolling over, gripping the pillow that still smells like Harper over my head. Everyone groans because I don't have clothes on. I don't care. It's my room.

"Well, it's too bad you're gonna die because I have some news that might interest you," Gus says, pulling a sheet over me like I'm a corpse.

I roll back over to look at him as he sits in the chair by my desk.

"What is it? Am I winning an award for the most fucked up?" I say deadpan, which makes Owen laugh.

"God, you're dramatic. Have you been reading more of Harper's romance novels?" Owen points to the stack I have on my desk.

Don't laugh. They're fucking addicting.

"What is it then? What's the *news*?" I ask, with a sarcastic eye roll.

"Harper's performing in three days. You know what this means," Gus says, and I sit up, alert like water just hit me in the face.

"Is she doing the water torture chamber?" I ask, and receive a nod. "Who is the guy watching her now? Why hasn't he stopped her?" I sit up even more and grab the file Gus has in his hands. "TINY!?" I shout. "Why is Tiny on this case? What the fuck, Gus!?"

"He was next in line," Gus says.

My back deflates against the headboard behind me. "Shit," I mutter, as I read his information in the file Gus hands me. He's probably scared Harper already. He looks like an angry bulldog even when he's asleep, and I speak from personal experience in seeing this.

"You're going to go with me to make sure Tiny doesn't mess this up," Gus says.

"I am?" I start to get up from bed and hit my foot on the wheel of Owen's chair.

"Whoa, whoa. Slow down. Slow down," Gus says.

But I can't slow down. I can't even breathe. Harper. I'm going to see her. This is my chance to be with her again. God. I'm revived, renewed. I pull on my boxers and grab a shirt from my dresser.

"Will I get to talk to her? Can I see her?" I ask, searching my dirty clothes for the least offensive smelling jeans.

Gus shakes his head no. "You're an observer, Reagan. For once, do what you're told. Please."

"I can do what I'm told, Gus."

I can, but not with Harper. Nope. If I see her, I'm not stopping until I can hold her again like I've been wanting to this whole time I've been away.

"She can't know you're there," he warns.

I nod, but she's gonna know I'm there.

"I have something for you, if you're up to it," Owen says, rolling his chair out to the hallway and into the living room. I follow him, and he points to the wall where he has a framed portrait of Harper and me from the park. It's us smiling in an embrace. Her forehead is resting against mine in black and white with the light from the lamppost shining down. It only sets fire to the urgency I feel in wanting to see her again.

"This is unbelievable, O," I say, and he smiles in a way that I've missed. He's back to being proud of his work. He shows me more on his phone, but this one hanging is by far the most perfect shot he took.

"Thanks, man." He nods, rolling his chair back as Dade steps in to get a better look at the picture.

"This is gonna be a real mood setter with the ladies," Dade says. "Having my best friend's lady looking like that at you. Shit. All sorts of expectations are going to be swimming around in their minds now. Thanks, Owen."

"I'm pretty sure your hand already knows the expectations here," Owen says.

Dade has no comeback, and it's an awesome sight. He laughs and gives his palm a conceding grin with a kiss.

1993

"Did you send her yellow roses?" Gus gives me his *what the fuck* face as we sit in the back of the auditorium.

I smirk.

"Dammit, Reagan." He shakes his head and turns to face forward.

The lights dim and rise twice. The audience quiets as people begin to fill the few empty seats. I'm eager to see Harper and get her reaction to the note I left on the flowers.

The lights dim all the way as the stage lights gleam and the announcer comes on stage to greet the audience with his top hat, tux, tails and cherub smile warming the crowd. I read the program for Harper's name and see she is listed right after intermission. I'm hoping I can ditch Gus long enough to see her before she goes on stage.

The same acts as before go on stage and perform with a slight improvement in their stage presence...and I do mean slight. If it wasn't for Harper being in this show, I am betting half the crowd would already be gone. Intermission comes, and I glance over at Gus who is studying the program with his leg shaking to a nonexistent beat.

"You okay?" I ask.

He nods, but I can tell he's nervous.

"Maybe you should get some air or check on Tiny. Make sure he's ready."

"You'd like that wouldn't you? Give you a chance to go find Harper and psych her out right before her performance?"

"It was worth a shot."

"You are an observer. Don't go see her." Gus stands, and I know I've put doubt in his mind by the mere mention of Tiny. He looks towards the stage, and I follow to see Tiny dressed as a stage hand in all black. He sees Gus and gives him a nod. I lower a bit in my seat, aiming the brim of my cap down so my face is hidden and duck out before Gus notices.

I flirt my way backstage, telling the cute stage manager I'm Harper's husband. She lets me pass without question. I search the open halls for the door I was told would have Harper's name on it. I find it and take a deep breath as I knock on the door. Her name is on a piece of white paper in silver writing.

"Come in," she calls, and I open the door. Her gaze finds mine in the mirror and she stops the powder puff on her cheek. My flowers are next to her, and the card is open on the vanity.

"Harper." I walk in, closing the door.

She stands and turns to me. She's more beautiful than ever tonight. "I had to see you. I'm sorry. I hope I'm not messing you up tonight by coming here, but I had to see you. I've missed you so much." I step closer, and she steps back.

"What are you doing here?" she asks.

I can't tell if she's surprised to see me or mad I'm here.

"I needed to see you. You got my flowers?" I ask.

She nods.

"And the note? Did you read it?"

She nods again. She turns her head away and back to me.

"What are you doing here?" Her voice cracks, and the back of her hand goes to her lips. I step closer.

This is it. She's breaking. Move closer.

"I've missed you," I say, and reach my arms around her and pull her into my chest. She releases into me with a sob, bracing her arms around me, squeezing me tight. "God, Harper." I moan, brushing my hands over the back of her head, kissing her hair. She tugs away from my chest, scanning my face.

"I've missed you, Reagan." She whimpers, and it breaks me in a new way to hear her say this.

"Angel." I kiss her lips and feel her longing for me. "I..."

A tap on the door interrupts as Mike walks in saying, “Five minutes,” looking down at a paper in his hands and then up at us. His face falls when he sees me holding Harper. “Oh...I didn’t know...” He stammers. “I didn’t know you had company.”

“It’s okay, Mike. This is Reagan.” She introduces us, pulling away to wipe a tissue under her eyes, gazing into the mirror. I shake Mike’s hand, and he studies me like I would study any guy holding onto the girl I love. I can see his admiration for her as he looks her way in the mirror.

“You, okay Harp?” he asks, and she nods.

“Okay. Five minutes,” he says looking me over from head to toe before stepping out of the room. I embrace her from behind in the mirror, and her eyes meet mine.

“I love you, Harper. I want you to know that. Even if you don’t believe it. It’s true.”

She tilts her head down and back up, turning to face me. “I needed time to think, and I do wanna talk. Like you asked in your note. Will you be here afterwards?”

“I’ll be here,” I say, brushing my hand over the side of her head. I kiss her one more time before letting go and turning to leave. She grabs my hand before I get to the door. She rushes me with a kiss, holding her hands to my face and releasing with a slow meaningful stare.

I hurry back to my seat, but Gus is gone. I sit down just as the lights flicker on and off. I study the stage noticing feet scurrying under the velvet red curtain. The announcer appears as the lights dim and the stage lights rise.

"We know you all have been patiently waiting for this next act," he muses, and the crowd cheers. "This next performer needs only two words to introduce the extraordinary performance you are about to witness. Houdini Harper."

The crowd explodes into cheers and clapping. I find myself whistling, full of adrenaline as Harper takes the stage. She's glowing in a dark cat suit outfit that's slick like wax against her curves. She stands next to the water torture chamber filled to the top with liquid, and she smiles for those taking pictures. She waits patiently next to it while flashes burst one after the other.

She lays down next to the chamber as two assistants walk on stage. The lid to the chamber lifts with a chain attached and lowers with their guidance down to Harper's legs. Harper lifts her hands for one assistant to cuff them together while the other holds the lid steady. Harper lifts her legs and the lid lowers to them. The top of the lid opens in two halves as her legs go through it and then closes with only holes for her feet to stick out of. The assistants latch the lid closed with padlocks, and the lid rises, lifting Harper in the air with it. The audience is dead silent as Harper is positioned over the top of the water. Her face is calm and poised. She looks ready, and I'm already holding my breath.

Harper signals the assistant with a flick of her head, and the lid lowers, submerging her into the water. She's still as she lowers, water spilling over the outside of the chamber. The lid sits flush with the top and the assistants lock it in place, stepping away from the chamber. A curtain lowers over the chamber, and the audience gasps. It rises after a few seconds to reveal Harper struggling in the water to get free. I can't tell if this is scripted or real, and I search the stage for Tiny. He's standing close with Gus right beside him.

The curtain lowers, and my breathing stops again. Seconds later, the curtain lifts and teases once more, only this time Harper is struggling harder and looks to be motioning with her head. *Something's wrong*. The curtain lowers again. I stand to signal Gus, but he can't see me. So I run to where I entered the backstage earlier. Everyone is glued to the performance.

"Something's wrong," I say to the stage manager, who shrugs me off.

"This is what she does. It's fine. She's fine."

"She's not fine, something's wrong!"

I rush the stage and pull the curtain open from behind to see Harper still, eyes closed. "Something's wrong!" I shout, and Tiny rushes the stage.

I shake the chamber, but it doesn't budge. "Where's the ax?" I yell to Tiny and Gus.

The other stage hands scramble to get the ax and hand it to me. I hit the glass, splintering it, but it doesn't break. Tiny takes the ax from my hands, and with two heaving blows, cracks the glass, spilling the water which floods out onto the stage.

The assistants unlock her legs as I hold her and lower her to the floor. "Harper!?" I scream, laying her flat, checking for her pulse.

"Harper?" I yell again, and press my palm to her chest and compress.

"Harper?" I yell again.

She doesn't move. I breathe into her mouth, watching the air expand her chest and resume compressing.

God, Harper, breathe baby.

I breathe again into her mouth, willing her to take in my air. Medics lean in just as Harper coughs up water. I fall on the back of my legs, relieved as the medics take over.

Tiny nudges my shoulder, and I grab his hand to stand up. Gus pats me on the back shaking his head in the rare *good job* way. The medics lay Harper on a gurney, securing her in place.

"It's time to go, Reagan," Gus says.

"No, I have to stay! I told Harper I'd be here," I say.

"No, Reagan. You can't stay. It's time to go," he repeats.

"No..." I hurry to Harper's side, gripping her hand, and she looks at me with a mask now placed over her nose and mouth.

"Reagan!" Gus calls.

"Harper, I'm here. I'm here angel."

She nods, trying to smile. Gus comes up behind me with his hands on the side of my arms.

"It's time, Reagan. Let her go."

"No!" I shake him loose, holding onto her hand. The medics begin to roll the gurney, and Harper pulls away as Gus holds me in place, not letting me follow. The tips of Harper's fingers touch mine, and I notice she isn't wearing her ring. My heart sinks even lower, realizing she wanted to talk to me because we're done. It's over. I struggle in Gus' grip, but resign as the sinking feeling takes over even further.

"It's over," Gus whispers, holding me tight.

I soften in his grip.

It's over.

Unlike every other case where I was fine to disappear as the hero, this one knocks me down to my knees when Gus releases me. I don't want to disappear.

2035

The sobriety chips are in my palm, and I hold a bottle of unopened whiskey in the other as I sit in my car outside the liquor store.

Fuck fate. Fuck everything.

I can't even remember wanting to drown myself in this as much as I do now. I know my time was limited going back. I just thought I would have more of it. More time to make it right. More time to see Harper and hold her again. Maybe savor it more. Remember what it was like to feel her wrap herself around me.

Just when I think I can't out fuck myself, I go ahead and do it. Maybe Harper would have done the trick if I wasn't there beforehand to confuse her and throw her off? Maybe I'm the wrench in that plan? Tiny would have handled it.

God, *Fuck fate.*

Gus was right. Gus was right.

His words about his own love interest and how he botched the case he was on swell in my mind among the thoughts of Harper and how I may never see her again. In fact, I'm certain of it.

I open the glove box of my car to throw the chips back in and pull out a copy of the postnup agreement I had revised to state everything I have be placed in Owen's name, and for my trust fund to be given to him if he wants it. I want him to have it. He gave me a chance to love again, and I want him to have a chance to find his passion. If that means burning the money in the front lawn, so be it. It means nothing to me. Everything I want is living and breathing in 1993.

I drive to the office for another case I need to handle. One last case since Harper's was technically not mine anymore, even though I handled it to the end. I greet the older ladies at the information desk who give me a solemn nod. Gus must have shared my woes with them.

I walk down the ramp and past the fiction shelves, slowing when I reach all the paperback romance novels that remind me of Harper. I reach the door near the periodicals and scan my hand over the security marker. It opens, and Gus is standing inside. He gives me a nod as he scans his eye in the side panel.

I don't talk as the cab descends. "You look like shit, Reagan," are the only words Gus utters until the doors open. I catch a glimpse of myself in the reflection of the shine in the doors and agree. I look like lovesick shit. Gus and I enter the office where Barney is sitting at the long conference table. He motions for me to take a seat across from him.

"You have a new recruit to show the ropes," Barney says, as he holds open a file folder and stares down at it. "Says this one was brought up on charges for disorderly conduct in a bathroom. You sure would know about that one, huh, Reagan?" Barney is joking with me, and I'm not amused. "I picked this one myself. I think you two will get along very well."

Great.

The door opens behind me, but I don't look to see who it is. I don't care. I just want to get this done and move on. I stare at the paperwork in front of me with my father's signature at the bottom, signing me away for another assignment to make amends for the last one I screwed up. I flip the page to see the time I have, and it says this case is going to take nine months. This is by far the longest case I've ever done, and I groan at the thought of it.

Barney steps to the door to greet the person entering and holds out a chair next to mine for them to sit. The gesture surprises me because there is no way he is holding a chair out for a fellow law breaker. I look over to see Harper taking a seat next to me. I'd forgotten what it felt like to smile. My cheeks expand to the point of hurting.

"Harper?"

Her face is warm as she regards me with a smirk.

"I couldn't let my husband go on another case without seeing his thug wife first." Her face lights up as she scans over me and winks when her eyes meet mine. "I'm straight up G now." She arches her brow and opens her coat to show me the shirt she is wearing. It has a picture of Dr. Dre and Snoop Dog on it.

My hand goes to my mouth as I cover my laughter.

I know Gus is in the room. I know Barney is in the room. I know a fucking police officer is the room, but I don't care. I reach for her with an urgency I've only seen in dramatic chick flicks and pull her towards me with a feverish kiss to her lips. It's over the top, and in every way conveys how much I've missed touching her and being able to show her how much I love her.

"We'll be outside. *Don't* get any ideas, Reagan. We're watching," Barney says as he makes his exit.

I open my eyes with my lips still attached to Harper's and shoo him out. Gus pats me on the back, walking past with the officer behind him snickering. I pull away, relief flooding over me and look into Harper's eyes, and I exhale.

"Angel."

About the Author

JL Pete lives in California with her three children as a writer at night and as an *any chance she can get to read* romance novel lover by day. After waking from a Channing Tatum inspired dream (yes that Channing Tatum) that stuck with her for a full day, she picked up a notebook and started writing her first novel. School pickups, drop offs and playdates be damned, she wrote her second and then her third. JL Pete brings her sarcastic humor, with a touch of sass, on love, romance and the straight up endearing antics that exist with a blossoming relationship in her latest novel *Call It Magic*.

Made in the USA
Middletown, DE
07 December 2017